THE PICTISH

BOOK TWO IN THE
DRAGON OF THE NORTH TRILOGY

BY

CHRIS THORNDYCROFT

Dragon of the North Trilogy Book 2: The Pictish Crown
By Chris Thorndycroft
2025 by Copyright © Chris Thorndycroft

All rights reserved. This book or any portion thereof may not be reproduced or used in any manner whatsoever without the express written permission of the publisher except for the use of brief quotations in a book review.

https://christhorndycroft.wordpress.com/

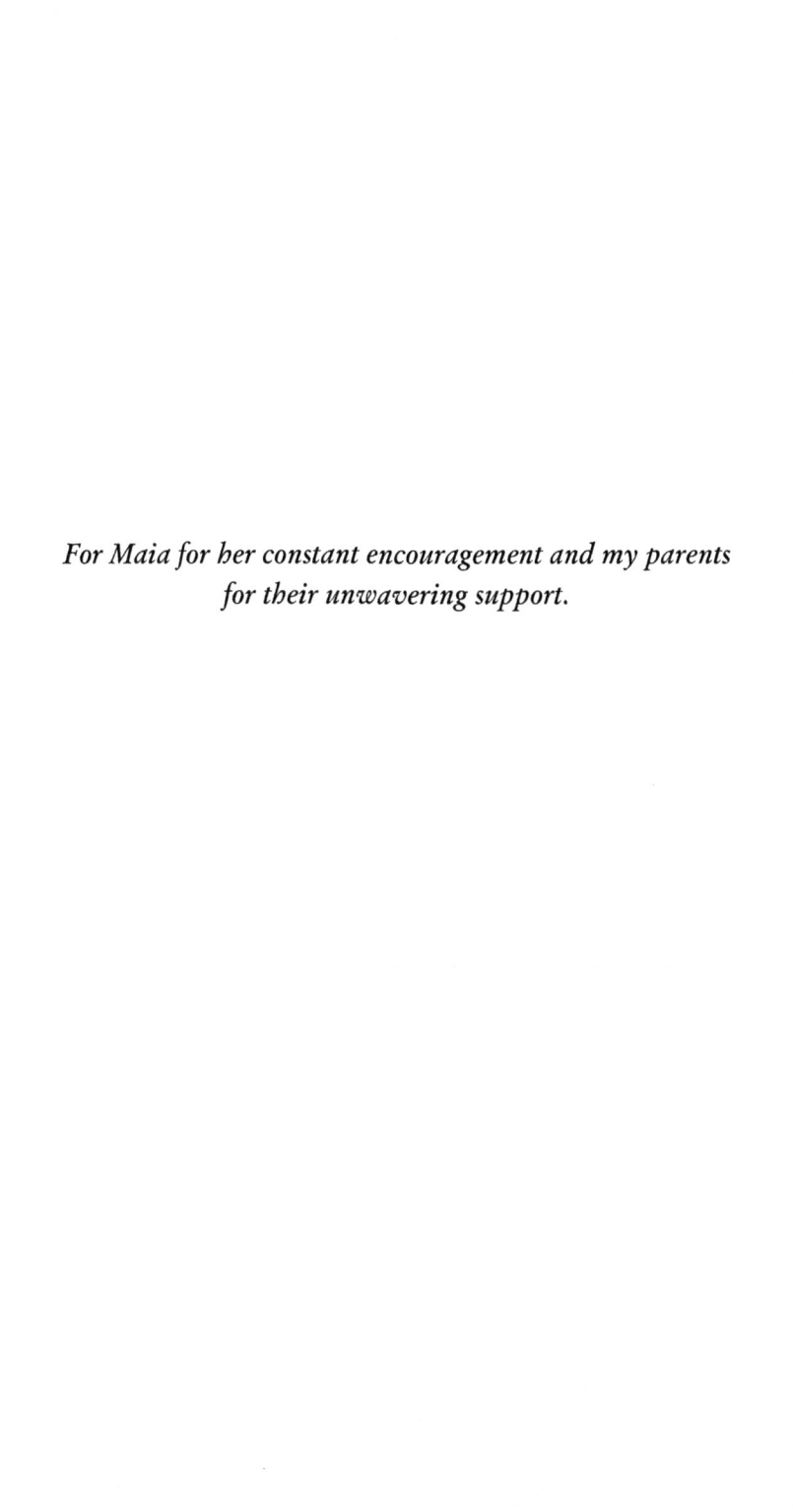

For Maia for her constant encouragement and my parents for their unwavering support.

Place Names

Latin	British	Modern English
Britannia	Albion	Britain
Mona	Ynys Mon	Anglesey
	Din Eidyn	Edinburgh
Eboracum	Cair Eborac	York
	Din Eil	Eildon Hill
Trimontium		Newstead
	Aber Teu	River Tweed
Cilurnum		Chesters, near the village of Walwick
Cambloganna		Castlesteads
Vindolanda		Near the village of Bardon Mill
Cataractonium		Catterick
Segedunum		Wallsend
Banna		Birdoswald
	Din Peldur	Traprain Law
Brocavum		Brougham
Onnum		Halton Chesters
Vercovicium		Housesteads
Brocolitia		Carrawburgh
	Aber Tina	River Tyne
Banovallum		Horncastle
Bremetenacum		Ribchester
	Din Guaire	Bamburgh
	Aber Clut	River Clyde

Descendants of Cunedag

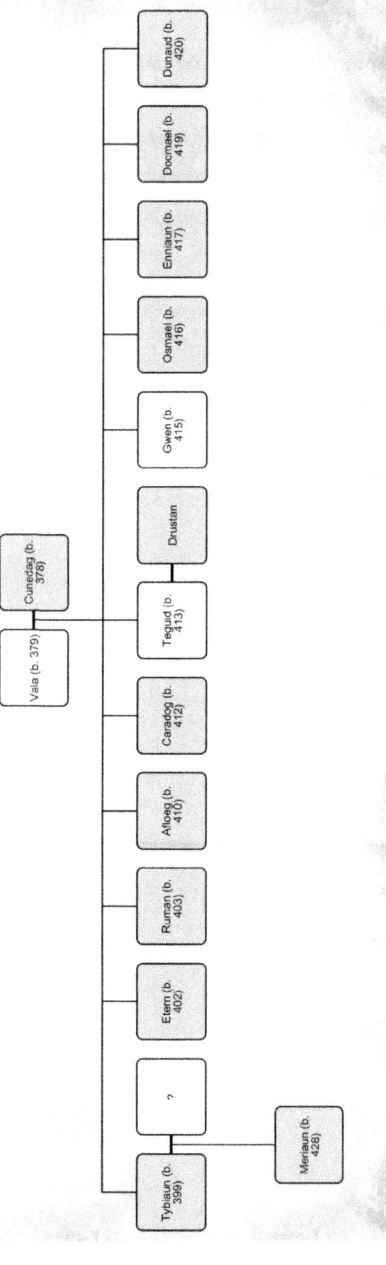

Chapter 1

Spring, 407 A.D.

A damp night hung over the streets of Londinium. It had stopped raining, but the tiled roofs and cobbled streets glistened by the light of the moon and the oil lamps that burned in windows. An unnatural silence dwelled in the streets and alleyways; a silence maintained by threat of violence. Peace held by a thread in the largest town in Britannia. The curfew had closed the wine shops and the brothels, and soldiers trod the cobbles in pairs, daring anybody to leave their homes in the dead of night.

Within the governor's palace on the banks of the River Tamesis, Gratianus, Imperator Semper Augustus, moved down the silent halls, his purple robes hanging from his corpulent body. Four months had passed since he had been proclaimed emperor and every night that he lived to retire to his chambers, he counted as a blessing. His predecessor had not been so lucky nor lasted nearly as long.

Marcus had been a common soldier from Londinium's garrison put forward as the figurehead of the rebellion by a collection of merchants and civil servants which had included Gratianus. It had been a reactionary measure to the fear which swept the diocese like a plague with the news that a massive barbarian horde had invaded Gaul during the last days of 406. It had been a harsh winter, and the river Rhine had frozen from bank to bank, allowing armies of Vandals, Alans and Suebi to walk across and strike at towns and forts within the empire.

It was perceived as a sign of the end of the world by the west and particularly in Britannia. If Gaul fell, they might well be next. Britannia's eastern shores had been plagued by

Germanic tribes for generations as it was and the military strength of the island had been severely reduced by Flavius Stilicho, Rome's magister militum, who had removed many of its soldiers to defend Italy from the Goths several years previously. If the barbarians turned westwards and crossed the channel, the Britons would not be able to hold them off.

So, in a panic, the ruling class of the diocese had plucked a likely soldier from obscurity and draped him in the purple. The plan was to control this simple military man who would be emperor in name only. It had been done before. Magnus Maximus who had led Britannia's troops into Gaul in a disastrous coup was often mentioned by those old enough to remember him. And a hundred years before that, there had been Carausius, who had set himself up as Emperor of Britannia and Gaul and had reinforced the Saxon Shore by building a series of forts along the south-east coast. The island had always been a hotbed of rebellion it seemed, but with Marcus, few had known the true nature of the man they had made one of the most powerful men in the west.

Emperor Marcus's reign had been short and sordid. Until his ascension to the purple, his appetites had been restrained by military life and a meagre salary. Now they were unfettered and all Londinium had suffered as the monster of lust consumed him, the sudden power of his position addling his mind more than the strongest wine. Wives and daughters were raped, property confiscated unjustly and any who protested were executed with brutal military efficiency. For a whole month, the smog of the execution pyres did not dissipate over Londinium until, eventually, those who had elected him had had enough. Marcus was dragged from his litter by an incensed mob, including several angry husbands and fathers, and beaten to death in the forum. Few had tried to save him.

With hindsight, a soldier was perhaps not the right choice for Britannia's emperor, so it fell to Gratianus who had been the treasurer of Britannia's chief province of Maxima Caesariensis to succeed where Marcus had failed. Gratianus had no military background and had spent his life with the clerks in the treasury, overseeing the collection of taxes and managing expenditure. To many of the conspirators who had instigated the rebellion, that made him the perfect choice. The diocese was in dire financial straits, after all. With barbarians holding Gaul in their grip, trade had all but dried up.

Gratianus had done his best to please his fellow conspirators by keeping their taxes low while discreetly raising taxation on those who had failed to show their support. Arrears were collected with ruthlessness where required, but always from those who had little power to do anything about it. It was a delicate game. If he was too harsh, then he might face rebellion from a different quarter; too lenient and the diocese would not have the funds it needed to keep itself running. But Gratianus was a shrewd man with much experience in placing the correct amount of pressure on the financial levers of government and, as such, was a more popular and successful ruler than Marcus had ever been.

Even so, Britannia was on the verge of civil war. Ambrosius Aurelianus, the Comes Britanniarum and highest military commander on the island, had wanted no part of the rebellion in the first place. He was a traditional Theodosian and loyal to the idea of Rome, despite it being a shadow of what it had once been, with a feeble-minded simpleton ruling it from Ravenna.

Aurelianus held the north of Britannia, including the great military town of Eboracum while a subordinate of his, Constantinus, had gone rogue in the south. Constantinus, a common thug risen from the ranks, had set himself up as a military dictator and practically held the commander of the Saxon Shore hostage.

Christ, Jesus! What a mess of everything people made, thought Gratianus as he headed towards the baths. With nearly every soldier in the diocese either pledged to Aurelianus or Constantinus, there were barely enough men to guard Londinium. If the two decided to go to war with each other, Gratianus would simply have to back one and hope he would turn out to be the winner. And he was the emperor for the love of God!

It had been a tiring day, and he longed for the hot steam and the soft touch of that pretty Illyrian slave girl. He wasn't above having his way with the palace slaves and saw in himself no comparison to the debauched rule of his predecessor. Marcus had disgraced himself by violating the daughters of noblemen. Slaves were human chattel and violating them offended no one.

The palace guards snapped to attention as he passed them. At least he still had his bodyguard, though that hadn't saved Marcus in the end. And if either Constantinus or Aurelianus decided to march on Londinium, he would be finished. The only way forward was to play them off against each other and it was to this end that Gratianus intended to apply his mind while his body relaxed in the baths.

After steaming himself in the laconicum, he pondered the problem. Feeling suitably hot to the point of discomfort, he got up, the sweat running down his flabby body in rivulets. He made his way into the cooler tepidarium where Vibiana, the Illyrian slave girl, waited with oil and strigil.

She wore a short tunica which hung from her slender shoulders by the thinnest of straps and the steam of the place made it cling to her damp breasts magnificently. She stood with her head bowed, awaiting her emperor to lie face down on the bench. He did so, heaving himself up and she drizzled olive oil over his broad back and began rubbing it into his fleshy folds.

Gratianus closed his eyes and enjoyed the firm and well-trained hands of the slave rub the tense knots from his shoulders. Afterwards, he would bend her over the bench and take her as he had done many times before. Then, a cup of wine before bed; the perfect way to unwind after a taxing day.

He opened his eyes as he heard raised voices in the corridors beyond the baths. Who dared to raise his voice in the emperor's palace as if it were the fish market down on the docks? Somebody was shouting something, and he couldn't make out the words. It seemed to be a proclamation of some sort. He closed his eyes again. The guards would deal with it and then he would make the troublemaker wish he had never been born on the morrow.

"I must fetch more oil, *Domine*," Vibiana said, bowing out of the room.

She was gone before Gratianus began to suspect treachery, his usually sharp mind sluggish by the lateness of the hour and the heat of the baths.

There was a clattering of sandals in the changing room next door. The doors to the baths were supposed to be locked. Who had opened them? Four of his bodyguard entered the tepidarium, swords drawn.

"What's going on?" Gratianus demanded, sitting upright, his head spinning with the sudden movement. "What's that noise outside and why are your blades drawn?"

He understood at once as they approached him without answer. In a panic, he slid off the bench and ran as fast as his fat frame could allow, into the caldarium. There was a door there that led into another set of changing rooms from which he might escape into the hallway beyond. He hurried over to it and yanked on the handle. It was locked! He spun around to see the soldiers approach. *Trapped!*

He turned to run. The floor was wet. He slipped. His feet shot out from under him and his massive bulk slammed down on the floor heavily. The back of his head smacked against the tiles, and he saw stars for a brief moment. When they cleared, he saw the helmed heads of the four soldiers standing over him, sword tips pointed down at him.

"Long live Emperor Constantinus!" one of them said before he thrust his sword point down into Gratianus's belly.

The usurped emperor gasped as the blade sank in. He was betrayed! He was undone! That bastard Constantinus had somehow outmanoeuvred him, yet he could never have done it alone. Who, of his co-conspirators had betrayed him? These questions flitted through his mind, almost as a distraction to the sharp pain in his gut.

Once the first blow had been struck, the other three soldiers overcame their nerves and stabbed down with their own blades, each of them wetting their swords in the emperor's blood. As with Caesar, no man must fail to redden his blade else he appear less guilty than his comrades. And, like a thousand tyrants before him, Gratianus died to make way for his successor.

From the doorway to the tepidarium, Vibiana the slave watched as the royal blood seeped across the floor, running between the tiles in a geometric pattern of crimson. A small smile touched her lips.

Thus always to tyrants.

Chapter 2

A great cheer rose from the horde of warriors who assailed the main gate, accompanied by the sound of splintering wood. King Cunedag raised his sword into the air as a triumphant and encouraging gesture to his men, joining their enthusiasm at this turning point in the siege. The main gate was down. With access to the lower enclosure, they could marshal their forces and prepare to take the upper part of the fortress where the enemy leadership was gathered.

The twin peaks of the great volcanic rock of Alt Clut towered above the attacking warband, its eastern peak crowned by a spiked palisade. Steep rock on all sides, the deep cleft in the middle was the only way up. This stronghold of the Attacotti had been a thorn in the side of the Britons for decades. Originally the royal seat of the Damnonii tribe, the invading Attacotti from Erin had taken it for themselves and forged a new Gaelic kingdom on British shores. Now, it was time to drive the invaders from the great rock and reclaim it for the Britons.

"In, you wolves!" Cunedag urged his men. "In and at them!"

There was a surge forward as hundreds of warriors pressed and shoved their way in through the shattered gates, trampling the arrow-riddled corpses of those who had fallen in the siege.

The boats beached on the seaweed-strewn sands at their backs, the leadership of the attackers watched as the lower enclosure fell to their men and Cunedag dearly wished he was in the thick of the fighting, not sitting astride his horse and watching it from afar.

"King Cunedag!" Cunlop bellowed over the cheering din. "Won't our men be vulnerable to arrows from the middle enclosure? Wouldn't it be better to hold them back until we are ready to storm the rock?"

Cunedag shook his head. "The rock face is too steep above the lower enclosure. Those Gaelic scum won't be able to loose arrows down on them without losing their footing into the bargain. Once they begin ascending the cleft, that's when every man will need a shield over his head for they'll rain rocks upon us."

Cunlop nodded. He was a young nobleman and inexperienced in war but, once the Attacotti were driven from these shores, he would become king of Alt Clut and the surrounding area. Cunlop was descended from the old Damnonii kings through a distant strain and had been chosen as the figurehead of this war against the Gaels. Long had the Attacotti raided the borders of their neighbouring tribes and stolen their cattle and their women, but it had taken the urging of Ambrosius Aurelianus, the commander of the Roman military below the Wall to go to war with them.

Cunedag and his Votadini warriors wouldn't have been able to oust the Attacotti alone and the neighbouring Novantae and the Selgovae were too weak to be of much help. So, a Roman vexillatio of six hundred soldiers headed by Cunlop had marched north to join the Votadini and smash the Gaels. Cunlop wore the cuirass and plumed helmet of a Roman officer but hadn't shown much in the way of tactical sense during the year-long campaign against the Attacotti. It had fallen to Cunedag to plan much of their fighting westwards, and it was down to him that only the royal seat held out against them now.

But it was in Rome's interest to place such a man on a northern throne, despite his lack of military sense. Cunlop was a Christian and had spent his twenty-odd years in comfort below the Wall growing accustomed to the Roman way of life. The lowland tribes north of the Wall formed something of a buffer between Rome's border and the more savage Picts who lived in the mountains further north. This was the abandoned province of Valentia which had once lain between the two Roman walls. Now it fell to tribal allies like Cunedag to hold it for them with occasional financial and military aid from men like Aurelianus.

The sound of slaughter reached them from behind the walls of the lower enclosure as the last defenders who had not had time to reach higher ground fell to the spears of the attackers.

"Victory!" said Cunlop.

"The first stage of victory," Cunedag corrected him. "We still have our work cut out for us in taking the rest of the fortress."

"I still think we could have just starved them out."

"That would have taken months," Cunedag replied. "They have enough food and water to outlast us. Our forces require constant feeding, and we have already stripped the surrounding lands bare. We are now reliant on meat and grain being shipped down to us by boat and already that is taking too long."

Cunlop pondered this in silence and Cunedag rode forward without saying anything further to him. The young nobleman irritated him but, he supposed, he would be a better neighbour than some Attacotti chieftain. They just had to get his royal backside onto the throne atop the rock.

His men parted to let him pass and he rode in through the smashed gates and surveyed the scene. The lower enclosure was mostly livestock pens, workshops and storage huts. None had been torched or looted as his men had been given strict orders to keep the destruction to a minimum. This was to become a British fortress once more and Cunlop had no desire to rule over a pile of ashes. Dead Attacotti warriors littered the ground and, looking up the cleft between the two great rocks, Cunedag could see the palisade at the top which guarded the gap, the middle enclosure beyond straddling the twin peaks. Ordinarily a series of winches, baskets and platforms were used to hoist men and supplies up the steep rockface but all those had been reeled in. The only way up there now was a hard climb. The slain Attacotti warriors had been left to die defending the lower enclosure. Such loyalty was both admirable and frightening.

He saw the flash of a helmed head as somebody peered over the top of the palisade before ducking out of sight. This was going to be a hard assault, and he knew that he would lose many men. His face grim, he returned to the main gate where Cunlop was congratulating the warriors who had taken the lower enclosure. How many of these poor fools would survive the next assault?

"Find whatever food you can in these buildings," Cunedag said to Murcho, his younger brother who was also his penteulu; chief of his warband. "Get our men fed and watered but keep them clear of those brewhouses." He nodded in the direction of the small, thatched huts where the smell of honey and heather could be detected, a sure sign of mead production. "I don't want our lads drunk until we have taken this fortress."

Murcho nodded and then began bellowing orders to the warriors. He had been a meek boy in his youth, but eager to earn praise and had always served his brothers well, first Brude and then Cunedag. Now, having seen over twenty-five winters, he was a good leader of men, fierce in battle and well-respected. Cunedag couldn't be prouder or ask for a finer penteulu.

Once the looted stores had been shared out and the wounded carried away to the boats on the riverbank, Cunedag called a meeting of his captains to discuss their plan of attack.

"Storming the cleft is going to be costly," he explained. "I want as many shields as possible brought forward and given to the men who will be making the climb first. This will be conquest by way of attrition, and it is important that we do not fall back or slow down our assault or all is for naught. We keep sending men up the rockface until we establish a foothold on the palisade. Once that is done, it is simply a matter of holding it while the rest of our warriors climb up."

"Just like storming the walls of any fortress," added Murcho with as much bravado as he could manage.

"Aye, a fortress wall two-hundred feet high!" added one of the officers of the vexillatio.

"Not got the balls for the job?" asked Murcho, testily. These Roman auxiliary troops were good at discipline and fighting shoulder to shoulder on the field of battle, but they lacked the Celtic spirit of hurling themselves into danger in the pursuit of honour.

"We're here to help Cunlop win his throne," the Roman replied testily, "not throw away our lives on a suicide mission."

There was outrage from the Votadini warriors at this and much name calling from both sides.

"Enough," Cunedag barked, commanding silence. "Our own men will storm the cleft with the Romans ready to climb up after them once the palisade is secured."

"We're sending our own lads up first?" Murcho protested.

"They're the better climbers," said Cunedag. "And we can hardly expect the same kind of ferocity from men who are in a strange land merely to follow orders and receive their pay."

The officer who had piped up looked affronted at the implied insult to his men but said nothing. With little further to discuss, the meeting adjourned and preparations were made for the assault. Every shield that was in good repair was brought to the foot of the cleft where the Votadini warriors were marshalling. Iron hooks on ropes were handed out and, contrary to his earlier orders, Cunedag made sure the men in the front lines were given a measure of mead to bolster their courage. He was asking them to climb into the jaws of death and they knew it.

But the warrior culture of the north prized courage above all things. That was the stuff great songs were made of; men marching to war and storming hill forts, climbing to the homes of the gods themselves to snatch victory with bloodied hands. And, as they drank their mead and beat their shields with their spears in an effort to summon every drop of courage, a druid from one of the coastal clans told them of how Bran of ancient legend had stormed Erin to free his sister, Branwen, who suffered terribly under her husband, the high king of the Gaels. War between the island of the Britons and the island of the Gaels was as old as the Dawntime, it seemed.

Cunedag wished old Gonar the high druid of his own clan was there. He'd tell them such stories that would make them be ashamed not to hurl themselves into the afterlife of Annun without a second thought. But Gonar was very old now and had trouble walking, much less marching with a teulu to war.

With a blowing of horns and a last great cheer, the brave warriors charged the foot of the cleft, scrambling up the shallow, grassy slope with their shields on their backs and hurling themselves at the black rock, bare feet and strong limbs grasping for purchase.

The Romans watched with awe as their comrades shot up the rock like cats up a tree, their lack of armour and lives lived on the wild, rugged moors and hills north of the Wall making them well-suited to the task. But they were not the only ones watching and, as Cunedag spotted the helmed heads of the enemy massing on the palisade above, he yelled out a warning to his men.

"Shields! Raise your shields!"

The painted linden boards rimmed with iron were unslung from backs and held overhead just as the first rocks and javelins came hurtling down from above. Cunedag winced as he saw first one, then another of his men dislodged from their positions as the missiles slammed into their shields, knocking them from the rockface to tumble to their deaths. A third man, struck by one of the falling warriors, joined them in their plumet to the rocks below.

"Keep climbing!" Cunedag roared. "Keep going! Do not stop!"

If only the top of the palisade was low enough to reach with an arrow, he'd give his men some covering volleys, but Alt Clut had stood as a stronghold for centuries precisely because it was damn near impregnable. It burned in his gut that he must stand and watch helplessly as his men inched further and further up the cleft, all the while rocks and spears were launched at them from their destination.

More men fell by the time they were close enough to swing their grappling hooks at the top of the palisade. They spread themselves across the cleft along the foot of the palisade to attack it from as many points as possible. Loops of rope went spiralling up and as soon as they caught, the defenders rushed to dislodge them, reaching over the parapet to cut through the ropes with their knives.

One of the men who had climbed with a bow and quiver across his back, lodged himself into a niche in the rock, bracing himself with his feet, and unslung his bow. Nocking an arrow, he let fly at one of the exposed defenders. The arrow sank into the man's neck, and he fell back with a cry. Cunedag grinned. Now those bastards would think twice before leaning out over the parapet.

His men started to climb, quickly and agilely, each of them desperate to reach the top before some Attacotti tribesman hacked through their rope. The bowman on the rocks below loosed arrow after arrow at any who poked their head up from cover, killing several with his deadly shafts.

"I will give that bowman his weight in silver when all this is done," said Cunedag, turning to Cunlop. "Are your men ready to climb once we have secured the top?"

"As ready as they can be," the king-to-be replied. "Though I don't have a head for heights myself."

"We'll arrange a basket to be lowered for you," said Cunedag. "We can't have the new king of Alt Clut breaking his neck before he is even crowned."

"You don't seem to mind risking your own neck, Cunedag," the young nobleman replied. "Are you really going up with the next wave?"

"I wouldn't have it any other way," Cunedag replied. "I won't ask my men to do something I would not dare myself and, had it been my own way, I would have climbed up with the first wave."

If there had been any intended criticism levelled at Cunlop, Cunedag left his side before he could respond and joined his men clustering at the foot of the cleft.

The first wave of attackers had started to reach the top and the fighting could be seen from the ground as men moved back and forth atop the palisade to the sound of clashing steel. The men on the ground were as eager as starving wolves to join the fray and none more so than Cunedag.

"Up and after our brave comrades, friends!" he bellowed. "Let not the sacrifices of the fallen be wasted! Climb, you dogs! Climb and avenge our countrymen!"

The Votadini warriors did not need telling twice and they launched themselves at the rocks, scrambling up with eager blades at their sides and grim determination written on their faces. Cunedag did not wait in line, pushing his way through the throng to race his own men to the top. Hand over hand he climbed until the ropes dangling from the palisade were within reach. Seizing one, he hauled himself up, feet spread wide on the timbers of the palisade as he walked his way up, grasping their spiked tips and heaving himself over.

He drew his sword as soon as he gained his feet on the wooden walkway behind the parapet. It was his old Roman spatha from his days as a decurion in a cavalry unit posted on the Wall. It had served him well over the years, its blade well-notched and worn by the grindstone. It was ostensibly a cavalry sword, longer than the old-fashioned gladius, but it worked just as well when its wielder was on foot. As soon as an Attacotti tribesman ran screaming towards Cunedag, he brought the blade up in a two-handed sweep which disembowelled the Gael and sent him tumbling from the palisade with his innards spilling loose.

His men spread out along the wall to give room to the ceaseless stream of Votadini tribesmen who were scrambling up, shortly followed by the Roman auxiliaries. The defenders were pushed back and retreated towards the roundhouses. Cunedag grinned. They had the palisade. The middle enclosure was as good as won.

He jumped down from the wall to the grassy dip where the homes and workshops of the lower-class tribesmen lay spread between the two peaks. He led the charge against what remained of the defenders, hacking down any who dared stand against them. More attackers swarmed over the palisade and the Roman auxiliaries quickly formed a shield wall which prickled with spears on their right flank.

What was left of the Attacotti defenders gave up and ran to the gates of the upper enclosure on the eastern peak, clearly hoping to make their last stand there now that the middle enclosure was lost. The Votadini pursued them until a volley of arrows sailed forth from the walls of the enclosure.

"Fall back!" Cunedag bellowed. "Get out of range of the walls!"

He didn't want to begin the assault on the final portion of the fortress until every warrior of his was over the palisade and a proper strategy could be formed. As it was, the day was won and the Attacotti chieftains must be in a blind panic, trapped on the highest peak with the rest of their so-called impregnable fortress in enemy hands.

Chapter 3

The trumpets blared as the ships from Rutupiae docked and the mooring lines were pulled taut. Londinium's harbour was garlanded with flowers and the crowds roared in delight as the troops clattered down the gangway.

First came the infantry cohorts, their helms polished, and armour scrubbed clean, freshly painted shields with the Chi-Ro symbol an eggshell blue matching the clear afternoon sky. Then came the sagittari with their Hunnish bows over their shoulders followed by the cavalry on sleek Arabian stallions. Such was the show of military might on display that some in Londinium might be forgiven for worrying that there wasn't a soldier left to guard the Saxon Shore.

All the town had thronged to see their new emperor disembark from his ship and their voices cheered as one in a great cacophony when he appeared astride a white stallion. He was a tall man, with dark curly hair and a handsome face. A veteran who had worked his way up from the ranks, he was in his forties now and had the bearing of a man well-seasoned in battle, no doubt with the scars to prove it.

Constantinus looked like a man who had been *made* to rule an empire and was a far more favourable choice with the people than that dull old *municeps* who had preceded him. Gratianus had been chosen by merchants and financiers with the express aim of safeguarding their interests. Constantinus was a soldier who had claimed the purple by right of arms and was what the frightened populace truly wanted; a warrior to protect them from the barbarians across the channel.

And, as if a reminder of what they faced, behind Constantinus came the *foederati*; Saxon mercenaries, bribed into fighting their own countrymen, although if what people said was true, what Rome called 'Saxons' were in fact made up of a dozen different tribal components including Angles, Jutes, Danes, Franks and Friesians. They were flaxen-haired for the most part and blue-eyed with much facial hair which, along with their breeches, instantly marked them out as barbarians. They wore mail and scale armour, and some had helms with eye-loops and cheek guards. All carried at their belts, the long, broken-backed knives called 'saexes' which allegedly gave the Saxons their name.

The street that led up from the harbour to the crumbling forum and basilica was lined with cheering people, held back by members of the town's meagre garrison. Unmarried women tossed petals from balconies as the column of soldiers passed by and Constantinus waved gallantly at the young women, no doubt winning many a heart that day.

On the steps of the forum, a gathering of the province's leaders watched the approaching column with sour faces. They were dressed in their robes of state, a sign that they were willing to play ball with this new usurper and accept him as their emperor, though they were loath to do so. These were the men who had draped their fellow politician Gratianus in purple robes and had thought to benefit greatly under his rule. Four months was all that had been allowed to them before the blades of his own bodyguard, bribed by somebody loyal to Constantinus, had ended his reign.

"Well, the people have their emperor, once more," said Silvanus, the treasurer who had taken on Gratianus's duties. "A soldier again. Let's just hope he is a better ruler than Marcus."

"Marcus was a thug from the ranks," said one of the younger politicians, a tall, thin man with dark hair. This was Vitalinus, praeses of Maxima Caesariensis and ruler of

Londinium. "This fellow is at least used to commanding power. And the people do seem to like him."

"The people don't know what's good for them," said Victorinus, the vicarius of Britannia. "That's why they need emperors and good ones at that, not soldiers showing off. Gratianus, for all his faults, was a man who understood how a province is run."

"Worried this new fellow might not take to you?" Vitalinus asked with a sideways smile at Victorinus. As the chief overseer of the diocese, the vicarius reported directly to the emperor and ruled in his stead when he was away. Victorinus had been appointed by the conspirators when Marcus had been proclaimed emperor as a way of keeping a steady hand on the despot's rule. His authority under Gratianus had been somewhat obsolete given the late emperor's focus on domestic policy but that might all change with another military man wearing the purple.

"None of our positions are safe," muttered Silvanus. "This Constantinus is little more than a renegade warlord. God alone knows how he'll shake things up."

That sobering thought quietened the tongues of the politicians as much as the approach of the emperor himself and they looked on with grim faces as he neared the steps of the forum.

Privately, Vitalinus was most pleased with the change in rulership. Gratianus had been an insufferable buffoon. His overinflated sense of importance at being proclaimed emperor had not led to such sadistic debauchery as Marcus of course, but it had been intolerable, nonetheless. He had even commandeered the praeses' palace – Vitalinus's own residence – as his own. He hoped that Constantinus, like Marcus, would prefer the more familiar military environment of the fort in the north-west corner of the town.

Constantinus dismounted at the foot of the steps and the congregation of politicians bowed as he ascended to meet them.

"A fine turnout to greet me," said the new emperor. "And I speak for the plebs as well as your fine selves. I particularly enjoyed the flowers. It is a marvel how you were able to gather so many summer blossoms at such short notice."

"We have Vitalinus to thank for that, Caesar," said Silvanus. "His efficiency is matched only by your own in summoning so many troops and having them prepared for a parade at the drop of a cap."

"I have only to stamp my feet, as Pompeius once said," said Constantinus with a smile. "As soon as word reached the Saxon Shore that the tyrant Gratianus had been murdered, my troops knew that they must strike while the iron was hot else some other fool got ideas. I was proclaimed emperor that very night and we began our preparations to depart the following morning."

"Your resourcefulness is a credit to you and a great encouragement to your subjects in these troubled times," crooned Victorinus.

"We stand on the brink of oblivion," said Constantinus. "Something Gratianus did not fully understand. He was content to hole himself up in the palace yonder and count coins while I shall prepare Britannia for war."

And, with those portent-laden words, the new emperor left the politicians and headed through the forum towards the basilica, his personal guard following him closely.

Bishop Lentilus and his gaggle of priests and deacons waited by the doors to the basilica which had once been the largest and most impressive structure of its kind north of the Alps. It had been partially torn down during the Roman reoccupation of Britannia after the rebellions of Carausius and Allectus and had been repaired as best as funds would allow and was still used for law courts and other large gatherings. Bishop Lentilus had his eye on it for the location of a new church.

Constantinus addressed his subjects in the apse of the building where the afternoon sun shone down through the high, arched windows. The most throne-like chair had been found for him to sit in while the others sat on simple folding chairs in a semi-circle around him, aping the Roman senate of antiquity.

"And what of Ambrosius Aurelianus?" asked one of the politicians.

"What of good Aurelianus?" asked the emperor.

"He holds the north just as you hold the south and he has been against the election of our own emperors since the start. One thing this diocese will not survive is a civil war."

"God knows, that is the last thing I wish for Britannia," Constantinus replied. "Aurelianus is a good soldier but a bit of a stick-in-the-mud when it comes to politics."

There was nervous laughter at this.

"But I am confident that it will not come to war between us," Constantinus continued. "I have no plans to remove Aurelianus from his position as Comes, in fact I require him to continue to do his duty. Somebody will need to defend these shores while I am in Gaul fighting the barbarians and I can think of nobody better than Aurelianus."

There was an outcry at this as the politicians who were so keen to please their new emperor found themselves confronted with something even they could not accept.

"You intend to sail to Gaul?" asked Silvanus the treasurer. "To war with the barbarians?"

"I do indeed, Silvanus," the emperor replied.

"And how many troops will you be taking with you?" asked Victorinus.

"As many as can be spared."

"But we are woefully undefended as it is," Victorinus replied. "Begging Caesar's pardon, but the fine display of military might we saw today is scarcely enough to defend the Saxon Shore as it is, and if you remove most of them to the continent, we will be wide open to attack. Then there are the Picts and the Scots to consider. Aurelianus and the Dux Britanniarum have been able to keep them behind the Wall these few years past, but again, Caesar plans to strip the garrisons, leaving us open in the north. We will be overrun on all sides!"

"My dear friends," said Constantinus with a patronising smile, "you fail to grasp the military sense in my plan. The best way to defend these shores is to never let the enemy set foot on them. By taking the fight across the channel, we can crush these savages while they are still celebrating their sacking of the Gaulish towns. And, as for the Picts, I will not be *stripping the garrisons*, as you put it. I will leave enough troops for Aurelianus and the Dux to continue to defend the northern frontier with the help of Britannia's allies in the north. Even as we speak, a new king – a Romanised, Christian king – is being placed on the throne of Alt Clut and the Scottish kingdom there is no more. That is one less enemy to deal with and I haven't been emperor two days yet."

"But this campaign …" inquired Silvanus. "How will it all be paid for? Already the property owners are overtaxed."

"Peace must be paid for," said Constantinus with steely eyes. "In the meantime, I would like us to turn our attention to the billeting of my men and the setting up of the imperial residence." He turned to look at Vitalinus. "I had considered using the principia in the fort rather than your fine palace, praeses, so you may rest assured that I will not be turfing you out of your bed as Gratianus did."

Vitalinus smiled at him. "I am most grateful, Caesar," he replied. "And I will make sure the fort is ready for you and your men immediately."

Later that evening, Constantinus visited Vitalinus in the governor's palace for wine and talk. The streets of Londinium thronged with late-night revellers. Constantinus had repealed the curfew and ordered the distribution of free wine for the populace. He wanted the plebs to celebrate their new emperor and drink his health.

"Today went rather well," said Vitalinus as he poured them both some wine in the privacy of a private chamber in the palace where even the slaves had been dismissed. "I think you suitably impressed both the plebs and the nobles."

"It's amazing what a bit of armour polish and a quick show of resolution can do," Constantinus replied as he accepted the cup of wine and lounged back on his couch. He was still wearing his ceremonial armour. It had been a long and trying day, but Londinium was secure, his men were billeted in the fort and his reign was off to a good start.

"I do believe those old fools in the basilica nearly soiled themselves when you announced your plans to invade Gaul. It really was quite amusing."

"Amusing or no, I would have thought that they had been better prepared for such a notion. Did they really expect me to sit on my throne here in Londinium and spend my days collecting taxes as Gratianus did?"

"Perhaps some of them had a hope that the purple might mellow a military man. Even Marcus entertained no ideas of expanding his borders. Supple flesh and the sting of wine constituted the limits of his empire."

"And my borders *will* be expanded with this invasion of Gaul," said Constantinus. "Once I have successfully driven the barbarians back across the Rhine, I will rule an empire larger than that of Carausius or Maximus. Honorius will be forced to recognise me as co-emperor of the West."

"Quite so, Caesar," said Vitalinus. He noticed his emperor's cup had run dry and leaned forward to refill it.

"And the bodyguard of the late Gratianus have been taken care of, I assume?" Constantinus asked him.

"Paid off and reassigned to various corners of your new empire," Vitalinus replied. "One had the gall to ask for more money with blackmail on his mind. He is currently feeding the fish at the bottom of the Tamesis."

"Very good. I am grateful for the loyalty of such men but would prefer not to have the killers of emperors around me."

"You are quite safe here, I assure you," the praeses replied. "Nothing happens in Londinium without my say so and the same can be said for much of Maxima Caesariensis."

"And the rest of the diocese?" Constantinus asked, showing an uncertainty that had been entirely absent from the confident whirlwind of a man who had swept into Londinium earlier that day.

"Surely you do not fear revolt?" asked Vitalinus with a faint hint of mockery in his voice.

"Not in the south," Constantinus replied. "The people love me and have long been grateful for my protection. Besides, the Comes of the Saxon Shore is terrified of me. No, it is the north that concerns me for it is an unknown quantity."

"You speak of Aurelianus."

"Oh, I have no concern that Aurelianus will try to usurp me while I am gone. He's not the type to make a grab for the purple."

"Indeed no."

"But how will he take the news of my election?"

"He has already suffered two usurpers both of which were wise enough to recognise him as Britannia's northern protector. When he learns that you too wish to keep him on as Comes Britanniarum, he will reluctantly carry on under your rule. He knows that the north will be lost under any other man, yet he is too much the loyalist to use his military strength to snatch power for himself. And in any case, he owes much of his success to me."

Constantinus smiled weakly. He was under no illusions that Vitalinus had long played the patron of both Aurelianus and himself, supporting both sides of what might have turned into an ugly civil war. It was only due to their differences in political temperament that had seen him elected to the purple and not Aurelianus who was far too loyal to Rome to accept such a thing. *More fool him*, he thought, before taking another deep gulp of wine.

"Threats to your reign originate much closer to home, I'm afraid," Vitalinus went on.

"Oh? How so?"

"You will need a new vicarius, one who is more loyal to you than Victorinus."

"That weaselly little fellow who was practically tripping over himself to please me in the basilica?" said Constantinus with a frown.

"He can't be trusted," said Vitalinus. "He belongs to that enclave of merchants and moneymen who quickly elected Gratianus before Marcus's corpse was cut down from the gibbet. And those money-grubbers are none too pleased to have a soldier giving them orders once more. Victorinus will serve their interests and not yours. May I put forward Chrysanthus as a suitable replacement?"

"The tribune?"

"Quite. He is that rare breed of solider who understands politics and he would make a very good overseer while you are away on the continent ... with my guidance of course."

"Of course. Very well. I leave it to you to make the arrangements. Chrysanthus will have my approval."

"And I would also like to suggest giving Londinium's basilica to Bishop Lentilus. His congregations have made do with a rather ramshackle church until now and I think it would be more fitting that the Bishop of Londinium minister to his flock in something a little grander under your new rule."

"No doubt favours are owed to good Bishop Lentilus," said Constantinus with a smile.

"I would not bore Caesar with the dull details," said Vitalinus. "Needless to say, an emperor needs the church's support as much as the army's."

"As a Christian I can appreciate that," Constantinus replied with a sigh as he swilled the remains of his wine around in his cup. "But as a divine emperor, I thoroughly resent it."

"Understandable," said Vitalinus. "But certain formalities must be upheld."

"Then the bishop shall have his new church."

"Excellent! Now, let us put aside the taxing duties of forging a new empire and celebrate a little. For what good is ruling the world if one cannot enjoy its fruits?"

He clapped his hands and, through a side door, a slave in a very short tunica entered, her face brightly painted, and hair parted in the middle to fall in loose curls on either side. She was perfumed and the scent of her carried across the chamber to tantalise and arouse Constantinus's wine-dulled senses.

"Vibiana here is expertly trained in pleasuring a man," Vitalinus said. "An Illyrian. I have had her in my service for several years now. I give her to you as a gift, Caesar, to mark your ascension to the purple."

Vibiana sank down onto the couch next to the emperor and placed a delicate hand on the hammered pectoral of his muscle cuirass.

"You are too kind, Vitalinus ..." he mumbled, utterly distracted by the deep-brown of the woman's eyes and the smoothness of her limbs as they coiled around his neck.

"Oh, please," said Vitalinus as he watched the couple with a glint in his eye. "The pleasure is all mine."

Chapter 4

"Rain hell upon them!" Cunedag roared as the arrows and slingstones streaked through the air from both directions.

The men atop the wall of the upper enclosure clustered above the main gate and launched everything they had at the attackers who ran up the steep slope, under the cover of shields and missiles from the Roman sagittarii and the Votadini slingers and bowmen.

The battering ram, which had been assembled from the timbers of one of the roundhouses in the middle enclosure, had been hauled up the side of the eastern peak, assailed by the defenders every step of the way. Now, it slammed against the gates, its sharpened tip, blackened and hardened by fire, crunching deep into the wood, splintering the iron-bound stakes.

Rocks tumbled down onto the upraised shields which protected the men carrying the ram from leather straps nailed to its side while they continued to pound away at the gate. A volley of arrows from the Romans thudded into both timbers and flesh atop the gate, knocking back the defenders and easing some of the heat off the ram team.

But the assault on the main gate was a diversion. The focus of the defenders was drawn to the ram and the clusters of howling tribesmen and stern-faced Romans who waited, just out of range farther down the hill for the gate to come down so they might charge the breach. None saw the small band of Votadini warriors who crept along the knife edge of the rockface at the foot of the enclosure's southern wall, their bare feet gripping the rock with the strength of hands as they worked their way along.

Murcho led them, a team of twenty men armed with grappling hooks and a steely determination to break the defenders' hold on the main gates. Cunedag had reluctantly dispatched his younger brother on this dangerous mission as he had not wanted to hurl his men against the walls in another bout of attrition which would claim more lives than it had to. But he dearly wished to be leading the men himself.

Glancing up at the wattle parapet atop the drystone wall, Murcho looked for any sign of enemy tribesmen passing overhead. He cursed. It would be impossible to see if twenty warriors awaited them atop the wall. They would be climbing up blind and trusting to Modron, the Great Mother, to protect them.

Then he remembered how their men had bravely hauled themselves up the cleft while the Attacotti had hurled down stones and spears at them and felt a touch of shame at the fear in his gut. Like his brother the king, he must inspire his men with courage. He was their penteulu, the chief of all Cunedag's warriors, and if their men had scaled a wall twice this height and under worse circumstances, then, by all the gods, he would clamber up this wall no matter what awaited them at the top.

"Here is as good a point as any," he said to his men, and they began to uncoil the grappling hooks from their belts.

Spreading themselves out, they braced themselves on the narrow ledge, the two-hundred-foot drop inches from their toes. Spinning their hooks, they let them fly at the top of the wattle parapet. They were well-practiced, and the hooks caught to a man. After giving his a tug to test its hold, Murcho began to haul himself up, his men quickly following his lead.

Like spiders they climbed the wall which, in contrast to the wooden palisade of the middle enclosure, provided ample footholds in between the stones and they reached the parapet with ease. Poking his head above the wattle, Murcho glanced left and right along the rampart. He grinned. All the defenders were clustered above the main gate. There was not a single sentry on any other part of the wall.

It was a simple but tried and tested plan and the story of how his brother and his Roman cavalrymen had taken back the fort of Cilurnum on the Wall nearly ten years previously inspired them all. Every fort had its weakness, and the game was to find it and exploit it.

Murcho and his men scrambled over the parapet and sank to their haunches on the stone walkway. Down in the upper enclosure, warriors hurried towards the gates bearing timbers to brace them against the blows of the battering ram. Women and the elderly cowered in the doorways to their roundhouses and children bawled in terror.

"The spears, quickly!" Murcho said to his men.

The bundle of ash shafts tipped with iron heads had been carried on the back of one of the strongest climbers and was quicky unrolled and the deadly weapons handed out. With such spears, they hoped to charge the warriors atop the gate and keep them at arm's length for long enough for the battering ram to complete its work. It would be a hot few minutes, but once the gates were down, they would have all the rcinforcements they needed.

They hurried along the wall, spears lowered and shields unslung from their backs, three warriors wide. Murcho was in the front line. Cunedag might have to keep his royal person safe in battle, but, as penteulu, Murcho wasn't about to march at the rear.

A shout from ground level alerted the defenders atop the gate that the wall had been breached and several on their left flank turned to meet the oncoming attack. None of them had shields. They had been propped up against the parapet so they had their hands free to hurl rocks down on the ram team.

"Albion!" Murcho yelled, bellowing the war cry of the Britons as they slammed into the left flank of the Gaels.

Spears slid into flesh as the Attacotti screamed and desperately tried to defend themselves with swords and long knives against men who could skewer them at a distance. They fell back, trying to avoid the jabbing spear tips while those at the back hurried to find spears of their own with which to thrust at this surprise contingent who had snuck up on them.

All the while, the gate was left undefended and the battering ram slammed into its broken timbers with all the more gusto.

Cunedag beamed as he saw Murcho lead the charge against the enemy atop the gates. "By Taran's thunder, he's done it!" he bellowed, drawing his sword. "Every one of you prepare to charge as soon as that gate is down!"

The warriors and Roman soldiers tensed themselves and gripped their spears, ready to hurl themselves through the gates and into the final Attacotti bastion that held out against them. This was it; the war could be over in moments.

With a splintering crack, the gates finally gave up their strength and one of them tumbled inwards while the other hung on snapped hinges. The Britons gave up a great cheer and, as one, ran up the grassy slope towards the gap in the enemy defences.

The ram team hastily hauled their tool of victory out of the path of the attackers and, plucking up their weapons, joined the charge. The men atop the gate abandoned the fight against Murcho and his warriors and ran down the steps to engage the sudden charge through the gates. They were outnumbered and, even reinforced by warriors from within the settlement, they hadn't a chance of halting the tide of Britons and Romans come to claim the fortress.

Swords, axes and spears thudded against shields and men screamed as they were cut down. Both Gaelic and British oaths filled the air which soon grew fetid with the stink of blood and ruptured bowels in the hot afternoon air.

The Attacotti defenders were butchered to a man and the roundhouses were ransacked, women, children and the elderly hauled out of their homes and forced at spearpoint into the centre of the enclosure.

"I couldn't have taken that gatehouse better myself," said Cunedag, grasping Murcho around the shoulders affectionately. "You saved many Votadini lives this day, Brother."

"I had your example to follow," Murcho replied. "Was it like this at Cilurnum?"

"Cilurnum was a mere auxiliary fort on the Wall," said Cunedag. "This is the royal seat of the Attacotti! And now, after more than two generations, it is in British hands once more!"

What was left of the tribal leaders of the Attacotti were dragged from the Great Roundhouse and forced to kneel at the feet of their conquerors. As the Attacotti weren't a tribe in the strictest sense of the word, they had no king or high chieftain. The word was a British corruption of the Gaelic *aithechthúatha* which referred to various vassal tribes, many of which had deserted Erin and sought independent kingdoms on British shores.

Their leaders were a sorry collection of old rogues who had likely ruled squalid little clans across the sea before forming some sort of coalition in Alt Clut. Any chieftains who had the Celtic spirit of dying in battle alongside their warriors had already done so and were currently being eyed by the ravens who wheeled overhead. These grey-haired old tyrants were beyond their fighting days and were all that were left of the Gaelic interlopers.

There was a druid among them who made much noise about sparing the lives of chieftains. He spoke British and claimed that to kill fellow nobles would be a crime against the gods. Cunlop, a Christian, was having none of it.

"Execute them all," he commanded of his Roman officers. "We can't have rogue chieftains running around the countryside stirring up rebellion to my rule and I have no desire to keep them here under lock and key. They have spent altogether too much time atop this rock as it is."

Cunedag and his men said nothing as the Roman soldiers carried out Cunlop's orders. The Attacotti chieftains wailed and begged for mercy as knives were placed to their throats and their heads forced back. None was given and all of them were soon coughing and gurgling as blood choked them and ran from the long gashes across their windpipes and jugulars.

"The druid too," Cunlop demanded.

But this was too much for the Votadini. Enemy chieftains were one thing, but killing a druid was an act of blasphemy and would surely call down the wrath of the gods.

"Be silent, you dogs!" Cunedag bellowed to his men. "This is King Cunlop's victory, and these are his prisoners to do with as he pleases! Do you not remember that I killed a druid myself in my youth?"

That quietened them. The story of Blathmac, the Attacotti druid who had stirred the northern tribes into rebellion against Rome nine years ago, was well-told. He had revived ghastly rites of cannibalism and had butchered many innocent farmers and shepherds as well as warriors taken prisoner to feed his warband. Some druids, it had to be admitted, were great blasphemers themselves and the Votadini quietened down as the Celtic priest was dispatched in the same manner as the chieftains he served.

The battle won, the enemy slain and the Rock of the Clut back in British hands, the warriors turned their attentions to cleaning up the carnage to prepare for Cunlop's coronation feast.

CHAPTER 5

Londinium's docks heaved with men and the air rang with bellowed orders. A steady chain of supply fed the holds of the moored transports with sacks of grain, amphorae of wine and casks of salted meat not to mention weapons, tents and disassembled artillery engines. Soldiers marched single file up the gangplanks and stowed their gear below decks while horses and their feed were loaded and secured with leather straps for their journey across the channel.

Ambrosius Aurelianus watched the massive operation from a balcony of the governor's palace alongside Vitalinus and several other officials. It was gut-wrenching to watch the military might of the island – such as it was – being loaded into transports for departure. It was a scene that was being repeated all over Britannia. These ships would sail down the Tamesis to Rutipiae where they would meet dozens of others from ports along the Saxon Shore before their voyage to Gaul. In addition to this, another fleet would be putting out from Segedunum, at the eastern terminus of the Wall, to join Emperor Constantinus's invasion force.

"And so," said Vitalinus with a smile, "Rome leaves just as she came, after four centuries of rule."

"You make it sound like Constantinus will not be returning, Praeses," said Aurelianus. "Have you so little faith in this usurper's war?"

"Oh, I have faith that he will make a great impression on the continent," Vitalinus replied. "He may even achieve recognition by Honorius, but make no mistake, Aurelianus, this day marks a change for Britannia. Our homegrown Caesar may return, or he may not, but I suspect that his attention will be focused on his continental territories for the foreseeable future. We must look to our own defences and rule this island as best we can in his stead."

"With what little he has left us," said Aurelianus as they watched the last of the horses being coaxed up the gangplanks.

"Come now, Comes, we must have faith in our own abilities. Have you not just brought me word that the Attacotti have been defeated and Cunlop now rules their territory as our ally? With him in the west and Cunedag in the east, the north is closed off to the Picts. And, as for the Saxons, the channel will be a hot zone for them now with Constantinus ruling both shores. I foresee a more peaceful future for this island."

"I hope you are right, Praeses," said Aurelianus. "All of Britannia hopes you are right."

As they watched the constant tramp of soldiers going up the gangplanks, Aurelianus did not see a glorious embarkation. All he saw was a rebellion against the true emperor to whom he had pledged his allegiance.

But, despite his loyalty to Rome, Aurelianus came from a family of usurpers himself. He was the nephew of King Aldroen of Amorica, a descendant of Cynan, the brother-in-law of Magnus Maximus. Cynan had followed the usurper on his ill-advised bid for the purple and Maximus had set him up as ruler of Amorica which became a refuge for many Britons after the failure of the rebellion. Now, Constantinus was attempting the same thing and, as far as Aurelianus was concerned, would meet a similar fate to Maximus. Rebellions always failed. Rome was eternal.

Later that afternoon, Constantinus himself came down from the fort to personally oversee the final preparations. The past few days had been an immensely busy time for the new Caesar and his underlings. New appointments had been made and new laws written up. Chrysanthus had replaced Victorinus as vicarius of the diocese and new taxes had been agreed on. The favours Gratianus had granted his wealthy friends were stricken from the tablets to the tune of much grumbling from the merchants and financiers. But this military campaign wasn't going to be cheap, and the money had to come from somewhere.

Aurelianus reluctantly joined Vitalinus and the other officials in the large dining hall of the palace to toast Constantinus and wish his imminent campaign all the best. With the emperor came his newly promoted generals, Iustinianus and Nebiogastes, two men whom Aurelianus knew as thuggish officers who were clearly giddy with their new-found status as the new emperor's *magistri millitim*.

Also accompanying the emperor were his own sons (products of some youthful indiscretions, for Constantinus had not yet married) who had been brought from obscurity and given positions of rank. Constans, his eldest, had spent much of his life in the clergy and had now traded cowl for cuirass despite having no experience of soldierly life. The younger son, Julian, had already embarked on a career in the military but having seen only twenty summers, had only reached the rank of optio. Hardly commander material, but both boys had been taken under their father's wing and were being groomed for high positions in his army.

"This wine is rather good," said Nebiogastes as he gulped down his second cup with vulgar haste.

"It is the last of my stock from Terraconensis," said Vitalinus. "I am down to my last amphora, but I decided that tonight merited the best to fill our cups with. Soon the trade routes will be open once more and we need not ration things with such severity." He raised his glass to Constantinus with a hopeful smile.

"Indeed, the reestablishment of trade with Britannia will be one of my first priorities," the emperor said. "That should ease the sting of my new taxes a little, don't you think?"

"I am sure the landowners and merchants will be thrilled, Caesar," said Vitalinus.

"Just be sure to keep them in line while I am gone," said Constantinus with a wink that was not entirely jovial.

"Surely Caesar does not fear a rebellion of fat merchants?" said Vitalinus. "They would not dare stir up any trouble that would put their countryside villas at risk. You have the support of the mob Caesar, that is what counts. Besides, we have Aurelianus here to protect us in the rare event of any disturbance. He will ensure Britannia's loyalty to their emperor, isn't that right, Aurelianus?"

Aurelianus forced a smile and raised his wine glass. "Hail Caesar," he said, the words nearly choking him.

Once Caesar and his entourage had departed for their ships and Aurelianus and all the other officials had retired to their quarters, Vitalinus sat in his private chambers by the light of an oil lamp and looked out of his window at the moonlit sky above the docks.

Noise rose from the restless town, and he could see the lights of the brothels and wineshops where the emperor's men were enjoying their last night ashore. Upon the morning tide, they would be gone with sore heads and the town would be curiously silent, its population reduced by over half. He greatly looked forward to the peacefulness of the void Constantinus and his army would leave. It would be much easier for him to continue his plans for the diocese without the constant military interruptions and obligations.

A side door to the chamber opened and Vibiana entered wearing a palla of dark, rough spun wool. This she removed to reveal a long, figure-hugging tunica of a pink material that clung to her curves and was pinned at her shoulders with gold clasps. Expensive jewellery provided by Vitalinus glinted in the lamplight.

"Ah, Vibiana," Vitalinus crooned. "I am sorry I kept you waiting. Our evening did go on a little and I couldn't have either our emperor or his staff seeing you in the palace."

"Think nothing of it, *Domine*," the Illyrian replied, bowing her head. "I am well used to coming and going like a shadow in the night."

"Indeed, it is just one of your many qualities. Come, sit with me and have some of this excellent wine."

Vibiana did so, settling in beside her master. Whatever could be said of Vitalinus, he at least lavished luxuries on his slaves.

"Tell me, my dear," he said, pouring her some wine. "How does young Constans see his father?"

Vibiana took a deep swallow of the wine, hoping that it would dull the experiences of the past week. As well as gifting her to Constantinus for his pleasure, Vitalinus had also arranged for her to pleasure his son who had been newly emancipated from the clergy. But, while the emperor had the usual sexual appetite of a middle-aged soldier, Constans showed a distinct desire to make up for his years of celibacy and had a taste for flesh that bordered on the gluttonous. What's more, the young cleric-turned-soldier had a decidedly sadistic streak which had left Vibiana's skin marked in several places in addition to the memories of the more monstrous things he had done to her. She had obeyed her master, but the very thought of Constans made her shudder.

"Constans is most grateful to his father for taking him from the monastery and giving him a position in his army," Vibiana said. "There was no resentment that I could detect."

"None at all?" Vitalinus asked, incredulously. "Not even for abandoning him to the church at a young age? Or for violating his mother who was from a noble family which was all but broken by the scandal?"

"None, *Domine*. I truly believe that young Constans is simply happy to see his life head down a different path."

"Well, that is disappointing," Vitalinus said with a frown. "I had hoped for some sign of the son wanting to overthrow the father. Perhaps I should have sent you to Julian, though the lad is barely weaned from his mother's teat and may even be a virgin, despite being in the army. Your, ahem, *talents* might have proved altogether too much for him." He smiled at her and raised his cup. She raised hers in return, though the smile on her face was forced.

"Time will tell, I am sure," Vitalinus went on. "It is, of course, very early in the game to hope for internal troubles, but no reign is without them. We must wait and be patient. You have done well, my dear. I knew I could count on you. And now …" he set down his wine cup and took hers from her hand and placed it on the low table next to his, "… I wish to reacquaint myself with the techniques you have so perfected to keep emperors and their sons wound around your little finger."

He leant in, nuzzling her neck, and pushed her back onto the couch, his hands running over her curves as he started to kiss the tops of her breasts. Vibiana stared at the ceiling as he pushed her tunica up around her middle and let her mind drift away to another time and another place, just as she always did when she could not bear the present.

As Constantinus's ships were setting sail from British shores for Gaul, Cunedag returned to his royal seat of Din Eidyn. He had made many changes since becoming king of the Votadini. The old Celtic style of hillfort with its drystone wall surrounding a collection of roundhouses had been the standard pattern for British settlements beyond the control of the Roman military for centuries. But, having grown to manhood on the Wall with its square fortifications and series of watchtowers, milecastles and gatehouses, he had seen the weaknesses in Din Eidyn's defences and had done his best to strengthen his royal seat.

The result was something like an auxiliary fort in design, built atop the old drystone wall with a higher palisade and regular square watchtowers as well as a massive oblong gatehouse. He had also removed the Great Roundhouse which had served as the *lys*, or 'court' of Votadini kings for generations, and built a much grander residence of timbers with a slanted roof and many chambers for him and his family.

There had been much grumbling at the changes to Din Eidyn, though never within earshot of the king. Few saw the need for all this 'Romanisation'. It wasn't as if Cunedag's father hadn't been fostered below the Wall and he had felt no need to radically alter the layout of his royal seat. But Cunedag was a far more Roman ruler than Etern had been. He was something of a hero below the Wall so it was supposed that such praise had gone to his head a little and made him feel more kinship with his adopted people than the tribe of his birth.

Nevertheless, Cunedag was a well-loved king, and his people were ecstatic to see his return and triumph over the hated Attacotti. His queen, Vala and their three sons, Tybiaun, Etern and Ruman, awaited him in the main enclosure. Vala was more beautiful to him than ever for their months apart and he lifted her off her feet as he embraced her, kissing her long and hard. The three boys, who were eight, five and four respectively, clamoured around them, trying to squeeze in and gain some of their father's affection.

"And how are my fine princes?" Cunedag asked them, scooping them together in a bear hug. "Have you been holding the fort, Tybiaun?"

"Yes, Father," Tybiaun, the eldest replied.

"Eisia's dog had whelps," said Etern, the middle child who had been named after his grandfather.

"Did she?" Cunedag said. "Well, that's good. Maybe one of them can be yours to train."

"Me too!" said Ruman, the youngest.

Cunedag laughed. "If there are whelps to go around, then you shall all have one. Now, who's going to let me into the Great Hall? I'm famished after the ride here!"

The three boys each exclaimed that they would be the one to lead the way and, beaming, the family headed towards the newly built Great Hall where the preparations for Cunedag's homecoming feast were well underway.

The stars looked down on much merriment within the high walls of Din Eidyn that night. Mead and ale had been distributed to the entire settlement and within the Great Hall, boar and venison sputtered and crackled as they were turned over the fire pits, their juices and the wine in which the cooks basted them, running down to sizzle in the embers. The tables were piled high with bannocks, baskets of summer berries and boards of butter and cheese.

The noble men and women of the Votadini, brought from every clan from the hills to the coast, sat at the tables, their faces glowing with the warmth of drink, heat and good company. A bard, under the tutelage and stern eye of Gonar the druid, recited his work in progress concerning the victory of the Britons over the Gaels of Alt Clut and several warriors roared at him when he got certain details wrong or failed to mention a warrior or deed they deemed important.

Shamefaced, the bard finished and scurried for cover, but nobody blamed him overmuch. The details of what had happened in the west were still fresh and constantly argued over by the warriors present. There would be time for the bard to become fully informed so that he might recite the tale properly and then their deeds would live on forever in the mouths of poets.

Also at the feast, was the king's sister, Alpia, and her husband Tegid along with their sixteen-year-old son, Tancorix, who followed the conversation of the adults with great interest. His younger sisters sat with Cunedag's sons, and they sniggered as they fed table scraps to the dogs under the table whenever their parents weren't looking. The adults were too engrossed in discussion of the highland tribes to notice much in any case.

"It is said that the Epidaii are also stockpiling food and weapons," said Murcho, gnawing on a chicken bone. "Though what their plan is, no one can tell me."

"You don't fear invasion?" Vala asked, turning to look at her husband.

"Not of us," said Cunedag. "The Epidaii are too weak to attempt such a thing alone. And no northern tribe would invade another without the support of the Uerteru. They are the ones holding power in the north."

"And what of the Uerteru?" asked Murcho. "Do they too marshal their warriors?"

"Who knows what goes on that far north?" said Alpia. "But if any highland tribe threatens Votadini lands, then they'll find me coming out of retirement to meet them on the field of battle."

"Since you turned from war to focus on motherhood, the north has breathed easy these past nine years," said Cunedag, winking at his sister.

She raised her horn in reply. "The feathers on my spear are gathering dust and yearn to soak up blood once more."

"But something bad *is* brewing," said Tegid. "Mark me. These are dangerous times. I've never known such a quiet in the north. It is as a lull before a great storm."

"Hardly surprising," said Alpia. "With the Romans stripping the province of just about every soldier, the Wall sits unguarded. It is only natural that the northern tribes start planning a few raids. We would be no different were it not for our king's alliance with Rome."

She smiled at her brother who lolled on his throne, a living contradiction. His hair was long and his skin was marked in several places with blue tattoos to pagan gods. He was a barbarian chief who wielded a Roman spatha and behind his throne hung his standard; a gold dragon embroidered on the red cloak of Padarn, his ancestor, the first Votadini prince to be fostered by Rome.

"Be that as it may, Alpia," said Queen Vala, "the northern tribes are faced with something of a problem. The lands of the Votadini and Alt Clut meet. The way south to the Wall is blocked by territories friendly to Rome, or at least, to Roman Britain. To reach the Wall they would have to trespass on our lands."

"That is true," said Cunedag. "But will it be enough to deter them? The prospect of striking deep into British territory must be a heady one for them."

"But the Wall has been poorly defended for years," said Murcho. "It's hardly less defended now than it was before this Constantinus set off for Gaul. Most of the forts were empty even when Cunedag was posted there in his youth."

"Also true," said Cunedag, "but what you fail to see is the symbolism of Constantine's departure. Something has changed in Albion and the northern tribes sense it. It's not just the reduced garrisons on the Wall. It's the lack of retaliation if they breach it. No Roman army is going to march north to punish them, not now every soldier is needed to guard the frontiers. If they make it past the Wall, then they can grab what they can without any fear of reprisal."

"Except from you, my husband," said his wife.

He sensed the concern in her words and clasped her hand under the table. For her, this was not just an academic conversation. Her family still lived in Eboracum, within easy striking distance of the Wall. Not that he was worried Eboracum could ever fall to a band of northern raiders, but there was no denying that times were changing. An era had come to an end and the future seemed so uncertain.

Part II

"And afterwards Alaric died of disease, and the army of the Visigoths under the leadership of Adaulphus proceeded into Gaul, and Constantinus, defeated in battle, died with his sons. However the Romans never succeeded in recovering Britain, but it remained from that time on under tyrants." – Procopius, *History of the Wars, Books III and IV: The Vandalic War*

CHAPTER 6

Spring, 408 A.D.

The ravens had already started to descend on the field of the slain, cawing and fighting over the best morsels. Melga, war chief of the Pictish tribes, surveyed the scene with grim satisfaction. To the east and the west, the great wall of the Romans stretched for as far as the eye could see, rising over hills and dipping out of sight only to rise again like a never-ending ridge-backed serpent.

For generations, this wall had defended the Roman portion of the island; an impenetrable barrier to the unconquered men of the north. Melga was of the wild Uerteru tribe who looked on the tribes of the lowlands which dwelled in the shadow of the Wall with derision. They had been softened and weakened by centuries of contact with Rome, allowing their children to be fostered by Romans in exchange for Roman favour, unlike the truly free tribes of the highlands.

A year had passed since the Britons had elected Constantinus as their emperor. A year since the new Caesar had taken most of the island's military strength with him to Gaul. The province was wide open, and the Wall was all but undefended. For the first time since the Great Conspiracy forty years ago, it was possible to strike at the heart of Britannia and this time, the Romans would be too entangled in their own affairs on the continent to do anything about it. All of Albion might be theirs for the taking!

Melga was no king, but he carried the favour of kings and commanded their men as a warlord the north had not seen since the days of Gartnait who had masterminded the Great Conspiracy. He had been chosen by the chieftains of the Caledonii, the Epidaii, the Venicones and his own native

Uerteru to lead their warriors south on a great plundering expedition that would shatter the last resolve of the Romanised Britons.

The notion of wiping out the lowland tribes first had been discussed. Melga would have taken great pleasure in punishing the treachery and cowardice of the hated Votadini and their neighbouring Novantae and Selgovae, but he had been overruled. Why waste time warring against petty allies of Rome when an entire Roman diocese lay waiting for them?

And even Melga, much as he hated to admit it, had a grudging respect for Cunedag, the new king of the Votadini. He had proved himself to be a real war chief of the old sort, fortifying his royal seat and strengthening his borders. Last summer, he had driven the Gaels from the shores of Albion and put that Roman milksop Cunlop on the throne of Alt Clut, tightening a bottleneck at the narrowest part of the island and making the path to the Wall all the harder.

But the Gaels, for all their harrying of the western Pictish coastline, had to be thanked for their timely intervention. The coast of Cunlop's new kingdom was under attack from the wolves of Erin who came to strike a blow for their fallen comrades butchered atop the Rock of the Clut. Cunedag and his warriors had marched westwards that spring to aid their ally, leaving the Votadini lands emptied of warriors. Striking while the iron was hot, Melga had marched south, through the lowlands towards the Wall while Cunedag's attention was on the west coast.

With sword and torch they had swept through Votadini lands, feeding themselves on stolen livestock and grain as they marched, slaying all who tried to stand against them. Soon, Cunedag would hear of their passing through his lands and would turn to pursue them, but they would be across the Wall by that point, and deep into Roman territory.

The Romans, predictable as ever, had rushed to defend their precious wall with their lives and now their bodies littered the plains on either side of the Wall and three of their forts were aflame, blackening the sky with their smoke.

The Wall had been all but unmanned for the past few years, yet pathetic plumes of smoke from their warning fires had gone up any way, sending the signal along the Wall that they were under attack. It didn't matter. Help would be too long in coming and wouldn't be much when it got there. The Wall no longer had the manpower it needed to function effectively as a border, instead trusting to Rome's northern allies to defend it. Little good that did when the lowland tribes couldn't even defend their own territories from the Gaels.

They had struck Cilurnum first; a cavalry fort with three-hundred men garrisoned there. The Romans had ridden out to meet them but had been overwhelmed. The survivors fled back behind the walls of the fort which soon swarmed with the blue-painted warriors of the north.

Reinforcements had eventually arrived as Melga's men were looting the stores of Cilurnum and the Picts had laughed to see a mere hundred riders approaching from Vindolanda. The Romans had cut a retreat when they saw the size of the Pictish warband who had taken Cilurnum but Melga sent out his cavalry detachments to hunt them down and butcher them. He would kill every Roman soldier he could to minimise the chances of his movement south being interfered with.

Then, he had split his warband into three; two flanks to take the auxiliary forts on either side of Cilurnum while he remained with the main body of his warriors. He wanted no enemy troops left to close the gap behind him. This was the most fortified part of the Wall and consisted mostly of cavalry units. With those gone, there would be nobody to pursue them as they marched south.

"The civilian prisoners have been corralled in the largest of the Roman buildings, my lord," said one of Melga's warriors as he climbed to the parapet to report to his war chief. "Slaves mostly. We searched the settlement beyond the southern wall, but it seems to have been abandoned some time ago. We might send the prisoners back north to serve our own people."

"I have neither the time nor the warriors to waste escorting slaves north," said Melga. "We have no need of these people. Kill them all."

"Yes, my lord."

The warrior headed back down to ground level and soon, the screams rising from the fort's headquarters could be heard, confirming that Melga's orders were being carried out. He hawked and spat over the parapet and then headed down to ground level to begin barking orders at his warriors to move out.

Within the hour, the long column of warriors passed through the open gates on the fort's southern wall, the smoke of burning and the stink of death behind them. Melga sat astride his sturdy highland pony and watched his massive warband move past. Many of them saluted their leader, this easy first victory a good sign of things to come. Within a couple of days, they would reach the great walled town of Eboracum, the longtime home of the iron legions who had now departed. They would strike hard and fast. The Picts moved light, bringing no baggage train with them. The bountiful lands of the south with their towns and farms and villages would provide.

Melga's tattooed face split into an ugly grin and he turned his pony south and rode to the head of his warband, the winds of victory in his nostrils. Let the south scream for their Roman masters! The Picts had entered the empire!

The boats burned on the shore, black plumes of smoke rising into the dull, iron-grey sky. They were crude vessels made of hide stretched over wicker frames and they burned merrily as Cunedag and his mounted warriors wheeled on the wet sand, the last of their torches and fire arrows spent, and galloped up the beach to where the Gaels were massing for a last-ditch stand.

With their boats gone, there was no way the invaders could return to Erin and therefore, no way they might return to Albion with more recruits next season. It was the policy of the Britons to leave none alive and the small band of Gaels – all that was left of a season's raiding party – knew it.

They mustered a brave defence, regardless, standing firm with shields overlapping, a solid lump prickling with spears. But Cunedag's men were veterans in the saddle and far outnumbered the Gaels in any case. They galloped towards them in a wedge formation, hurling their javelins at the last moment to break up the shield wall and open the enemy ranks up like an oyster for the knife.

Men screamed as javelins punctured wood, mail and flesh. Some fell, the long shafts embedded in their guts, their shields falling from their hands, opening wide gaps in the shield wall.

And into those gaps, the Britons thrust their spears. Yelling war cries, Cunedag and his men drove deep and hard into the enemy flanks, smashing their shield wall and scattering them like sheep. Hooves trampled those not quick enough to get away and, as spears became lodged in bone and mail, the Britons drew their long cavalry swords and began hacking at the fleeing enemy, cutting them down as they ran, their blood sinking into the sand.

It was over in moments. This last band of Gaels, who had raided with such confidence earlier in the season, had been driven back to their boats and butchered without mercy. There could never be mercy for those who plundered British shores and made slaves of its women and children.

Holding his reddened spatha aloft, Cunedag bellowed his victory. Another battle won. Another victory for the free tribes of the north.

They rode up the grassy dunes towards the rest of the warband where King Cunlop sat astride his white stallion. Cheers greeted them from those who had watched the final battle from afar.

"Another great service you have done me, King Cunedag," said Cunlop. "I do believe my people favour you more than they do me."

If there was a hint of jealousy in the younger man's words, Cunedag thought it best to ignore it. "Your territories are safe once more, King Cunlop," Cunedag replied.

"Until next season," Cunlop replied wearily.

"Next season they will find us ready once more," said Cunedag, sharing his fellow king's fatigue at the seemingly endless situation they found themselves in. "Until every wolf cub in Erin is used up, they will find us ready to meet them."

It was on the return journey to Alt Clut that a rider approached the war band, his mare in a lather and exhaustion on his face.

"My king!" he cried, causing both Cunedag and Cunlop to look at each other. But the rider was Votadini and had ridden for nearly two days without rest to bring dire news from Cunedag's kingdom. "The northern tribes are on the move, my king!" said the rider, sliding out of his saddle and kneeling at Cunedag's feet. "A massive warband, nearly three-thousand strong!"

There was a collective intake of breath at this and much concerned murmuring. Cunedag demanded silence while he got the story in full from the rider.

"They must have waited in the north, gathering their forces until you rode west to fight the Gaels, my lord," said the rider, revived somewhat by the nozzle of a mead skin pressed to his lips.

"Which tribes?" Cunedag asked.

"All of them! The Picts are united!"

Cunedag said nothing but his mind was doing cartwheels as it tried to make sense of the situation. 'Picts' was a Roman word for just about anybody who lived north of the Wall and referred to the old custom of warriors painting and tattooing themselves with ritualistic and tribal designs as a way of channelling the fury of beasts and the sprits of ancestors. The lowland tribes had long since abandoned such barbarity over the course of their gradual Romanisation but among the northern tribes, beyond the ruins of the second Roman wall, the custom continued and now even the lowland tribes referred to their more savage neighbours as 'Picts'.

"All of them ..." Cunedag repeated, the words spelling doom for Albion. The Picts had once been a patchwork of warring tribes but, in recent centuries, had been galvanised into something more along the lines of a single nation, united by their hatred of the southerners and the Gaels who continually raided their coasts and settled in their western territories. The withdrawal of the Roman military provided a target too tempting to pass up. Now, every Pictish tribe was looking to share in the plunder of a Roman territory.

"How could they pass through our lands undetected?" asked Murcho in disbelief.

"Because we weren't there to detect them," said Cunedag glumly. "How could I have been so foolish as to leave our back gate unlatched?"

"Do you suppose they are in league with the Gaels?" Murcho asked. "Those dogs from Erin have attacked with more ferocity than usual this summer. Perhaps it was a ruse to draw us from our lands."

"Their ferocity was an answer to our recapture of Alt Clut last season," said Cunedag. "No, the northern tribes hate the Gaels more than they hate us, even. I do not see them as being in league with them. Just opportunists, waiting for the moment to strike."

"They cut through Votadini lands like a streak of lightning," the messenger from the east said. "Burning and looting on their way. They take only what they can carry and are fleet of foot."

"Aye, they'll be at the Wall by now. Most likely making for Vindolanda or Cilurnum."

"But that's the strongest part of the Wall," said Murcho. "Damn near every cavalryman is posted in one of those two forts."

"Exactly," said Cunedag. "With a force that size, they could take those forts with ease and leave no defenders to block their way if they head back north. In one stroke, they might have wiped out the entire northern defences. Damn!" He slammed his fist into the palm of his hand with savage force that made the messenger wince. "Cunlop, you must ride on to Alt Clut alone. We are for the Wall."

Within three days, the Votadini force came within site of the smouldering ruins of Cilurnum. The bloated ravens, disturbed by their approach across the field of the slain, took off sluggishly into the acrid sky. Cunedag glared at the sacked fort that had once been his home. The dead auxiliary soldiers who littered the ground and walls had been his comrades.

"It's unthinkable …" Murcho murmured beside him. "Cilurnum taken …"

He need not say more for the significance was lost on none of the men who rode under Cunedag's dragon banner. Ten years ago, this had been the fort Cunedag and a small host of cavalrymen had taken back from an invading Attacotti force and held against a massive warband to prevent them from crossing the frontier and entering the empire. History was repeating herself with a grim sense of humour. This time they were too late and an even larger warband had crossed into Britannia Secunda.

"Here lie the bodies of my comrades," said Cunedag, dismounting and looking around at the dead, eyeless faces of the slain. "The riders of the Second Asturum, my old unit, and I see the standard of the Fourth Gallorum come up from Vindolanda too. Brave fools to throw themselves into the fray for they numbered less than two hundred."

"The signal fire was lit," said Murcho, glancing at the burned-out tower atop the principia.

"But who would come?" said Cunedag. "Other than the dead we see here. If only the First Sabiniana were still posted at Onnum, the day might have been saved, alas, they have long since departed for the continent."

It grieved the Votadini king more than he would allow himself to show to see the faces of many he had known in his previous life. His old commander, Candidius was there, where he had fallen from his horse, skewered through the belly by a spear. And none pained him more than the lifeless corpse of Morleo, his own foster-brother and prince of the Selgovae lying nearby, hacked and stabbed to death with the trampled and bloodied draco standard of the unit not far from him.

"Damn fool insisted on staying with the unit," he said to Murcho as he cradled the young prince's head in his hands, fighting back the tears. "He could have returned to his people as I did but he felt that he had no place among them. His eldest brother now rules the Selgovae with at least two more in line ahead of him. I must bring word to them of his death."

Further dismay was caused by the discovery of the corpse of Titus Gemellus, the Dux Britanniarum himself, surrounded by his bodyguard. It had been his responsibility to hold the frontier, despite the woeful lack of manpower, and he had laid down his life in doing his duty, ever the honourable Roman soldier.

It was all too much for Cunedag who had come of age among these men and the tears streaked his ash-grimed face as he howled at the sky and the cruelty of the gods. He should have been here to fight alongside Gemellus and Candidius and Morleo and all the rest of them, not hunting down packs of roving Gaels. But Albion was an island beset on all sides. One front couldn't be contained without losing ground on another. Rome was increasingly turning its attention in on itself while its outlying provinces burned.

"I will arrange funeral pyres," said Murcho. "Though, many of these men were Christians, I'll wager. How best to honour their beliefs?"

"There is no time," said Cunedag. "While we stand around here wondering how all this came to pass, the ones responsible are marching south and doing the same again to other settlements. Eboracum lies three days ride from here. It will be the choicest target and the Comes himself will be in danger."

"Are you saying that we are to march into Roman territory?" asked Murcho.

"Aye, that is what I'm saying," said Cunedag. "The ones who did this are free to cut and burn to their heart's content and Ambrosius Aurelianus will need our help if the whole of northern Britannia isn't to fall to the blades of those scum.

Saddle up! Leave the dead to the ravens. Mayhap they will fly south with us, and we will glut them a second time!"

CHAPTER 7

They rode hard for Eboracum, stopping only when the horses were exhausted. Like the Picts, they had no baggage train but unlike the Picts, they had no warriors on foot. Cunedag had left all his unmounted warriors with Cunlop, knowing that speed was of the utmost importance. With any luck, they might reach Eboracum before its gates fell to the painted horde though what good three hundred Votadini horsemen might be against three-thousand Picts, he did not like to contemplate.

Tegid and his young son, Tancorix rode with them. At seventeen winters, the lad had proved himself a good warrior in the recent campaign against the Attacotti and now his mettle would really be tested in defending the south from the Picts. Cunedag kept his nephew close to him, treating him almost as a son as his own sons had not yet come to age.

Through the morning mist of the third day, they sighted the walls of the provincial capital nestled in the hills. The legionary fort was on one side of the river and the colonia on the other side, with a stone bridge connecting the two. Smoke rose from both sides of the river, but it was the smoke of hearth fires and bakeries, not the burning of homes. No invading warband was camped outside its walls and the town seemed to be at peace.

"No sign of the enemy," said Murcho as they drew up their horses on a wooded hill above the road that led down to Eboracum's gates. "I don't understand it. We didn't pass them on the way south. We would have noticed."

"It seems that our foe has other targets in mind," said Cunedag. "Eboracum, for the time being, is spared. Come, let us see what the Comes has to say. Hold the standard aloft! I don't want them mistaking us for Picts. In Roman eyes, there is little difference between us."

Leaving his men to make camp in the hills, Cunedag, Murcho and a small delegation rode up to the fort's northern gate, the dragon banner fluttering above them. Sentries atop the gatehouse bellowed challenges but somebody must have recognised the dragon standard for the gates creaked open and Cunedag and his men rode in.

At once, it felt like a homecoming to Cunedag who had been trained within the walls of that very fort. Across the river lay the residence of Praeses Colias, Vala's father and the man who had fostered him. A huge feeling of relief washed over him to be within Eboracum's walls and he hadn't realised how concerned he had been to find so much that was familiar to him under siege. But there was still a niggling worry about where the Picts were now and what their plan was.

"I must speak with the Comes Britanniarum directly," he told the fort prefect. "The Picts have crossed the Wall and have entered the province."

"You don't need to tell us that," said the prefect a little testily. "They passed by not two days ago. Christ be praised they did not try to take the fort and the town as I daren't contemplate our chances against that painted horde. Even with the reinforcements we've received."

"What? You have been reinforced?"

"Aye, the Comes received word from the Wall that Cilurnum had fallen, and he called all units to converge here and reinforce us. I had thought that was why you were here …"

"No, I got word of the Picts marching through my territories and when we discovered that they had broken through the frontier, I decided to head south and lend whatever support I could to Eboracum's defences."

"Well, your presence here is much appreciated, though I don't know where the Picts have gone now. I would offer quarters for your men and horses, but with so many mounted units come down from the Wall, I don't have the space. You are welcome to take over the old canabae below the southwestern walls. Nobody lives there now, and the fort can shield you somewhat should the Picts return."

"Thank you, I'll send someone to see to it. But where is the Comes?"

"Across the river discussing defence measures with the praeses. Shall I send an escort with you?"

"I'm quite capable of finding my way, Prefect."

After sending Tegid and Tancorix to convey his orders that the rest of the teulu should make their camp in the old canabae, Cunedag, Murcho and the rest of his delegation passed through the fort and crossed the river into the colonia.

Those old streets with their stalls and smells and shouts of hawkers were like echoes of childhood to Cunedag. Many eyed him and his men with caution as they made their way to the governor's residence, nervous at the sight of barbarians in their midst. Most probably took them for common mercenaries come to help defend them from the Picts.

The governor's residence had changed little over the years, and Cunedag even recognised many of the slaves who scurried about to see to their needs. He had not trod those mosaiced rooms since he had married Vala ten years ago and was overcome with a rush of emotions. These only intensified as Fulvia, his foster mother swept into the room, imperious as ever, with only a touch more iron in her black hair than he remembered.

"Cunedag! Oh, thank God and all his angels for delivering you to us in our most desperate hour!" the old domina cried.

"I came as soon as I was alerted to the Picts moving south," Cunedag replied, kissing his foster mother on the cheek. "Unfortunately, I was engaged with the Scotti in the west otherwise they would never have slipped through Votadini lands."

"A courageous thought, though I fear they would have broken through regardless, even if it did come to that," said a voice from the doorway to the atrium.

Ambrosius Aurelianus entered the room with Colias behind him. The Comes Britanniarum wore his parade-ground armour, though it was dulled as if having been worn for several days without being polished. "These Picts were undoubtedly counting on your attention being focused on the west coast," Aurelianus went on. "And they could have taken Din Eidyn within a day if they chose to, so it was favourable that you did not stand against them."

Cunedag did not take offence at the Comes's lack of faith in his ability to halt the Picts. At three-thousand strong, they could have swarmed his royal seat like ants and the fact that Aurelianus recognised this, meant that he did not place any blame at Cunedag's door for not preventing the invasion.

"Cunedag, my dear boy," said Colias, taking his foster son by the hand and embracing him. "I am glad that you are here."

"As am I, *domine*," Cunedag replied. "Though I bring sad news from the north."

"Cilurnum fell, I know ..." Colias said.

"That's not all. The Dux is dead. I saw Gemellus's body myself. And ... Morleo was slain too."

Fulvia let out a sob at his words and covered her mouth. Morleo had been something of a favourite of hers. He had been the more mild-mannered of the three foster sons.

"We had suspected that Gemellus had died defending Cilurnum as nobody had heard from him since the battle," said Aurelianus. "But this is sore news all the same and I offer my condolences to you all for the loss of Morleo. He died a hero of Rome."

"What has happened here at Eboracum?" Cunedag asked. "The fort prefect said that the Picts merely passed by without attacking."

"Thank Christ that they did for I don't know if we could have held out against them," Aurelianus replied. "We gave them as good a show of force as we could muster, and I think that persuaded them to seek other places to plunder rather than get bogged down in a lengthy siege."

"I understand you have called all available troops to you," said Cunedag. "What is your plan?"

"To ride out and smash the Picts," the comes said simply. "Once I have enough men under my command. Can I count on your support?"

Cunedag nodded. "My three-hundred riders are yours to command. What else do you have?"

"I have called the remaining eight cavalry units stationed on the Wall. Then there are the irregular units like the Taifal vexilliato from Banovallum who are on their way as we speak."

"That makes us just under five-thousand men," said Cunedag. "It's enough, but it's tight odds."

"We must use the terrain to our advantage and conduct abrasive operations until they are weak and desperate enough to be drawn into battle," said Aurelianus. "They have little cavalry which gives us an advantage there. I intend to send out hit-and-run detachments to starve them and pick off stragglers and scouting parties. Little by little we can whittle them down and, with any luck, halt them before they reach Londinium."

"Londinium?" Cunedag exclaimed. "Surely, you don't expect these wretches to strike that far south? The very capital of the diocese?"

"This is no raiding party, make no mistake about that," said Aurelianus soberly. "Three-thousand Picts is a force large enough to bring Britannia to its knees and, with our glorious new emperor in Gaul with damn near all our troops, I have no doubt that they know it. We are this island's defenders, gentlemen. We had best start thinking about *how* we are to defend it."

Three days later, the British host left Eboracum and marched south. It was slow going as they were forced to bring a baggage train to feed the soldiers on the march, the countryside having been stripped bare by the passing Picts. Many farms and villas had been looted and burned and the landscape resembled one of ghosts and ashes, with the survivors having fled south.

As they camped on the night of the first day's march, an old shepherd was brought to Aurelianus's tent. He had approached the camp at dusk, keen to trade information for food as all of his flock had been taken by the ravaging enemy and he had lost his livelihood. Aurelianus heard him out and then gave him food, drink and a place to sleep.

"If what this man says is true," Aurelianus said to Cunedag upon calling him to his tent, "the Picts are somewhere to the east of us. They'll be making for the crossing at Petuaria. The road from Eboracum to Londinium crosses a large estuary called the Abus Fluvius at that point. There was once a fort and an amphitheatre there, but now all that remains are ruins and a collection of hovels clustered around the ferry point. If they cross that river, then they'll enter Flavia Caesariensis. Lindum will be their next target. It's not nearly as well-defended as Eboracum. After that, it's a straight line down to Londinium with plenty of places to loot along the way. We must stop them at Lindum."

"Has there been any news from the Taifals of Banovallum?" Cunedag asked.

The comes shook his head. "They may try to cross the river, but they risk running into the enemy. My guess is that they're heading northwest to try and meet us."

"If we wait for them, then we risk letting these bastard Picts swarm across the river," said Cunedag."

"My thoughts exactly," said Aurelianus. "We must hold that crossing point, no matter the cost. On the morrow, I will take my forces south to blockade Petuaria. I want you and your warriors to head south-west and cross the River Usa where you can. Then curve south-east and try to meet up with the Taifal vexillatio. We will need a strong cavalry charge if the Picts descend on us."

"If they do, you might all be wiped out," said Cunedag, "while we traipse around to the south of the river looking for the Taifals."

"That is just a risk we'll have to take," said Aurelianus. "Besides, I am confident we can fortify what's left of the old fort down there and form a bottleneck that will make the Picts think twice about storming us. If we can hold the river for as long as it takes for you and the Taifals to ride north, you can cross the river and join us."

CHAPTER 8

Londinium had been in a state of panic for four days. When word had reached them that the Wall in the north had fallen and that the Picts were swarming down through Britannia Secunda, some of its wealthier residents had seriously considered piling their riches into boats and taking their chances in Gaul. It had taken much persuasion to stop them fleeing like rats from a sinking ship with promises that Ambrosius Aurelianus and all the power of the north would prevent the invasion from reaching too far south.

But the truth was far from certain. Vitalinus seethed as he read the latest report from the north, handed to him by Chrysanthus. All correspondence passed through him before the vicarius was allowed to send word to Constantinus about what was happening in Britannia. It was the only way Vitalinus could ensure that the emperor did not rush home to fix its problems with the troops he was supposed to be fighting the barbarians in Gaul with.

Things had been going so well and now all was in jeopardy by this sudden invasion. Why had that fool Cunedag not stopped them? That was why Britannia had lavished such favour on their client king, allowing him to rule his tribe and lending British troops to help control the region and now he had let three-thousand Picts wander through his own backyard and enter the diocese!

It had crossed Vitalinus's mind that Cunedag, for all his background in the Roman military, had thrown in his lot with the wild men of the north and was complicit in the invasion but Aurelianus, in his reports to Chrysanthus, had claimed that Cunedag remained loyal to Rome and was helping him harry the Picts, for all the good that was doing. It was a wonder they had spared Eboracum, but now they were on the border of

Flavia Caesariensis. Why not smash them in open battle? That was what all in Londinium wanted to know.

But Aurelianus had confirmed everybody's worst fears about the Emperor Constantinus's war in Gaul; Britannia no longer had the forces needed to defeat invading warbands. The comes was attempting to harry the enemy by cutting off their access to food and toying with them as a cat might with a mouse. *More like a mouse with a cat.* It was taking far too long as far as Vitalinus was concerned. If he did not want his plans ruined utterly, he would have to nip this problem in the bud using his own, discreet means.

Vibiana entered his study noiselessly on slippered feet and, at a motion from Vitalinus, reclined on the silk couch in the corner.

"You wished to see me, *domine*," she said.

"Yes. Forgive the earliness of the hour, but word has reached me from the north. The Picts grow closer by the day."

"Are we in danger?"

"No, not if we use our resources cleverly," Vitalinus said, leaning back in his chair. "I have a job for you of the utmost importance."

"I am ever willing to serve, *domine*."

"This leader of the Picts, Melga, has more cunning than we are used to seeing in a northern savage. We must know his intentions. We must place a spy in his camp."

Vibiana's eyes widened as she tried to control the fright that her master's words put into her.

"I wish you to travel to Lindum," he went on. "I will provide you with an armed escort of course, for the roads are unsafe for a woman in these troubled times, but once you are within the town, you will be on your own."

"Why Lindum, *domine*?"

"Because, as far as we can predict the mind of this painted savage, Lindum will be his next target, and it will fall to him too. Aurelianus has not the men to stop him and Melga will be looking for a fortified place to lodge his warband."

"But *domine*!" Vibiana cried. "I'll be captured! Misused by those northern barbarians!"

Vitalinus smiled. "My dear, I *wish* for you to be captured."

Her face paled. "*Domine?*"

"How else will you be able to pass information to Aurelianus on what Melga is planning? Come now, Vibiana, have confidence in your skills. I will ensure that you are bedecked in costly fabrics and ornaments, and you are already prettier than any harlot to be found within Lindum's walls, we can be sure of that. Melga will see your quality and claim you for himself, I have no doubt of that."

"But he's a savage!"

"As all men are, deep down. We are, at our core, base creatures. And you, my dear, know how to play men to your advantage whatever their creed. Tempt him, Vibiana. Ensure that he takes you into his bed and once you are there, then you will be as precious to him as all the loot in the southern towns. Go now and prepare yourself for your journey. We have little time."

"Yes, *domine*," Vibiana replied, meekly and, as she turned from her master, he did not see the look of utter loathing that crossed her face.

Cunedag was pleased to meet his old comrade, Asaros, and his Taifal cavalrymen in the marshy lands on the western side of the River Trisantona. These were the men he had commanded in the last war against a Pictish and Attacotti confederation ten years ago. They were fine horsemen and deadly with their eastern bows, able to nail a target from the saddle at a gallop and their horses were the finest Cunedag had ever seen.

"Well met, Cunedag of the Votadini!" said Asaros, clasping his hand as the two leaders greeted each other.

"Glad to see you can still ride," said Cunedag. "I feared you had all turned into farmers in the peaceful lands south of Lindum."

"Ha!" the Taifal commander sneered. "We are kept busy enough defending your shores from Saxon pirates. They arrive by the boatload every summer seeking land and plunder and their settlements spring up faster than we can burn them. I doubt you see more action than us in the north!"

"It's good to have you with us, Asaros," Cunedag said with a grin. "The situation is indeed dire in the north. Aurelianus holds the crossing, but he is sorely undermanned. Three-thousand Picts lurk somewhere to the north of him and will descend at any moment. We must ride for the river with all haste to reinforce him."

"Would it not be better to ride around to the west where the river thins and come upon Aurelianus's left flank? That way we might prevent the enemy slipping past him and entering Flavia Caesariensis farther upriver. Besides, you have already come that way, I think, and know that is safe."

"True, that way is safe, but it takes too long," Cunedag replied. "And I don't believe the enemy will try and circumvent Aurelianus. They outnumber him and he may need our help sooner than we can give it to him. The North Road leads straight to the crossing, and we can be with him in a day."

"As you say," Asaros replied. "The road is as straight as the crow flies so we may gain some advantage in speed."

Once the horses were refreshed, they set out immediately towards the North Road that led up from Londinium. They reached the settlement on the southern bank of the Abus

Fluvius on the evening of the next day and found it empty of nearly all its residents. They knew what loomed north of the river and apparently had not the confidence in the Comes Britanniarum to hold the crossing against the barbarian tide.

"Damn cowards have even left the ferries unmanned," said Asaros as he galloped through the sorry collection of thatched houses and muddy streets to report to Cunedag.

"Would you wait around with three-thousand Picts on the other side of the river?" Cunedag asked him.

"We're here aren't we?"

"Yes, but we are warriors, Asaros. The inhabitants of these hovels are the same as those of dozens of similar settlements we have passed in the wake of the Picts. They make their livings off the land and when the land is stripped bare by the ravaging wolves from beyond the border, they have nothing, not even their lives in many cases. These poor bastards decided to get out with what they have ahead of time. I do not begrudge them that for there could be few warriors among them. Simple farming and fishing folk most likely."

"Well, you may have kind thoughts in your heart for them," said Asaros, "but I at least begrudge them leaving the ferries for us to man ourselves. My people are not great watermen."

"It's only a river, not the Northern Sea," said Cuncdag with a grin. "We'll hold your hands if you get seasick."

Asaros grunted at this and then occupied himself with ransacking the abandoned homes for food. There was little to be had. Cunedag had been right; the inhabitants of the small settlement had got out with whatever they could carry. There was no time to be lost in any case, as there were only three ferries in working order and it would take them some time to float their men and horses across.

Cunedag decided to be in the first ferry so he could personally bring the news to Aurelianus that both he and the

Taifals had arrived. He was also keen to see if there had been any movements of the Picts sighted. They had not attacked the crossing, that much was clear, for no smoke or stink of death carried across the river which it certainly would have done had Petuaria fallen. That was something at least.

As the ferry was moored on the northern bank and Cunedag led his stallion down the ramp and onto the jetty, he could see that Aurelianus had been busy. The settlement was a little bigger than the one on the south bank and the presence of British troops had clearly inclined the residents to stay. As a result, Petuaria was a bustling community full of industry. The clink of hammer on anvil could be heard from the blacksmiths' forges as armour and weapons were repaired. There was laughter and song from wineshops and men, women and children hurried up and down the muddy streets, carrying messages and running errands.

Aurelianus himself had set up his headquarters in the old principia of what had once been the fort, long since abandoned. The town walls, which were in a poor state of repair, were being reinforced with rubble from the derelict buildings and the largest gaps were barricaded by timber palisades constructed from felled trees from the woods that surrounded the town.

"You are building a new Eboracum from the ruins of a settlement, it seems," Cunedag said as he entered the principia to find Aurelianus poring over a map table set up in the cross hall.

"I am glad of your return, Cunedag," said Aurelianus, looking up from his maps. "I was told that somebody had got the ferries in order again. The Taifals are with you?"

"Yes, we met them in those godsforsaken marshes northwest from Lindum. You have things well in order here."

"I have been given the rare gift of time in your absence, so I made the best use of it and fortified our position."

"Any news on enemy movements?"

"Nothing but scouting parties sneaking close to see what we're doing. I believe we are succeeding in making them wary of crossing the river. It would be a nasty battle here and both sides would lose a lot of men. This Melga is no headstrong fool. That is something at least."

"How are our stores?"

"Food is scarce," Aurelianus replied glumly. "Petuaria is only a small town and can't feed us all. There is game in the surrounding woods, but my hunters run the risk of running into their enemy counterparts."

"I will send out my own men," Cunedag offered. "They are used to moving faster and with less noise than Roman soldiers."

Three days later, a detachment of Cunedag's hunters came upon the remains of the Pictish camp.

"And you're sure it was a large camp?" Aurelianus quizzed the returning soldiers. "Large enough to host three-thousand men?"

"It spread for as far as the eye could see," the lead hunter replied. "They weren't cooped up in a small place like we are but spread out across the hills. We saw the campfires and detritus of a massive warband."

"Well, we found their camp at last, it seems," said Cunedag. "Though nobody was at home."

"Where could three-thousand Picts have gone without us seeing them?" Morleo wondered aloud. "Back north, do you suppose?"

"No," said Aurelianus, a grim expression on his face. "They didn't come all this way south just to turn around at the first sign of a river held against them. I fear we may have been duped into entrenching ourselves here while leaving our left flank open. I want scouting patrols to head west. Check the crossings at the River Usa. Find out if they have circumvented us. I hope to God we have not sat here like fools while they marched around us!"

Cunedag took on the responsibility of finding out if the enemy had indeed marched west, as he and his men had so recently travelled those roads themselves.

"I said we should have gone the long way around," Asaros said as they rode towards the snaking trail of the Usa. "This Melga played the comes for a fool!"

"If we had, then we would have run into the brunt of the enemy warband," Cunedag replied. "They would have obliterated us, so it's just as well we followed my plan."

"Aye, but we might have been able to turn back and get word to Aurelianus that the enemy was heading south. He would have known of their trickery days ago!"

Cunedag said nothing as they continued riding at as fast a pace as the horses could manage. He was angry with himself for Asaros spoke the truth. They should have known of the Picts' movements but instead had sat on that riverbank waiting for them to attack. This Melga was a canny one and that, Cunedag knew from experience, was the worst kind of enemy. They soon picked up the trail of the enemy's passing. Looted farmsteads and the remains of a large camp on the southern bank of the Usa told them that they were on the right track.

"They'll be making for Lindum," said Cunedag as the trail the next day seemed to turn south-east, cutting across the marshy lands that surrounded the tributaries of the Abus Fluvius. "Even if we caught up with them, there is little we can do to stop them. Lindum is doomed, I fear."

It was a melancholy camp that night as Cunedag sent a rider back to Aurelianus to tell him of Lindum's impending fate. The passing warband had left little food in the area and the men ate the last of their rations by their campfires, knowing that the war was going to be all the harder now that the enemy was behind the walls of a provincial capital.

Chapter 9

Melga looked around at the crumbling town of Lindum with a wide grin. For the first time in his life, he had entered a Roman town, and he had entered it as a conqueror.

The town consisted of two portions which straddled a slope that ran down to the riverbank. The upper part was the old legionary fort in which the basilica and forum now sat, with a massive gate at the top of the steep slope which led down to the lower part of the town; a sprawling settlement of wineshops, brothels, bakeries, wharves and warehouses which had grown below the old colonia.

Many of the inhabitants had fled with what little they could carry as the Picts had approached the town and whatever garrison it currently boasted had thrown down their weapons and departed with the civilians rather than attempt any futile defence. Melga had claimed the provincial capital of Flavia Caesariensis without a drop of blood being shed. It was almost disappointing.

His warriors were making up for the lack of fighting by looting the town and drinking whatever they could get their hands on. The frugal days of empty bellies in the woodlands above the Abus Fluvius were a distant memory now that the wineshops and warehouses were being raided. Those foolish civilians who had stayed were desperately trying to ingratiate themselves to their new overlords by providing the keys and locations of secured stockpiles of wine, beer and food, not to mention handing their women over to the Picts as if they were sacrificial offerings to these gods from the north who might look on them with something other than disdain if every single one of their appetites were fulfilled.

Melga turned the old Roman headquarters in the upper part of the town into his personal residence, the well-ordered rooms and geometric aesthetics a sharp contrast to the smoky hillforts and thatched roundhouses he was used to. Wine was brought to him, as were women whom he corralled in a pen in the forum like livestock to either be given to his men as favours or to sell as slaves. He would indulge his own desires later, picking the best-looking of the women for his bed once he was confident that the town was secure and the sentries were in place.

There was plenty more to organise too, and he allowed himself a cup of the stinging Roman wine that was so different to the heather ale and mead of the highlands while he listened to reports and gave orders like a king in a ruined court at the end of days. He lolled on a high-backed chair draped with furs and silk cushions while looted gold and silver from the town's church and fine residences was piled at his feet as his lion's share of Lindum.

It was just as he was starting to tire of the administrative details when two of his men entered the room with another captive. At once, Melga could see that this one was unlike all the rest. She was clearly a harlot of some sort; even Melga recognised how these Roman whores dressed. She wore a tunica of saffron silk which left her arms bare and stopped short of her ankles which were gilded with jewelled ornaments. This was no brothel whore but some wealthy man's full-time mistress.

"We found her skulking in one of those big houses overlooking the river," said one of his warriors.

Melga leant forward in his throne and beckoned the woman with a crooked finger. She walked over to him, feigning confidence, with her head held aloof. Oh, this one was used to being treated far above her station!

"What's your name, whore?"

"Vibiana," said the woman, again with a haughty tone that defied her status.

"Where is your master?"

"He fled, the cursed coward," Vibiana spat. She spoke British with a curious accent and Melga realised that she was not from these shores.

"And he left you behind?" he said, his suspicions aroused.

"Yes, damn his bones," the whore went on. "He was only interested in taking his valuables. I said to him; 'am I not valuable?' but he was fleeing to his mother-in-law's estate in the south and said that he could hardly bring his concubine with him!"

"Understandable, I suppose," said Melga, finding her story plausible enough. "But it must have stung him terribly to leave behind such a beauty as yourself."

She shrugged. "He had grown bored of me of late and I of him. But Fortuna has laid a different path before me. I would much rather please a king than a grubby merchant."

She smiled as she said this, her whole demeanour softening and she approached Melga with swaying hips and a coquettish tilt of her pretty head. Great Mother, she was actually flirting with him!

Melga was too smart to fall for the charms of a woman who clearly wanted to please whoever held the power of life and death over her, but he found himself softening to her, nonetheless. This whore had guts! More guts than anybody else in Lindum, it seemed.

"Where are you from, Vibiana?" he asked her.

"I was born in Illyria."

"Oh?" Melga had never heard of the place. "And how did you come to these shores?"

"My mother worked in the household of an administrator in Salona. He sired me on her and I was raised in his household until the age of twelve. After that, he had no desire to keep me, so I was sold to a brothel on the coast. From there, I was purchased by a merchant who traded with

Britannia. I was brought here and then given in payment to my last master for several amphorae of wine."

Melga tutted at the callousness of men. "I would have sold you for more than a few amphorae. In fact, I may not sell you at all. You are a finer jewel than any of this base stuff my men have looted from the cellars and coffers of Lindum. I think I'll keep you for myself."

Vibiana smiled, and, at a flash of those surprisingly healthy teeth, a burning lust for her blossomed in the battle-hardened Pict's chest. He seized her arm and yanked her down onto his lap. He could feel the quickening of her pulse beneath her fair, soft skin. She was scared of him, certainly but, he allowed himself the indulgence of thinking, just for a moment, that some of it was arousal.

Hooves drummed on the earth like the rolling peal of approaching thunder. Cunedag led the charge, his spearpoint the tip of the wedge that would pierce the enemy's heart as they desperately tried to get into a defensive formation.

Cunedag's scouts had spotted the Pictish camp not ten miles from the walls of Lindum. The invaders had been confident enough to light a cookfire despite the Britons having slaughtered two of their hunting parties in the past few days. These ones didn't seem to have got the message and were lounging around over their breakfast on a bright and sunny morning, a selection of dressed game hanging from a pole nearby.

Cunedag yelled death at them as his spear slammed into the neck of a Pict, sliding over the rim of his buckler, and bursting through the back of his head in a shower of crimson. Their line, such as it was, shattered and the thirty-man cavalry charge rode over the Picts, trampling them and stabbing at anything that moved.

Several survivors turned to flee but the mounted men soon cut them down and, seemingly before the first war cries of the charge had dissipated into the trees, it was over. Around fifteen to twenty Picts lay dead, their bodies tossed about haphazardly with their blood seeping into the forest loam.

"You'd think they'd send out larger hunting parties," said Murcho as he cleaned his spear tip with a bit of rag. "Or at least not sit about eating breakfast when they know a large war band is nearby."

"Picts don't do a whole lot of thinking," said Tegid. "And talking of breakfast …" He helped himself to a ladleful of the stew that bubbled over the fire.

"Well, here's some meat for us to take back to our men, at least," said Tancorix, indicating the cadavers of two roe deer and a boar. "Already dressed for us. They must have been hunting in these parts for a couple of days."

"That's not all!" said Murcho as he investigated the piles of gear that had been left in the shade of the trees. "Look here! It seems our Pictish friends took a few prisoners."

In a makeshift pen of woven branches, three men sat on their haunches, bound and gagged and looking up at the Britons with pleading eyes. They had the short-cropped hair of soldiers and the strong bodies to match.

"Cut them loose," said Cunedag. "Let's see who they are."

Their bonds and gags removed, the three men revealed themselves to be Britons and grateful ones at that. "We fled Lindum before it fell to the Picts," said one. "But were captured two days ago by these men here you have so efficiently slain, for which we are eternally grateful. May you perhaps be men who serve Ambrosius Aurelianus, the Comes Britanniarum?"

"We fight with him," Cunedag replied. "Though we are free men of the north. I am King Cunedag of the Votadini. But one question remains; why did three able-bodied men with soldierly looks to them flee Lindum instead of staying to defend it? I must warn you; Aurelianus takes a dim view of deserters."

"We are no deserters, Lord Cunedag," said the man, his back straightening with pride. "The truth of the matter is that we fled Lindum in order to find Aurelianus. We serve Vitalinus of Maxima Caesariensis and have travelled from Londinium on a mission of a clandestine nature."

Cunedag and Murcho shared a look. Here was something interesting.

"Go on," Cunedag said to the man.

"Well, Vitalinus has seen fit to place a spy within the camp of Melga the Pict. We escorted her north and were ordered to seek out the comes to bring word to him of her presence in Lindum."

"*Her* presence?" Cunedag said.

"She is a harlot in Vitalinus's service," said the man.

"You took a harlot into enemy territory and just left her there?" Cunedag exclaimed.

"She is no ordinary whore!" the soldier said. "A high-class piece if ever there was one. Vitalinus had her decked out in fine silk and gold to pose as some wealthy noble's wench. The idea is to tempt Melga into taking her into his bed so that she might get word to you of his plans via a second spy who has the opportunity to go beyond the town walls."

"A risky plan," said Cunedag. "Melga may just ravish her and then kill her. Or just kill her, depending on his mood."

"You should see this wench, Lord," said the man with a conspiratorial wink. "A man would be a fool to toss her aside, even a Pict. Uh … begging your lord's pardon …"

"I am no Pict so you can relax on that front," said Cunedag.

"Right," said the soldier, clearing his throat. "Well, what I mean is that she is clearly a whore of quality. And, as for looks, she'd give Aphrodite a run for her money. We had to escort her north and it was a ball-aching few nights on the road sleeping in her company, eh, lads?"

His two fellow soldiers nodded their assent with juvenile grins.

"Well, you've headed in the wrong direction if you wished to run into Aurelianus," said Cunedag. "He's to the east of the town, blockading the river to stop any reinforcements or shipments of grain entering Lindum. We intend to starve the Picts until we come up with a plan to take the town, but this spy of yours might play her part in that. You will come back to my camp, and I'll see that you are fed, and we can discuss the matter further."

The soldiers seemed grateful for that, seeing Aurelianus's ally as just as good as Aurelianus himself. They had already suffered much and had narrowly escaped a brutal interrogation at Melga's hands for their captors had intended to bring them back to Lindum for questioning. All they wanted to do now was pass on their message and then get back to Londinium, leaving the wild north to its business.

Cunedag saw that they were fed and provided with ponies to take them back south the following day. He extracted the last details of Vitalinus's plan from them, learning that this harlot, Vibiana, would sneak written messages out of Lindum using one of the fish traders. The Romans had built a dyke to connect the River Lindis with the River Trisantona to the west and, every morning, this fisherman headed up the dyke where he would meet a man of Aurelianus's, pass on his message, and return to the harbour with a boatload of trout.

It seemed like a lot of risk for very little reward to Cunedag, but none of the risk was his and he may yet learn something from this plucky strumpet so, he agreed to receive the fish trader's dispatches in Aurelianus's stead. Every morning, he sent a man down to where the dyke met the Trisantona. For the first few days, no news came from Vibiana. The fisherman was met by Cunedag's man every morning and all he could do was confirm that she had been taken in by Melga and was currently seeing to his needs up at the principia in the upper portion of the town. If there was any news to share with her allies beyond Lindum's walls, then she wasn't sharing it yet.

Cunedag doubted the mad plan would yield any fruit and had to focus his attention on other means to take the town. A full-on assault would be foolhardy as, despite being somewhat outnumbered, the Picts now had walls to hide behind and artillery engines to hurl rocks and *scorpio* bolts at them.

There was much discussion on the possibility of sneaking into the town, as Cunedag had heroically done at Cilurnum and Murcho had managed at Alt Clut. Cunedag would have liked nothing better than to sneak in, overrun the walls and open the gates to let in the rest of his teulu, but they could barely get close enough to Lindum's walls to look for any gaps in their defences.

"The only way we can find a way into the town is from somebody already within its walls," said Murcho. "I think this spy of Vitalinus's might be our greatest asset. If she can help us get in, the town will fall in a day."

"If she hasn't already been killed with her hide decorating Melga's new residence," said Tegid. "For we've heard no word from her yet."

Vibiana dreamt of her childhood in the hills above Salona. It was a frequent dream and such a pleasant one that she often worried that it was nothing but a pleasant fiction, invented by her mind to convince her that there was something better out there, something she may one day return to.

Her family had been poor but that hardly mattered in her dreams which were all sensory; the smell of the Adriatic Sea, the way the sunlight glinted off those deep blue waters, the cries of the fishermen and the taste of olives ripened in those green hills where the wild ponies ran. She thought she remembered brothers, once upon a time, at least two, both older than her. Everything before her brief term of service in the household of her mother's master was vague.

It had been a sweet but teasing false start to her life and she hadn't even known that her family were slaves. She must have been five or six when her mother had brought her down into the town of Salona where she was put to work scrubbing floors and peeling vegetables. Since that day, her life had been a succession of drudgery and exploitation that had grown ever more sordid and unbearable.

She remembered her mother dying. That event stood out in her memory like a wound that would never heal. It can't have been long before her twelfth birthday because she didn't remember much of her time in domestic servitude after that. She had been sold on and then on again, making her way, eventually, to these gloomy shores where life was perpetually cold and grey. She barely remembered the sun, the real sun; the one that warmed the hills of her homeland. Only in her dreams. But she swore long ago that one day she would return to Illyria and walk in the hills of her childhood again.

She awoke, startled by angry cries in the street below the window of the ruined principia. Melga's warriors were at each other's throats again and it sounded like blood would be spilled sooner or later. Most of the food was gone and, with the river to the east blockaded by the Britons who also lurked in the woods to the north, the Picts had fallen to fighting and brawling among themselves over the last scraps. Tensions were high as the nature of their predicament began to set in.

For her part, Vibiana wasn't starving, at least not yet. She pleased Melga enough for him to lavish what small luxuries he had on her. She slept in a small chamber near his own and ate of the food he had hoarded for his own consumption. It wasn't much, but it was better than the conditions in the lower part of the town.

The argument in the street had indeed turned to violence and the sound of a man being gutted by a Pictish blade could be heard, his gasps and cries to his gods rising to Vibiana's window. She sighed and got out of bed, annoyed by the distraction to her thoughts.

She had been mulling over her options ever since she had left Londinium, the town that had been her home for most of her adult life. Although she was a slave to be used and passed around for the sexual pleasures of men, her life in Britannia's capital had been one of relative comfort. Vitalinus, seeing much potential in her as a spy, had seen to her education and she had wanted for nothing. So why then had he sent her north on this godawful mission to warm the bed of a filthy heathen?

Not once, in her years of doing his bidding, had he sent her so far from Londinium. She was used to pleasuring politicians and clergymen in the villas and bath houses of Londinium. Now she was taken nightly on a filthy wolfskin by a brute of a man who, although lacking the sadistic perversions of many of the more civilised men she had spent her time with, was a crude savage, nonetheless.

Was Vitalinus tiring of her? Was this his way of casting her aside on a mission that could well be the death of her in the hope of gaining some small advantage in this northern war? She tried to think of ways she had displeased him and could find nothing. She had served him well, loyally, even, as far as a slave can ever show true loyalty. It all felt like a ghastly punishment for some undisclosed crime.

And yet, being so far from Londinium and Vitalinus gave Vibiana a strange sense of freedom she could not remember feeling in all her life. She wielded power as Melga's concubine. Here she was, a woman in a town full of barbarian savages and not one of them would dare touch her. Although she was still Melga's slave, Melga was but a man after all and she feared him far less than she feared Vitalinus. A savage mind lacked the cruel cunning of a wholly civilised one. Vitalinus had spies who watched his spies and all of Londinium was tangled in his sticky web. Melga was but a simple barbarian who recognised only primal strength. And he was besotted with her. That made him weak and vulnerable to manipulation. *Could it be done?*

The winds of change were sweeping Britannia in any case. Three usurpers had been named emperor in less than as many years and now it looked like there would be war between the latest pretender and the true emperor of the West. Vibiana had played her part in the shift of power by opening the bathhouse doors so that the guards of that grotesque Gratianus could slay him (was that why Vitalinus had sent her north? Did she know too much at last?).

She was convinced that Britannia was doomed. Constantinus's campaign seemed a fool's errand to her, and the island was now stripped of her legions and left open to barbarians on all sides. The whole diocese might burn within the year. If she was ever going to make good on her promise to herself, if she was ever going to make her dream a reality, then she had to act now.

Her homeland called to her. It was so vivid in her dreams that she felt as if she could almost touch it, and yet it seemed so fragile that she feared it might vanish beyond her grasp for all time. She had never been in more danger than she was now, but if she did not risk her life in making her move, then she risked losing her dream of freedom forever.

Her mind was made up. She was going to betray Vitalinus.

Chapter 10

The following week saw little change other than that Melga sent out fewer hunting parties. That meant that they were doing something right, and it brought much pleasure to the Britons to think of the Picts slowly starving inside the walls of the town they had taken.

The fisherman finally brought word to them that Vibiana had come up with some useful information. In his desperation, Melga was sending some of his men to the small town of Causennae about a day's ride south of Lindum in the hope of ransacking it of food. To keep the Britons' focus on Lindum, he was going to feint by marching a large body of troops north to look like a retreat. When attacked, the body of men would head back to Lindum where the town's watchtowers would cover them. By the time Cunedag realised that it was a ruse, Melga's men would have returned from Causennae with whatever food they could grab.

Cunedag and his captains pored over Vibiana's sealed letter in the confines of his tent. It was written in a woman's hand and, though some in the tent claimed that this was no more than the imagination of others, there was a faint whiff of perfume to the small roll of papyrus. Cunedag considered how precious an agent she must be to Vitalinus to spend money educating a whore.

"Melga must really be desperate," said Murcho. "To go to this much effort not to attack us, but merely to procure some provisions for his men. We've got a real stranglehold on that town. All we need do is squeeze a little harder!"

"I would much rather take the town by force of arms," said Cunedag. "Starving an enemy is a slimy way to win a victory and there are still people within Lindum who are little more than prisoners of the Picts. I would not starve them into the bargain."

"I'll bet Melga is keeping this pretty Vibiana's arse nice and plump," said Asaros. "It's a wonder she's keen to help us outwit her master! Do you not think it unwise to place our trust in a spy we don't know and a whore at that?"

"We have no reason not to trust her," Cunedag said. "Her master in Londinium is desperately hoping that we drive the Picts back across the wall. This spy may well be hoping that we swiftly take the town and remove her from Melga's clutches. And I'd dearly wish to oblige her if I only knew how. But she has thrown us a bone and we must do what we can with it, though it will mean dividing our forces. If we are not to betray our knowledge of Melga's plan and the spy in his midst, we need to make a show of falling for it. I will take the bulk of the teulu north to engage the enemy when they leave the town. Murcho, I want you to take a hundred men south and overrun this foraging party."

"You want me to take the smaller contingent?" Murcho asked, his face a little hurt. "I *am* your penteulu, Brother."

"And that is why I trust no other to lead my men on the more dangerous mission. Besides, I must be seen to be at the head of the larger force, else Melga will know that we have not fallen for his bait."

"Thank you for your confidence," said Murcho, his pride restored. "Though it still seems like a lot of effort just to wipe out a foraging party."

"Aye, it might not aid us much in taking Lindum, but it will whittle Melga's forces down for us a little," said Cunedag. "And you never know, we might be able to winkle some useful information about Lindum's defences from them so be sure to take prisoners."

Two days later, Murcho led his contingent of one hundred riders south along the road that led first to Causennae and then on to Londinium. Well before the end of the day, they had reached the outskirts of the small town and Murcho led them into the woods that clustered to the west of the road. All they had to do now was lie in wait.

Night had fallen by the time his scouts returned from where he had posted them on the road and informed him that a band of twenty to thirty Picts was riding down from the north.

"Hardly challenging odds," Murcho said to his men with a grin. "But remember, this is not to be a slaughter. The king wants prisoners to interrogate."

"Do we attack them on the road?" one of his men asked.

"No. We run the risk of most of them fleeing back north or vanishing into the woods if we do that. We wait until they are in the town itself, then we close in behind them and trap them."

They mounted up and, muffling their bridles with their fists, moved through the trees towards the road. The Picts were hardly being subtle about their raid and Murcho supposed they had no reason to. Causennae was all but deserted and posed no challenge to thirty warriors looking for plunder. They sang and laughed as they rode down the road towards the town, oblivious to the hundred Britons who waited in the woods, listening to the drumming of their horses' hooves on the road.

Once the sound of their passing had vanished, Murcho led his men out of the trees and onto the road. He set a leisurely pace to give the Picts enough time to breach the gates of the town. He wanted them well and truly within the trap before he sprung it. It was almost too easy.

As the walls of Causennae came into view, the Britons could see that it had fallen to the enemy band without a fight. The gates stood open and there was no sound of fighting from within.

"Come on, men!" Murcho yelled, raising his spear into the air. "In and at them! And get prisoners!"

They broke into a gallop and thundered through the gates of the town. Murcho had expected to run into the Picts as soon as they entered and catch them while they were distracted with their looting, but an eerie silence hung over the darkened buildings.

"Something's not right," said one of Murcho's men. "Where are the town's inhabitants?"

Murcho said nothing as they rode down the deserted main street that ran from north to south. There didn't seem to be a soul about and the Pictish warband that had descended on the town seemed to have melted into the shadows.

"Turn back," he said. "This isn't right. We're walking into a trap of some kind. Back!"

They turned their horses around and headed back towards the northern gate but before they reached it, they could see that it had been barred against them. Bowmen appeared on the rampart of the gate house and spearmen emerged from the shadows on either side of them. Murcho knew that this had been a terrible mistake.

"Throw down your weapons, Britons!" called a voice from the shadows. "And you may yet live!"

Murcho glanced at his men. *Do we have a chance?* Their eyes seemed to ask him. *How many of them could there be?* Murcho's thoughts dwelled on his brother, and he knew that he couldn't let him down. He couldn't afford to get captured and used against Cunedag. He would rather die. And his men saw that in his eyes and understood. There would be no surrender.

"Kill as many as you can!" Murcho yelled, raising his spear.

His men roared their defiance as arrows sailed into their ranks from the gatehouse. Then, the Picts in the shadows charged.

"I can't understand it," said Tegid. "Do you think they suspect that we know of their intentions?"

It was close to the end of the second day since Murcho and his men had ridden south and Cunedag had taken the rest of the teulu north to await the Picts' false withdrawal from Lindum. They had camped on a wooded rise near the North Road so they could quickly descend on the Picts as they headed north. Even though it was a ruse, and the Picts would fall back to Lindum as soon as they came under attack, Cunedag wanted to slay as many of them as he could. The less Picts defending Lindum, the easier it would be to take the town when the time came for it.

But they had waited all day and there was no sign of movement on the road north. The afternoon had dulled to dusk and there was no noise but the breeze and birdsong in the treetops. Something was wrong.

"Maybe they've postponed their retreat until tomorrow," offered Tancorix.

"Maybe," said Cunedag. "But I don't like it all the same. Dispatch a rider south to meet with the penteulu. I want to know if that foraging party has headed south, though if the road north is quiet, I'm guessing the road south will be too."

His orders were carried out and a scout galloped south, following the woodland trails and staying well clear of Lindum. As night fell, Cunedag couldn't sleep for worrying about his brother. He had sent him off with a mere hundred men. What if they had all been outwitted? What if the words of the spy were a lie? If anything happened to Murcho, he didn't know if he could ever forgive himself.

Murcho could barely see out of his right eye, so badly swollen it was. Blood streamed from a gash in his scalp and from where the tight rope dug into his wrists. Although his legs were tied together beneath his saddle as they rode north towards Lindum, he desperately tried to keep himself from sliding to one side for he knew that he would be dragged for some distance before his captors halted his horse.

All his men were dead. He fought back tears of rage and grief and tried not to think of all the lives that had been lost under his command. That he still lived while the bodies of his men littered the streets of Causennae burned like a hot brand to his soul. They had fought as hard as they could, his loyal warriors surrounding him to the last, dying where they stood as the press of Picts surged in on them.

It had been a trap. Causennae had been deserted long before they had arrived, its inhabitants pushed out by a large Pictish band who had lain in wait for the Britons to ride in, following the thirty-man raiding party which had been the bait. What fools they had been! That bitch of a spy was clearly working with Melga and had sent out information that had cost the Britons a hundred good warriors, not to mention the capture of their penteulu, brother to King Cunedag himself.

Murcho tried to think of a way to end his own life before they reached Lindum for he knew that he would be tortured for information on his brother's strength and position. It wasn't the agony of torment that he feared, only the failure of his resolve. If he gave Melga anything that could be used against Cunedag, then his failure would haunt him for eternity in Annun.

The southern gates to Lindum swung open to admit the victorious warband. Many empty saddles returned for the Britons had fought valiantly and that at least gave Murcho some pride in his men. As the gates slammed shut behind them like the slamming of a tomb's lid, Murcho was led up the main street to the upper portion of the town, jeered at by the Picts every step of the way. Some even threw things; refuse in the form of animal bones and other less pleasant things but nothing hard enough to endanger the young prince's life. He was too precious to their master to risk injuring more than he already was.

As they approached the principia, he was hauled down from his horse and a noose was looped over his head so he could be dragged about like a collared wolf. Up the steps to the principia he was hauled and into the cross hall which was bedecked with Pictish banners. The gaps between the columns were piled with loot and supplies.

A man lolled on a throne at the head of the hall. He was around forty, with black hair touched with grey and the hard, compact body of a man who had not allowed middle age to slow his fighting lifestyle. This, Murcho assumed, was Melga.

He was dragged to the Pictish war chief's feet and made to kneel. He tried to raise his head to look his enemy in the eyes, but it was forced down by the butt of a spear. All he could see were Melga's sandaled feet and the slender, slippered feet of a woman standing next to him.

"Prince Murcho mab Etern of the Votadini!" Melga said. "Brother and penteulu to King Cunedag. Welcome to Lindum!"

There was laughter around the hall at this and Murcho closed his eyes on his tears, unable to bear the shame.

Chapter 11

The torches flickered in their niches around the principia as the sounds of the returning war party celebrating their victory rose from the streets of the town. Vibiana looked out over the lamplit houses of Lindum; a Roman town now the sordid play-pit of northern barbarians.

"Vibiana," Melga said from his throne. "I'm sure I can find something more interesting for you to look at than the debauchery of my men. Come here!"

Vibiana felt the tug of her lust for freedom somewhere deep within her, such an old pain that it was almost a companion. She had burned many bridges to get where she was and now, at the last, she found that she was no closer to freedom than she had been when she had been brought to these shores.

Melga was drunk, having celebrated the success of their plan along with his men. He lolled on his fur-lined throne, a jug of wine hanging from his grip, occasionally spilling crimson onto the mosaiced floor.

She approached him, thrusting down her distaste as she had learned to do when she had been not much more than a child. The professionalism of her trade which had been honed and sharpened by several masters took over her body, yet if anybody took the trouble to look deep into her eyes of late, they might see a flicker of despair that had not been there a year ago.

Melga leaned forward and grabbed her jewelled wrist, pulling her towards him. She stumbled on one of the furs that carpeted his dais and fell clumsily into his lap. He gripped her around the waist with an iron-hard arm and, taking a swig from his wine jar then setting it down on the table beside his throne, he cupped her breast with a massive paw.

"We have much to celebrate tonight," he said before kissing her neck with his wine-stained lips.

She feigned arousal, as she had been taught from a young age. "Your plan was a stroke of genius, Master," she purred as she ran a delicate hand down the rough stubble of his cheek.

"Oho! Don't seek to flatter me, my dear!" Melga said. "We both know that the plan was yours, and that you concocted it to earn my favour! Though I am glad that you were keen to seek sanctuary with me. Do I not reward loyalty more than your slippery former master?"

"He is a worm compared to you, Master," said Vibiana before she kissed him full on the lips.

As they held the kiss, her mind curled in on itself in agony. To trade one debauched master for another! Was this to be her lot in life? To go round and round in a hellish circle? At least this savage Pict did not pass her around his associates as Vitalinus had done. It was a small mercy to be kept as the private plaything of a man but there it was. She had long grown sick of being a tool used to buy favour or extract information.

Melga tore his lips from hers, the pressing concerns of politics diluting his burning lust. "But we must do what we can to keep Vitalinus on our string," he said. "If he believes that you are still loyal to him, then we can use him to our advantage."

"Cunedag must be dealt with quickly," Vibiana said. "Else word will reach Londinium that he was tricked. Vitalinus suspects nothing but he may begin to wonder if he learns that Cunedag was so easily outwitted."

"Aye, he will die within days, my dear," Melga said. "And then the north will be won. With that dog Aurelianus encamped on the riverbank to our east, we can leave him in the mud and march south on Londinium. And I will personally peel the hide from your former master's back and decorate his own palace wall with it!"

"I would dearly like to see that, Master," said Vibiana. "But how are we to defeat Cunedag? He still outnumbers us, even after our butchery of a hundred of his men at Causennae."

"We have his brother!" Melga said. "We will learn all we need to from him. I am letting him sweat tonight and tomorrow, my interrogators will work on him with knife and hot pincers. That is, if you are not able to coax the information from him first."

"Me, Master?"

"Oh, I have no doubt my men can work the truth from his screaming lips, but torture can so often only result in half truths. Sometimes a softer touch is more effective. And who could resist your delicate attention?"

For a moment, Vibiana's mask slipped, only for a fraction, too quick for the drunken Pict to notice.

"I want you to go to him tonight," Melga went on. "He'll be tired. In pain. Frightened. I want you to make all of that melt away, so he thinks only of his lust for you and then I want you to find out where his brother is camped and how large his warband is. Learn everything you can from him even if you have to pleasure him a dozen times."

Vibiana forced a smile on her face. "As you command, Master."

"But first," Melga said, running a tendril of her perfumed hair through his thick fingers and smelling it. "I wish you to pleasure me. It has been an eventful day, and I can think of no better way to unwind than with a jug of wine and a beautiful whore."

Vibiana closed her eyes as she let him take her there on his throne. If she had any hope of survival, she would have slipped a dagger into that bulging neck of his and taken great pleasure in watching him bleed out. But getting out of the city alive and reaching the coast was more than she could manage. So, she was forced to play this game for her own survival. But it was a game she had been playing for as long as she could remember, and she was so tired of it that her mind felt driven to desperate thoughts.

Murcho opened his eyes as he heard a key in the lock of the door at the far end of the corridor. Moonlight shone in through the barred window of the small storage room which had been converted to a prison cell. His hands were manacled and chained to a peg in the wall and his whole body, tired and aching though it was, tensed at the sound of somebody approaching. Had they come to torture him already? He had thought that they would have at least waited until the morning or perhaps it *was* early morning, and he had dozed off? Time seemed to play no part in his life anymore.

Another key turned, this time in the door to his cell, and it grated open. Squinting in the light of the jailer's oil lamp, Murcho could see the tall figure of a woman entering his cell. It was the woman he had seen at the side of Melga earlier that night. Vibiana the spy. *Vibiana the traitor.*

"Leave us," the woman said to the jailer, and he complied without comment, which told Murcho that this woman, slave though she was, held some command over the Picts who served her master.

The door grated shut and Vibiana placed the oil lamp on a small stone shelf. Its flickering wick gave them both enough light to see each other's faces. Vibiana carried a bowl of something in her other hand and she approached him, leaning down to peer at his wounded head and swollen eye. He realised that it was a bowl of water and that she had come to tend his wounds.

It was a trick, that was obvious. Melga surely had physicians or medicine men in his following who could treat him. Why send his personal concubine other than to use her sexual allure to pull information from him? It was better than the torturers, but he knew they wouldn't be far off once he had rebuffed this whore's attempts.

"Those bastards really didn't go easy on you, did they?" Vibiana said as she dabbed at the dried blood that encrusted one side of his face.

He pulled away from her, not because of the pain of her touch but because he was determined not to let her play her game. This bitch had betrayed them and caused the deaths of a hundred of his men. If she thought they could get along then she was sorely mistaken.

"Come now, Murcho," she purred. "A big strong warrior like you can sit still and let himself be taken care of, can't he?"

"Not by you, you traitorous whore!"

She looked genuinely shocked by his words, and she set down the bowl and cloth. "Some wine then?" she said. "I could call for some …"

"I will neither sup with you nor be treated by you!" Murcho spat. "We trusted your information! And that information led to the butchery of a hundred good Britons! Have you no shame in betraying your master?"

A thunderous look briefly crossed her pretty features. "Shame?" she demanded. "My only shame was that I waited so long before I made my escape from him! Vitalinus has had me on his string since I was a youth. It took an invasion from the north and Vitalinus's own folly for me to find a chance to escape his clutches."

"And yet you ran into the arms of another brute who will only use you as Vitalinus did."

Vibiana closed her eyes and Murcho knew that he had struck some deep part of her soul. "Yes," she said at last. "But I am alive, and I am far from Londinium which is infested with Vitalinus's agents. I would take my chances with the wild Picts than remain in that rat's nest of politicians and assassins. You have no idea what it's like for a woman trying to find her place in a world of men who want only war. Life must be so simple for you. Ride out, kill, conquer and take what you can. We women must use subtler tools and always we are the tools of men."

Murcho said nothing, her speech having robbed him of words. He knew he couldn't trust this spy who turned on her master at the change of the wind, but there seemed to be a truth to her words that he could not deny.

"Well, I suppose you know why I am here," she said at last. "My new master has sent me to extract information from you; namely the whereabouts of your brother's warband. He told me to make love to you if that was what it took, but if you won't even let me treat your wounds, I would think that's off the table. But if you change your mind …"

"No," Murcho said. "Nothing will make me betray my brother. Especially not the attentions of a whore."

His insults lacked the conviction they had a moment ago and it looked like she was well-used to such contempt. He apologised anyway and immediately felt foolish for doing so.

Her eyes softened and she looked touched by his apology. "I have been called far worse, believe me," she said.

"I don't doubt it."

"I am sorry about your men. I did not wish them killed. The plan was to snare your brother by luring him to Causennae but he sent you in his stead. I only did what I had to in order to secure Melga as my protector."

"Some protector," Murcho snorted. "You do realise that he'll kill you or give you to his men as soon as he tires of you?"

"Yes. I am not naïve, dear Murcho. But what else can a woman in my position do? I have often thought about how I might escape his clutches and flee this land but how is a penniless slave to make her way to the coast and buy passage anywhere? Do not be fooled by these costly silks and gold ornaments. They, like my body itself, are my master's property. I wonder, would your brother look upon me with more mercy than Melga?"

"He'd skin you alive for betraying him and costing the lives of so many of his men."

"And what if I were to help you and your brother take Lindum?"

Murcho squinted at her, trying to read her face. "Why on earth should I trust you?"

"Because it may be the only chance for both of us to get out of this alive," she replied. "And because you have no chance of taking this town without my help. Surely, I have shown you how much I despise my current situation and yours is little better. What say you we work together to bring about Melga's undoing and free ourselves?"

"How could we manage such a thing?" Murcho asked, still cautious.

"I can get word to your brother. Melga can't read and doesn't check my dispatches in any case. I can tell your brother one thing and Melga another without him suspecting."

"So, we can have my brother and his men ready, but how to get them inside the town walls?"

"Leave that to me. But when the time comes for it, can I count on you to put in a good word for me with your brother? The deaths I caused were not intentional. Only his capture was, and I am sorry things turned out the way they did."

"If you get him and his men into Lindum," said Murcho, "then I'm sure he will see past your previous treachery. I once sided against him with our older brother, Brude, and he forgave me when I realised the error of my ways."

Vibiana smiled. "Then perhaps we have more in common than you previously thought. Now, what are we to tell Melga?"

"Tell him?"

"I have to give him something, else he will send his torturers tomorrow to extract the information I could not."

Murcho repressed a shudder, but she was right. He had to give her something, even a lie, else face torment tomorrow. "Very well," he said. "My brother is camped on the western bank of the River Trisantona. He has over a thousand men under his banner, including the local militias and garrisons of the forts we have passed by on our way south. Those numbers ought to keep your Pictish master cowering behind these walls."

"Aye, they would," Vibiana said, her eyes wide at the size of the nearby warband. "But are those numbers truth or lie?

He smiled at her. "Does it matter? We have enough warriors to take the town. The next part is up to you."

Chapter 12

When news reached Cunedag that Murcho's entire contingent had been wiped out, his rage and sorrow knew no bounds. He confined himself to his tent and drank himself into a stupor while his men listened to him raging at the gods and the world in general for their cruelty. The worst thing was, that Murcho's body had not been among the fallen, leaving him to ponder his brother's fate or what torments he might be enduring at the hands of the Picts.

On the third day of his mourning, Vibiana's fisherman brought a sealed dispatch from Lindum which was hastily brought to Cunedag. The distraught king of the Votadini doused his head in cold water and tried to sober himself before he opened it, knowing that it was likely more lies from the slut who had betrayed them and caused the death of his brother.

But the contents of the letter were more sobering than any other cure for drunkenness. She spoke of Murcho, claiming that he had been taken alive and was currently in a cell in Lindum. She explained her position as a spy in Melga's following and expressed her regret for her part in the ruse which had cost him a hundred warriors. She then told of how she and Murcho were working together to allow Cunedag entry to the town.

"Lies and more lies," said Tegid. "This bitch has tricked you before, my king. Do not allow your hope for Murcho's survival to cloud your judgement."

"Am I to give up hope that he is alive, then?" Cunedag demanded. "This may be a pack of lies, as you say, or it may be the only chance we have to take Lindum and save Murcho's life into the bargain. How can I disregard it, yet how can I trust it?"

"A hard choice. What else does the whore say?"

"That she will arrange for us to enter the lower town from the docks one week from now. She suggests that we come downriver in boats under the cover of darkness while she takes care of the sentries on the southern wall."

"A trap," said Asaros. "Tegid is right. She seeks to lure us into the town where Melga's men will be waiting with nowhere for us to flee to. Burn that letter and let us think of another way to take the town."

"There is no other way," Cunedag said, scrunching up the letter in his fist.

"Then at least ask this woman to prove that Murcho lives," said Tegid. "Demand proof of his survival before we agree to anything."

"That is good advice," said Cunedag. "Fetch a scribe. I will send this Vibiana a message of my own."

It took three days for the reply to come and Cunedag wasted no time in making preparations to act on Vibiana's instructions if she turned out to be in earnest. There were two approaches to Lindum from the west. One, was the River Lindis which curved to the east as it reached Lindum and the other was down the overgrown dyke which connected the Lindis to the Trisantona. If he wanted to get his warriors into Lindum and storm its harbour quickly, then he would need to use both approaches.

He split his warband into two and sent one half of it south-west to procure boats from the settlements on the River Lindis while he personally led the rest of his men to the point where Vibiana's messenger met his own man on a bend in the Trisantona. From there, they could head into Lindum's harbour in barges covered with hides as if they were cargo.

When Vibiana's message arrived, Cunedag took it into his tent to read in private. At the first line, his spirits rose for it seemed to be written by Murcho himself.

Dear Brother,

Vibiana tells me that you have requested proof of my life. You always were wise and cautious, Cunedag, and I would be worried if you had agreed to her plan without securing confirmation that I am truly alive. To allay your fears, let me remind you of an episode in our youth of which all but you and I are ignorant. Do you remember when you took father's favourite spear to practice your throwing and you lost the white heron's feather from its collar? This was not long before you left us so you couldn't have been more than twelve and I nine. You knew father would know you had taken his spear by the loss of the feather, so you had to procure a new one or risk a beating. I gave you my feather which mother had given me to play with. It wasn't a very good match, but you hoped father wouldn't notice and he didn't! You gave me all your honey cakes for a month in exchange for that feather but, in truth, I was happy to give it to you to spare you a beating.

Youthful nonsense, dear brother, but a fond memory I hope you share and can take as proof that I live. I don't know how far we can trust Vibiana, but I do know that you must be running out of options. Lindum must be taken, and this seems to be our best bet. Trust her at least this much.

Your loving brother, Murcho.

Tears welled in Cunedag's eyes as he finished reading the letter. It had been written in the same female hand as the others, but the words spoke the truth, and it had been Murcho who had dictated them. He was alive!

He left his tent and began bellowing to his captains. "How many boats have we?" he demanded.

"Three barges with enough hold space for twenty men apiece," said one.

"Not nearly enough! Find more! I don't care if you have to travel as far as Eboracum! I want every river barge available to transport our men to Lindum."

"Are we to go ahead with the plan, my king?"

"By Modron's pretty tits, we are!" Cunedag bellowed, happier than he had been in days. "My brother lives!"

Melga suspected nothing, Vibiana was confident of that. But that didn't mean that the atmosphere within the walls of Lindum was at all pleasant or easy. Food was almost non-existent and Melga dared not send out more foraging parties for the countryside was thick with Cunedag's men, and he believed it to be thicker still with the inflated numbers Murcho had given him. He was trapped. He could go no further unless he wanted to face Cunedag and Aurelianus in open battle and the road to Eboracum was blocked so he couldn't even escape back north. It put him in a sour mood and Vibiana found herself in an ever more precarious position.

It had been at her urging to keep Murcho alive. Melga had wanted to execute him rather than waste precious victuals on a prisoner who had already given up all the information he had. But Vibiana insisted that the Votadini prince may yet be of some use to Melga, particularly if Cunedag should attack the town. A political prisoner was not to be thrown away so hastily, even if food was running out.

The Picts had taken to eating rats now that there were no more dogs and cats left in Lindum. The horses would be next, though that would be desperation indeed for their meagre cavalry was already outnumbered by Cunedag's mighty host. But it was only a matter of time. Fodder was scarce too, and the horses were beginning to look as skinny as the men.

But the time had come for Vibiana to put her plan into action. The arranged night for Cunedag's move on the town had fallen and she had to get the gates to the harbour open else all would fail. She just hoped that the Votadini king would get his men onto the waterfront in time.

The main thrust of her plan was to divert Melga's attention to the woods northwest of the town, having told him that Cunedag was moving his troops closer in preparation for an attack. Melga had fallen for it and had doubled the sentries on the northern walls and moved many of his warriors into the upper portion of the town, leaving the lower part and the waterfront, critically undermanned.

There were still sentries on the southern wall who might raise the alarm when they saw boats approaching from the west and the south, but she had to hope that Cunedag would take care of them quickly and efficiently.

The only other thing she had to ensure was that Melga didn't use Murcho as a hostage once he learned that he was under attack. It had been Vibiana's idea to keep the Votadini prince as surety against his brother's aggression and it would go badly for her if Melga had him beheaded atop the gate of the upper town in view of Cunedag and his men. It was a dangerous plan, but Murcho had to be freed from his cell and hidden somewhere in the principia.

An oil lamp lighting her way and a Pictish sword hidden under her tunica, Vibiana made her way down to the cells. The guard was drunk, having supped greedily at the jar of wine she had given him earlier that day, and slumbered at the small table in the corridor, his head slumped forward. The keys to the cells and the latch key to Murcho's manacles hung from a peg in the wall.

As she reached for them, the jailer awoke and mumbled something, eyes rolling drunkenly in their sockets as he tried to focus on her. Without thinking too much about it, Vibiana picked up the nearly empty wine jug and brought it crashing down on the jailer's head, shattering the red pottery and dousing the man's skull in wine so that he slumped face-down on the table, senseless. Violence was not a tool she generally employed but tonight was a night that demanded extreme measures.

Taking the keys, Vibiana let herself into Murcho's cell. He had awoken at the sound of smashing pottery and squinted at her as she set down the oil lamp and began to work the lock of his manacles with the latch key.

"What's going on?" he demanded.

"I'm setting you free, what does it look like?" she said. "Tonight is the night. I hope you haven't forgotten."

"Forgotten, no. But it is hard to keep track of time in this darkness. Has my brother taken the harbour?"

"Not yet is my guess, or we would have known about it by now. But he should be on his way. We must pray to Christ that he comes tonight, or neither of us will live to see the dawn."

"I trust in my own gods, not the crucified carpenter."

"Perhaps we have need of them all. Come, on your feet and take this!"

She helped him up and handed him the sword she had smuggled out of the cross hall. Murcho buckled it around his waist and then unsheathed it to inspect the blade by the light of the lamp.

"Taran's fire, woman! This blade is as blunt and as rusty as any I've seen!"

"I wasn't exactly provided with a fine selection," Vibiana replied testily. "Most swords in the town are in the hands of your enemies."

"This one must have been set aside for sharpening," Murcho muttered as he sheathed it. "I'd do better to knock someone on the head with its hilt than try to stab them. Never mind. What's the plan?"

"To hide you in one of the upper chambers of the principia," she replied. "When your brother breaches the walls, Melga will seek to use you as a bargaining chip. He must not find you."

"I'd rather join in the fighting."

"You may yet, if Cunedag reaches the principia. Until then, you are to do as I say, or your brother will find both of our corpses when he breaks down these doors."

The dyke that the Romans had cut to connect the two rivers was perilously overgrown and the foliage on both sides scraped and scratched the sides of the barges as they were poled down the waterway towards Lindum.

Cunedag sat at the stern and squinted as the lights of Lindum came into view beneath a moonless sky like the pinpricks of fireflies. The oiled hides that covered the cargo hold before him concealed thirty of his warriors with keen blades and keener hearts. The four barges that drifted in the wake of the first contained similar contingents; a hundred and fifty warriors heading to Lindum's harbour with the aim of spilling Pictish blood and taking back a British town.

He only hoped that the other two points of his three-pronged attack were making similar progress. As he approached Lindum from the east, the rest of his teulu would be making their way up the Lindis from the south in whatever vessels they had got their hands on: barges, trading vessels and even coracles. From the west, the army of Ambrosius Aurelianus would be striking camp and marching towards the western walls of the town.

Cunedag had sent a message to the comes about his plan of attack and requested the support of the Romans. If they were to take Lindum with the minimum of bloodshed, then the attention of the enemy within must be spread thin in all directions. Vibiana had said that she would convince Melga to expect an attack from the north while the true attack would come from the south with a large distraction in the form of Aurelianus's men approaching from the west. If all went to plan, the Picts wouldn't know where to look once the arrows started to fall.

But all relied on timing. If the barges from the east arrived too early, the town would be alerted before they had adequate reinforcements from the south. And if Aurelianus's army attacked the western walls before Cunedag's assault on the harbour began, then the Romans would face heavy losses.

No cry of alarm rose from the walls as the barges entered the harbour. Whatever sentries had been posted there were either asleep or drunk. The harbour itself was silent, the hulks of traders bobbing gently against their moorings, most having been stranded at Lindum by Aurelianus's blockade of the Lindis to the east.

Cunedag leapt onto the stone wharf and helped moor the vessel while the other four barges followed suit along the waterfront. Somebody in the harbour wasn't asleep and issued a challenge.

"What goes on here?" the figure demanded as he approached. "Where's this lot come from? It had better be food for we've little desire for anything else here in Lindum."

The harbour man was a Pict by his accent and a hungry looking one at that.

"Oh, don't worry," Cunedag told him. "These barges carry a cargo that will be the salvation of Lindum."

The Pict looked confused, but his face soon turned to panic as the hide covering of one of the barges was pulled back to reveal thirty British warriors with glinting spear tips. His eyes goggled and he turned to make a futile dash to the gatehouse of the town before a spear hurled from one of the men in the barge struck him between the shoulder blades and felled him.

"Any sign of the boats coming upriver?" Cunedag asked Tegid as his men silently clambered out of the barges and onto the wharf.

"I'll send a man to wait on the southern bank," Tegid replied. "They can't be far off. Do we start our assault immediately?"

"I have no doubt we can take the southern wall with the men we have, but it's holding our ground once the whole town is roused against us which has me concerned. It's a chance we'll have to take. I hope by all the gods, they will be here to reinforce us soon!"

They had brought ladders with them and grappling hooks for scaling the town walls. It was the work of moments to lay siege to the wall on both sides of the gatehouse but before they had emerged from the warren of warehouses, wine shops and shanty hovels that clustered below the town, the alarm was shouted atop the walls that they were under attack.

No going back now, Cunedag thought to himself as his men ran at the walls bearing ladders between them. Arrows began to flit back and forth from both sides and more Picts began to appear atop the walls as the alarm was carried through the town. *Come on, lads!* he pleaded. *Don't leave us with our balls in the wind!*

Chapter 13

The words hit Melga like a punch in the gut. They were under attack from the south? How could that be when Cunedag's warband was somewhere to the north? Perhaps it was the army of Aurelianus making its move from the east at last? But how could they get right up to the walls before being noticed? Something about all this did not smell right.

"How large is this force which has taken the harbour?" he demanded of the trembling warrior who had brought the dire news.

"We estimate a hundred and fifty to two hundred warriors, lord," he replied. "They snuck into the harbour on barges and swarmed the wharf before the sentries knew what was happening."

Barges? That meant that they had come from the west, either up the River Lindis or down that damnable dyke. With Aurelianus blockading the river to the east, the dyke and the river winding south-west had been their only source of food and even that was meagre as few traders and fishermen wanted to try their luck in a town overrun by northern invaders. It could only be Cunedag's men who were attacking but why so few? Even two hundred was only a part of his full strength. A diversion? Was an attack from the north imminent?

"Lord, should we send all our troops to reinforce the southern wall?"

"No!" Melga snapped. "Else we leave ourselves open elsewhere. Send three-hundred men to hold the wall. That should be enough to deal with this puny tactic of Cunedag's. Another attack is coming, have no doubt about that!"

The warrior headed off to see to his orders while Melga readied himself for battle, shrugging on a mail shirt and strapping on his helm. By the time he had left the principia and made his way to the northern wall, another one of his men came running bringing news which came as a seconding thundering blow.

"Lord! A force is approaching from the west! Hundreds of riders and men on foot! They carry the standards of the Romans!"

A great pit opened within Melga's soul. *Aurelianus marches from the west while Cunedag attacks from the north and south!* It was what he had been most afraid of; a joint attack by these two respected war chiefs. He had enough numbers to give any attacker a bloody nose, but his men were half-starved and penned in like cattle. Could they survive this? And what of the attack from the north? When would that come?

It occurred to him that he had been played for a fool. Surely Vibiana would not dare …? But the more he considered the possibility, the more he began to believe that it was true. After all, she'd been planted in Lindum to trick him and had then betrayed her former master. Such a woman could never be trusted. She'd do anything for her own gain. As the realisation set in, a rage unlike any he'd ever known gripped him.

"Get those bastard gates open!" Cunedag bellowed as his men swarmed the wall like ants.

The fighting atop the rampart was furious with more and more Picts running down from the north on both sides to reinforce their beleaguered comrades. Every inch of ground was hard won and paid for in blood and Cunedag knew that he may well run out of warriors before the lower portion of the town could be taken. Where the hell were his reinforcements?

He had warriors on either side of the great gatehouse and the fighting in the middle was thickest with the defending Picts being whittled away one by one. Soon the Britons would have control of the gatehouse and when that happened, Cunedag was ready to rush the breach with the rest of his men. But how long would they survive without reinforcement?

Eventually, the Britons atop the gatehouse signalled that they had control of the structure and that the gates would be opened as soon as they were able. Cunedag bellowed to his men to form up and get ready to charge.

Although it had been a hard fight, Cunedag knew that they were only facing a fraction of Melga's defending forces. Why had he sent so few to reinforce the south? Had Vibiana's ruse of diverting Melga's attention north worked? Or had Aurelianus arrived from the east?

Either proposition pleased him, but they would still have a hard fight of it if they didn't receive the reinforcements from the south. He pushed the thought from his mind as the gates creaked open.

"Albion!" he roared, and the war cry was taken up by his men as they charged the gates.

There were Picts on the ground, newly come down from the upper portions of the town, and they hurled themselves at the attackers in a wall of blue warpaint, small buckers and savage defiance.

Cunedag slammed his shield into that of a Pict and then thrust the tip of his blade into the guts of his opponent. "Push them back!" he yelled. "Push them!"

"My king!" one of Cunedag's warriors atop the south-eastern corner of the wall cried. "The Romans are attacking the east gate! Aurelianus has come!"

Cunedag's men gave a great cheer. There was more cheering when word came from the harbour that several boats could be seen rowing up the Lindis. Cunedag breathed a sigh of relief, ignoring the stench of death all around him. This was a good day! His reinforcements had arrived!

Vibiana hurried up the stairs, an oil lamp in one hand and the hem of her bunched-up tunica in the other. The sound of fighting was all around her and the lights of burning buildings glowed in the pre-dawn.

When it became clear to Melga that he had been tricked, Vibiana knew that it was time to make herself scarce. He was in a rage and the whole principia was hurrying to block all doors. The Britons had taken the lower portion of the town and were marching up the hill, butchering any Pict who stood in their way.

She found Murcho looking out of the window in the chamber upstairs in which she had hidden him.

"It's over," he said as she entered. "My brother has all but taken the town."

"His men are at the gates of the principia," said Vibiana, "while Aurelianus takes the eastern wall."

"And me sitting in here!" Murcho yelled in frustration.

"Keep your voice down!" she hissed. "If Melga has not already learned of your escape, then he soon will do for he grows desperate now and will be thinking to threaten your life to keep your brother at bay."

"I would rather be down there fighting for my freedom than waiting here for Cunedag to give it to me!" He drew his sword and tested its sharpness once more.

"Don't even think it!" Vibiana snapped. "I have not risked my life so you can throw your own away! We wait here and you may yet get your chance at fighting if Melga finds us."

"Fighting for my life with my back to a wall rather than down in the streets is a poor choice," Murcho said.

There was an increase in the commotion beyond the gates to the principia and several Picts ran across the courtyard to reinforce their comrades who held the gates. Bowmen clambered onto the tiled roofs to shoot arrows down at whoever was in the street on the other side.

"I can practically see them!" Murcho said. "The time has come for me to act! I can shame myself no longer by waiting here!"

"Murcho, no!" Vibiana said.

"My people need me! I am their penteulu! I must aid them as I can!"

Vibiana watched helplessly as Murcho swung one leg over the windowsill. He turned to give her a parting look. "Remain here. I will see to it that you are rewarded for aiding me when all this is done."

Vibiana said nothing but her mind cursed the reckless principles of young men as he slipped through the window and onto the sloping, tiled roof of the portico.

Hurrying along, he dropped down into the bushes that lined the colonnades, sword drawn and ready for combat. Picts clustered around the gate, too many for him to take, but one man stood alone, his back to the main building.

Melga.

His chief enemy was but a few paces from him, watching his own doom creep steadily closer, unaware of the dull, but still deadly blade at his back. If he could just take him down, it would make up for all the shame of his being captured and held prisoner while his own men stormed Lindum.

Keeping low, his Pictish blade gripped in a sweaty right fist, Murcho moved towards his enemy. A forearm around the throat, a sharp jab under the ribs would be all that was needed.

But Melga was a warrior older and more experienced than Murcho. He had been crept up on before and had never let himself be off his guard because of it. Somehow sensing the youth's attack just as he made it, he twisted out of Murcho's grip and drew his own sword in one fluid movement.

"How, by all the gods, did you escape?" he demanded as he recognised his own prisoner before him. "And where did you get a blade?"

"You have a spy in your midst," Murcho boasted. "Who was a great aid to me."

"That slut, Vibiana," said Melga, taking little time to guess who he meant. "I suspected her of treachery. A pity I didn't cut her throat the minute I met her. No matter. I will deal with her once I have dealt with you, and in a similar fashion too."

He lunged at Murcho, his blade far sharper, sliding close to his abdomen. Murcho, no slouch in the training yard, batted the blade to one side and the courtyard rang with the slither of metal.

Several of the Picts at the gate turned their heads to stare in the direction of the duel that was happening at their backs, confusion written on their faces. Murcho ignored them. He might have a hard fight on his hands once he finished Melga but, by that time, he hoped that Cunedag would have the gates down and the odds would be evened a little.

Melga showed a fierce determination to cut down the young upstart who had escaped from his custody and he hacked and slashed at Murcho with such savagery that the younger warrior felt himself soon tiring after several days in a cell with very little food.

He realised that he must conserve his strength and let Melga wear out his own, but it was a hard task as the bigger, more experienced warrior kept up a barrage of attacks that Murcho struggled to fend off.

He let Melga drive him across the courtyard towards the colonnades on its eastern side. If he could get him between those stone columns, he could limit the powerful swings of his enemy's sword arm and use some cover to his advantage.

But Melga seemed to sense what he was doing and worked his way around Murcho's unprotected shield arm, forcing him to turn to defend his left flank. With dismay, Murcho realised that he was being herded back into the centre of the courtyard. There was no escape from this enraged Pict. The only thing for it was to try and outwit him with a feint …

He thrust and drew back, hoping that the big warrior would go for it. He didn't. It was like he could see Murcho's intentions before he moved, his years of experience making him more than a match for the young penteulu.

His sword clanged down on Murcho's own, the vibrations making his arm ring up to the elbow. His weakened arm was knocked to the side, too far to bring it up to defend himself from Melga's next blow.

The chieftain roared in exaltation as he rammed the tip of his blade through Murcho's belly, gripping the hilt with both hands as he pulled the blade up through his guts and lifting him up by his straining ribcage.

Murcho gasped, his sword tumbling from his grip to land on the gravel of the courtyard along with several pints of his own blood. Pain flooded his being along with the agonising knowledge that he had lost.

Melga ripped the blade free and Murcho sank to his knees and then toppled over, the world swimming before his eyes before it vanished utterly.

Vibiana clamped a hand over her mouth as she saw Murcho fall. She had watched the whole fight from the window in the upper chamber of the principia and had been willing the youth to cut down Melga, or at least hold his own until his brother's men could bring down the gates and come to his rescue. Now he had been slain with his countrymen but yards from him, separated only by a door and a handful of Picts. It was more than she could bear.

There were roars of triumph as the gates were finally breached and the Votadini warriors spilled into the courtyard, pushing back the defenders. The clang of swords echoed off the stone pillars and screams filled the air as the Picts were cut down. Melga had fled back into the main building, leaving the corpse of Murcho lying in a pool of blood in the centre of the courtyard to be found by his countrymen whose yells of triumph soon turned to cries of dismay at finding their penteulu dead.

Vibiana ducked out of sight from the window and hastily tried to make plans. Everything she had hoped for had unravelled. The Britons would kill her for sure now. Her safety had depended on Murcho's survival, but his foolish pride and boyish arrogance had put paid to that. There would be nobody to put in a good word for her now, and Cunedag may even suspect her involvement in his brother's death.

She had to leave somehow. She had to get out of Lindum before the Britons conquered it utterly. With no money or food, she wouldn't last long out in the wilderness of the north but to stay in Lindum was as good as a death sentence. Pulling her shawl over her head, she hurried from the room and made her way downstairs where the shouting of the remaining Picts echoed from room to room.

There was a door that led from the kitchens to the street behind the principia, but it would undoubtedly be locked. Hoping to God that the key would be somewhere in the kitchens, Vibiana hurried through the shadows, unseen by the panicked Picts as they dragged whatever furniture they could get their hands on to pile against the main doors.

The search for a key proved fruitless as she rummaged through the cupboards and swept the detritus off the tables in a desperate attempt to find a way out. She glanced up at the small, barred window and wondered if she could squeeze through it. If she found a way to remove the wooden bars …

she froze. Somebody had entered the kitchen, their footfalls on the flagstones making her spin around.

"Well, well," said Melga. "The traitorous little whore thinks to make her escape amid the chaos she has caused."

A cold chill swept over Vibiana. She was trapped!

"I should have you screaming under my knife for what you did!" said Melga. "Setting Murcho free and sending him to murder me? Oh, you are a clever thing!"

"That was not my intention, Master," she said, trying to keep her voice level. "I thought only to spare his life should you think to kill him. I had no idea he would attack you ..."

"I'm sure! As I said, your screams would fill this house were the current circumstances any different. As it stands, I have a different use for you." He produced a key from a cord of similar keys around his neck. "I believe this is what you were looking for? Come, we'll leave this house together and you'll be my hostage. I may have need to sell the Britons' spy back to them if my progress north is hindered in any way."

Vibiana understood. He meant to escape! He was leaving his men to hold the principia for as long as they could while he tried to escape back north. The powerful war chief of the Picts was little more than a coward!

But she'd play his game for as long as she could if it meant her survival and her escape from Lindum. Many things could happen on the road. An accident, a knife in the dark ...

Melga grabbed her by the arm, and she did not resist as he unlocked the door and dragged her out onto the street beyond.

It was little more than an alley filled with refuse from the kitchens, but it was silent and dark. Closing the door behind them, Melga led Vibiana down the street to where it met the western wall. His plan was clearly to reach the northern gate and then flee the town either on foot or, if luck was with them, by procuring a horse while the fighting continued in the south.

"Halt!" came a cry from the other end of the street.

Melga spun around, pulling Vibiana painfully with him. Several Britons had rounded the corner, apparently seeking another way into the principia.

Melga snarled and drew his sword as the Britons advanced with spears held low. The distraction caused him to loosen his grip on Vibiana's arm and she took the opportunity to kick him as hard as she could in the breeches. He gasped and doubled over, not quite letting go of her but she was able to wrench her arm away and take off down the street.

The Britons charged the Pict who, still recovering from Vibiana's blow to his manhood, swung his sword wildly at them. The sound of fighting echoing off the buildings behind her, Vibiana continued towards the northern gate, wondering, not for the first time, at the folly of men who must always pick violence over subtlety.

Chapter 14

Cunedag knew that something was horribly wrong before he even entered the captured principia. His warriors, bloodied and tired, clustered in the courtyard, their faces sombre despite their victory. The town was taken and the Picts – what few that were left of them – had surrendered.

They parted to let him pass. Something lay in the centre of the courtyard for his inspection. As he approached, he saw that it was a corpse beneath a cloak somebody had draped across it. Why all the glum faces over one death? Did not the whole town reek of death?

He knelt down and pulled the cloak from the head of the corpse and at once knew the reason for the black cloud that seemed to hang over his men, despite the light of dawn that was breaking over the bloodied streets.

Murcho was slain.

His brother, his penteulu, was dead.

"What … what happened?" he mumbled as a sob choked him.

"We're not too sure," said Tegid. "Though there is a sword in his hand. It seems that he met a good end."

Cunedag did not want to hear it. His brother was supposed to be a prisoner. Captured but safe. Not fighting for his life within the enemy camp. How had it come to this?

"My deepest condolences, my king," said Tegid. "We'll get to the bottom of this. We'll find out what went on here. It seems that our lads have captured a high-status prisoner. It may be Melga himself, though none of us know him to identify him."

"Show me," said Cunedag in a tight voice as he rose.

Tegid led him into the main building where several captured Picts had been herded and forced to kneel on the hard floor at spearpoint, their hands bound.

"This is the man," said Tegid, leading Cunedag over to a large Pict with skin marked by many tattoos and ritual scarring. He was in his forties, with lank, black hair that fell about his bloodied face in greasy tendrils. He had obviously given a good account of himself upon his capture for his forearms were brown with dried blood and his swollen face told of a brutal beating into submission. Cunedag's men had clearly suspected whom they had.

"Are you Melga?" Cunedag demanded.

The man looked up at him through one eye, the other swollen almost completely shut. "Are you Cunedag?"

"Yes. I am King Cunedag of the Votadini. Who are you?"

"I am Melga of the Uerteru, war chief of the northern tribes."

That he had waited until he had an audience with Cunedag before willingly giving his name suggested that he wished to die only by the hand of a fellow chief.

"What happened to my brother?" Cunedag demanded. "Who slew him?"

Melga grinned and Cunedag could tell that the man now had a death wish. "I did, but you can reserve your hate for the one who set him against me. I would have been happy to keep him a hostage, but your bitch of a spy set him free and put a sword in his hand. I had no choice but to defend myself."

Cunedag ground his teeth as a black rage consumed him. *Vibiana*. The spy and turncoat had played them all for fools. She had most likely sent Murcho against Melga in order to mask her own escape. "Where is she now?" he asked.

Melga shrugged. "She fled when I was captured by your men. If she is still inside the town, then I do not know where she is hiding."

Cunedag turned to Tegid. "Secure all the gates. Let no woman leave and then start searching the town for her. I want that whore brought to me!"

"What of the prisoners, my king?" Tegid asked.

Cunedag did not even pay Melga a last glance. "Hang them from the town walls," he said.

Aurelianus and his army entered Lindum just as Cunedag's men were securing the principia and moved from street to street dispatching what Picts they could find in hiding with ruthless Roman efficiency. By the time they reached the principia, they were met by the sight of twenty-odd Pictish corpses dangling from its walls, black-faced and bloodied, the shit running down their legs.

Aurelianus found Cunedag sitting with Tegid, Tancorix and Asaros in the cross hall, cleaning their weapons and eating what meagre stores had been found in the kitchens.

"I see you have taken it upon yourself to enforce your own brand of justice on prisoners of war," Aurelianus said, removing his helmet and joining them. "Is Melga among them?"

"Aye."

"I would have preferred it if you had left that task to me."

"Who took the principia?" Cunedag asked without looking at him. "Who took the town itself?"

"You wouldn't have got far without our assault on the east gate," Aurelianus said.

"Our penteulu, the king's brother, was slain," said Tegid hastily as a way to dampen the simmering tension between the two war leaders.

Aurelianus's face softened as he understood the Votadini king's foul temper. "My condolences, Cunedag," he said. "Was he …"

"Executed? No," Cunedag replied as he finished honing a vicious edge on his blade before inspecting it and sheathing it. "He died with a sword in his hand, such is the mercy of the gods. But how he came to die is a question I am still pursuing. The eastern section of the town? It is secure?"

"Aye, there isn't a Pict left who is not dead or in chains."

"What will you do with your prisoners?"

"That remains to be decided. Some will be executed, that is inevitable, though Roman policy usually spares some and sends them back to their homelands with the message of what happens to those who attack the empire. It is never a good idea to slaughter them all for it only stokes the fires of vengeance. Send some back humiliated and thankful for their lives, that has always been our way."

Cunedag grunted.

"Well, I must see to my men," said Aurelianus, rising. "There will be little food left in Lindum so we must not stay here long. We march south once the men have rested and seen to the wounded. Yourself?"

"Back home," said Cunedag. "Though there won't be much to feed us on the trail north."

"No, I suppose not," said Aurelianus. "Still, once you cross the Abus Fluvius, things may improve. They've had most of the summer to recover from Melga's war trail. We'll see each other tomorrow if you don't drink too much tonight. But if we don't, good work here, Cunedag. Britannia thanks you as does Rome."

"Another service I have done for them," said Cunedag without looking at him. "Add it to my slate."

Aurelianus said nothing and left.

As soon as he was gone, Cunedag turned to Tegid. "I want you to lead our warriors home," he said. "Take Murcho back to Din Eidyn and deliver him to our family so he may be buried with all the honours of Votadini royalty. You are to lead the tribe while I am gone."

"Gone, my king?" Tegid asked. "You are not returning with us?"

"I still have work to do here," Cunedag said. "I will come home as soon as I am able."

"You're going to look for her, aren't you?" Tegid said. "She's long gone, my king. Our riders have scoured the roads for a mile in all directions. She slipped past us. Let it go."

"Would you let it go if it was *your* brother?" Cunedag snapped. "Murcho was betrayed by that whore. She threw his life away as if it were a bargaining chip. The life of my penteulu, a prince of the Votadini, cast aside as a distraction!" The other warriors looked at their leader with concern for a hot rage burned in his eyes none of them had seen before. "I will not rest until I find that bitch and make her pay for what she has done."

"There is no way of knowing where she has gone," said Tegid. "She wouldn't have returned to Londinium, for she knows that word would reach Vitalinus of her treachery."

"Though she did help us take Lindum," said Asaros. "In the end."

"That won't be enough for Vitalinus to trust her," said Tegid. "He'll know that his spy is just as slippery as he is, and it would be more trouble for him to let her live. Mark me, she will steer well clear of Londinium."

"She'll be heading for the coast," said Cunedag.

"How do you know?" asked Tegid.

"She is foreign to these shores. The men who escorted her here said she was from Illyria, wherever the fuck that is. My guess is that she'll seek to return there but she'll need passage. It is in the coastal towns I must look for her. But I can't do it alone. I need two volunteers. He glanced at Tancorix. His young nephew had distinguished himself in the battle and had earned several notches for his spear. "You, Tancorix? Will you come with me to avenge your uncle and penteulu?"

Tancorix frowned as he considered the prospect. "With all respect, my king, it may be a fool's errand but, if I am a fool, then at least I hope I am a loyal one. I'll come with you."

Tegid placed his hand on his son's shoulder and smiled on him with pride in his eyes.

"I will also come," said Asaros.

"You, Asaros?" Cunedag asked in surprise. "Have you not your own people to accompany back to Banovallum? And this is not your fight …"

"Maybe not," the Taifal commander said. "But we Taifals understand the burning desire for vengeance. Let the Romans think with what's between their ears. We act on what is in our hearts and your brother was a good man and a promising leader. Betrayal has a foul aftertaste that can poison a wound if not washed out. I will gladly help you in this task."

Cunedag gave him a small smile. "Thank you, Asaros. You have proven to be a loyal friend as well as an ally these years we have known each other. We will leave at dawn, while Aurelianus's centurions are still beating his men awake with their vine sticks. I want to reach the coast in two days. We may overtake her on the road, in which case our task will be quickly accomplished, though I suspect she will be cutting across country. We must remember that she is cunning as well as treacherous."

"We'd best get some rest, then," said Asaros. "We have a long hunt ahead of us."

Chapter 15

Summer had faded to the golden hues of autumn and the morning mist hung over the fens and reedy estuaries like the breath of ghosts. The shore fort of Othona, with its round projecting walls of ashlar striped with red brick loomed above the mist that clung to its feet and obscured the thatched Germanic hovels that clustered around its walls.

Othona sat on a small peninsula and guarded the mouth of the Colonia Fluvius which led up to the town of Camulodunum. One of a series of forts built along the 'Saxon Shore', it was part of a defensive network designed to repel the Germanic raiders, but the raiders had become settlers in recent years and in the towns on the south-east coast, the languages of the Saxons, Angles, Jutes, Frisians and Danes were more common than the Latin or British of the natives.

Cunedag, Asaros and Tancorix stood on the southern bank of the river and watched the small fishing boats and oyster gatherers. Othona stood just across the peninsula and within it, was their quarry.

It had taken them two long months to find her. They had moved in a southerly direction down the Saxon Shore, going from fort to fort, looking for word that a woman was seeking passage to the continent. Ordinarily, it might have been an impossible task, but, with the war in Gaul, regular shipping had not yet picked up due to the constant threat of piracy from Saxon or Gaulish brigands who prowled the Northern Sea. And things were not going well for Constantinus and his rebellion on the continent. Iustinianus and Nebiogastes had both been killed and, having lost both of his generals, Constantinus was currently under siege in southern Gaul by Saurus the Goth, an ally of Emperor Honorius.

If Britannia's homegrown emperor was defeated, the island would stand alone, cut off from the empire, with most of its troops gone. If they were not overrun by barbarians, then it would be an army loyal to Honorius who would be their salvation and what mercy might they expect from the emperor they had defied? It would be the aftermath of Carausius's rebellion all over again in which public monuments had been pulled down as punishment while the smoke of the execution pyres marred the skies.

Cunedag and his companions found the situation on the Saxon Shore worse than it was in their homelands to the north. The commanders of the shore forts were attempting to fight fire with fire and had started recruiting Saxon militias and allowing them to live within the walls of the very forts that had been built to repel them. It was an appalling state of affairs; Romans paying the enemy to protect them from other enemies.

One Saxon, a brute of a man known as Wulfnoth, had risen to a position of some power in Othona, second only to the fort prefect, Julius Atratinus. Cunedag and his men weren't there to worry about Saxons infiltrating the Roman military but there was something about Wulfnoth which drew their attention. Word had it, that he currently had a consort foreign to these shores, who had brains as well as looks and that he rarely made a decision without consulting her first.

Such were the mysteries of the barbarian mind, thought many Romans, that a man would shame himself by letting a woman have any influence over him. It may well be some flaxen-haired harlot from Germania but something about it all made Cunedag think of Vibiana. It would certainly be like her to worm her way into the mind of a barbarian who had the power to protect her. After all, she had done the same with Melga. Why not a Saxon seadog?

But identifying her would be tricky as few had ever set eyes on her. Getting to her would be even trickier. As Vibiana had done in Lindum, this advisor had nestled herself within the fort with hundreds of soldiers protecting her. The only way to even get close was to pose as mercenaries looking for pay in the coastal militias.

And that was what had led them to be watching over the estuary that chill, autumn day, while the mist shrouded the sea like a portent of doom from the continent. They were on patrol; one of many such patrols they had been sent on since they had come to Othona looking for employment. They had been readily accepted as wandering thugs from the north looking to earn a crust and, as each of them had a barbarous tongue and nothing about them to suggest that they were deserters, even the Romans had accepted them, none the wiser that one of them was a king.

"I say we make up some story that will gain us an audience with Wulfnoth," said Asaros. "I grow tired of playing soldier. We must learn if it truly is Vibiana tucked away in that fort."

"Aye, and every day we waste, is a day that bitch might slip through our fingers," said Tancorix.

They had seen Wulfnoth only from a distance. Their own commander was one of his subordinates and they were too far down the chain of command to speak with the Saxon chief in person. They needed a way to gain his attention.

"Smugglers," said Cunedag after some thought. "We could say that we spotted a vessel putting in upriver to unload its cargo. It'll be gone by the time we report back to the fort, but Wulfnoth will at least want to hear about it from us."

"Smugglers?" Asaros asked sceptically. "Isn't that a little far-fetched? Hardly any ships put in around here because of the unrest in the channel."

"And those that do, pay their customs to Wulfnoth," said Cunedag. "That's why it's perfect. He'll be very interested to learn that a ship is slipping through his stranglehold on this peninsula."

"Aye, it's a good enough plan," said Tancorix. "Let's just hope that it leads us to where we want to be led."

They headed back to Othona and passed through its gates as the afternoon sun was melting the morning mist away. They reported their lie to their captain and, as Cunedag had predicted, were summoned to the principia within the hour.

They found themselves in a luxuriously decorated office with arched windows that looked out over the marshes beyond the fort's walls. There was much fine furniture in the room, which indicated that, though trade had dried up recently, the post of guarding the coast came with its perks no doubt in the form of bribes and creamed profits. A red curtain hung in the doorway to another chamber. It was pulled closed and secured with gold rope, suggesting that whatever was behind it was not for visitors' eyes.

Wulfnoth was a tall man, a common trait of his people, but thinner and less muscled than most. Despite his reedy frame, he seemed rangy enough to be a good fighter and clearly had the brains to match. He sat at the prefect's desk while the prefect himself occupied a silk couch in the corner of the room. Cunedag at once understood the situation. These two characters needed each other. It was reciprocal; Julius Atratinus needed the protection of Wulfnoth's men and Wulfnoth needed the Roman prefect to make his presence in Othona legitimate and free from interference from the Comes of the Saxon Shore who must be biting his nails in his villa to the south-west at the number of barbarians he must suffer in his army. Between the two of them, Julius Atratinus and Wulfnoth had this peninsula pretty much tied up, including trade going to and from Camulodunum.

"What's all this about smugglers making landfall in my territories?" Wulfnoth demanded. He spoke British with a thick accent. "Who dares? And how did they slip into the estuary? Are my men asleep on the headland?"

"As to that, lord," said Cunedag, "we cannot answer. All we can report is that we saw a small trading vessel unloading barrels on the southern bank of the river."

"And you did not challenge them?" Julius Atratinus asked from his perch on the couch.

"If we did then we would not be here to report it to you," said Cunedag. "They had half a dozen men with them. Armed."

"Germanic?" Wulfnoth asked, one blond eyebrow raised.

"Gaulish, I would hazard. Undoubtedly it was wine in those barrels. There are thirsty throats further west and the local muck is fit for only cleaning pots and bathing wounds. We Britons are not natural wine drinkers."

"As I have gathered," said Wulfnoth. "Even your mead leaves much to be desired."

"Are these men here to discuss the quality of British drink?" Julius Atratinus snapped. "What of the smugglers?"

"We do not know how they got in, but they must be gone by now," said Cunedag. "Smugglers don't waste time waiting around."

"True," said Wulfnoth. "But they often use the same drop points again and again. If they believe them safe. Did they see you?"

"I think not. We were at a good distance and, as I said, had no desire to get any closer."

"Well, their eyesight must be commended even if their courage cannot," said the prefect. "I suggest that they accompany a larger body of warriors to that same spot next week and that they stay in the vicinity for as long as it takes for the smuggling vessel to return."

"I will instruct my own warriors, not you, Roman!" Wulfnoth barked.

At this, the prefect's face paled, and he realised that he had overstepped the mark in his anger at losing out on customs. And, in that moment, Cunedag saw who it was who really ran Othona.

"Return to your duties," Wulfnoth said to them. "I will call for you if I need further assistance."

"Well, that was fruitless," said Asaros as they left the principia and headed for the ale shop to wet their throats. "If Vibiana is the woman who has shacked up with Wulfnoth, then he must have sent her on an errand."

"Not necessarily," said Cunedag. "Did you not see the curtain? Or smell the unmistakable scent of a woman's perfume in the air. I doubt the smell was coming from either Wulfnoth or Atratinus, and I have a mind that I recognised the scent."

"You think she was there?"

"I'm all but certain of it."

The ale shop was a grubby hovel in the Saxon portion of the vicus where Germanic tongues flavoured the air and tall, flaxen-haired mercenaries quaffed the local brew, jostled and joked with each other and occasionally broke out into songs of their homelands across the waves.

Cunedag and his companions acquired a jug of ale for a few beads and a bit of broken silver which passed for currency among the people of the coastal settlements since salaries had dried up some years back. They found a secluded spot away from the drunken antics of the raucous Saxons and discussed their next move while passing the foaming jug back and forth.

With nothing productive coming from the evening other than dizzy heads from the strong Saxon beer, they headed for what passed for their quarters down by the docks. It was as they were passing behind the stone warehouses that lined the waterfront that they realised they were being followed.

"Watch your step," Cunedag said.

"I see them," Asaros replied. "Are they mad to test us or just drunk?"

But Cunedag didn't think they were drunk. They quickly rounded a corner and entered a narrow alley, only to find it blocked by three large Saxons who played with the hilts of the seaxes menacingly.

"What's the trouble, lads?" Cunedag asked them as the three who followed them brought up the rear and hemmed them in. "We've nothing of value on us. Or is this a personal matter?"

"Somebody just wants a word with you three," one of the Saxons said. "Follow us."

There wasn't much of a choice in the matter, and they were led around the front of the warehouses and into one of them. The warehouses weren't much used since shipping had dried up and their gloomy interiors were bare and silent. *The perfect place to dispatch three men who had fallen afoul of somebody without causing a ruckus on the street*, Cunedag thought grimly.

There was somebody back there in the gloom and, as they came forward into the pool of light thrown down by the high, barred windows, Cunedag smelled them before he saw them. It was that scent again, a woman's perfume. It belonged to a figure almost wholly concealed in a rough spun hooded cloak which was far too clean to present a genuine picture of poverty, despite its owner's intention. And it failed to conceal the shapely form of a woman's body beneath.

"You three claim to have seen a smuggling vessel unloading its cargo some distance upriver," the woman said. "Why tell such lies? What have you to gain?"

"Who says we're lying?" asked Cunedag. "And who are you?"

"An interested party," the woman replied.

"Well, we're not lying. We did see a vessel. And now, let me ask you a question. What makes you so sure we're lying?"

"Because no ships have come into the estuary in the last week."

"How do you know?"

Cunedag could see little of her face, but what little he saw was smiling. She wasn't going to give too much away but it was clear to him that Wulfnoth's little bitch was involved in something her master knew nothing about. Why else accost him and his companions in an alley and drag them here to squeeze the purpose of their lies out of them. They made her nervous for some reason. He must find out what that reason was.

"Wulfnoth does not like secrets among his men," she said.

"Wulfnoth doesn't? Or you don't?"

"I do Wulfnoth's bidding."

"Does he know you're here, interrogating his men?"

The mouth beneath the hood turned into a snarl. "These men here follow my orders. And I could have them find out exactly what you three are up to using their own brand of questioning. Have you ever seen what those long Saxon knives can do to a person's skin? They really are highly versatile tools."

"Have you ever been to Lindum, lady?" he asked her.

The question came out of the blue and caught everybody in the warehouse by surprise. The woman froze as a statue, and they locked eyes. And Cunedag knew they had found Vibiana.

"Get them out of here!" she snapped.

"Don't you want us to find out what they know about these smugglers?" one of the Saxons asked, looking befuddled.

"Just get rid of them! They are no more than fools playing games. I will not waste my time on them further!"

They were hustled out of the warehouse and left alone on the docks while the Saxons retreated back to their mistress.

"That was a dangerous play, Uncle!" Tancorix breathed. "Letting her know that we know who she is. She might have had us killed on the spot!"

"It was the only way to get her to confirm what we have suspected all along," Cunedag replied. "Wulfnoth's whore is Vibiana. And she didn't have us killed because she was frightened of what we might say in the presence of Wulfnoth's men. She might hold their leash, but she is afraid of their bite all the same. We'll be followed and watched from now on."

"I can't figure how she was so sure that we lied about the smugglers," said Asaros.

"Because nothing happens in this estuary without her knowing about it," Cunedag replied. "She's got a better idea of what goes on in these waters than even Wulfnoth does. And we must find out why."

Chapter 16

Over the next few days, every spare moment not spent on duty was spent finding things out down at the docks. There was little activity but there were plenty of sailors and dock workers who had nothing better to do than loaf around, hoping that the sea lanes would open up once more and soon. These were desperate times and only the desperate remained. Drunkenness and fighting were commonplace and finding things out was not easy without drawing attention.

They eventually learned of a Briton who was involved in some sort of racket that saw him pocket several denarii a month. Coinage was scarce in Albion and the word was that the denarii came from Gaul and that he must be involved in smuggling. He also had regular business up at the fort where none saw who he spoke to or what it concerned. Cunedag had a mind that it was Vibiana who received him in the privacy of the principia, remembering that it was not unlike her to conduct her clandestine business right under the noses of her masters.

It was decided that they would have a quiet talk with this man and Cunedag set Tancorix to following him. He rarely wandered alone, however, and was always in the presence of two other Britons who looked to be strong fighters or, at the very least, able dockside brawlers.

Getting to their man was hard, but Tancorix had located his sleeping quarters in an upstairs room above a warehouse in the northernmost part of the docks. Being a man of some wealth, he occupied the room alone while his two companions slept in the warehouse below.

Cunedag, Tancorix and Asaros watched and waited one night as the rain hammered down from a blackened sky while the Briton and his two companions left the ale house and headed to their quarters. When the oil lamp had gone out in the upstairs window, they hurried across the street and down the alley that ran behind the warehouse.

Clambering up onto the roof, they did their best to break into the upper chambers without waking the men slumbering below. The rain, despite making the rooftiles slippery underfoot, did a good job of concealing any noise. Using a length of iron, they prised apart the wooden bars on a window and snuck in.

The Briton's door was predictably bolted but was of no sturdy construction and Cunedag and his companions were able to force it open with the minimum of noise. The Briton was awoken by their entrance and leapt out of bed to reach for a knife on a side table. Cunedag reached him first and knocked him back down onto his pallet with a boot to the chest.

"Help!" the Briton yelled.

"Damn him!" Asaros seethed. "We'll have those two brutes on us any moment!"

"Be ready for them," Cunedag replied. "I'll make sure our friend here doesn't try anything."

Sure enough, the other two Britons were roused from their slumber and charged the stairs which were barely wide enough for them to run abreast. Swords clanged out on the landing and the two thugs were summarily dispatched by Tancorix and Asaros who promptly returned to the room, cleaning the blood off their blades.

"Now then," said Cunedag, grabbing the trembling Briton by the neck of his tunica. "We'll be free from interruption, so let's have some answers from you."

"Wh ... who are you?" he stammered.

"Interested parties in your smuggling racket."

"I've no smuggling racket!"

"Come, now," said Cunedag. "We know you've been pocketing denarii from Gaul every month. Where does it come from?"

"You can have it!" the Briton said, pointing to a pouch on the same table he kept his knife on. "Take it, please!"

"We don't want your money!" Cunedag said, drawing the knife at his belt with deliberate slowness. "We want information. Where are the vessels landing? And how often?"

"There's an inlet behind an island upriver," the Briton explained. "The island is reachable by a causeway at low tide. The lookout on the headland is bribed to look the other way on the sixth day before the nones and the eleventh day before the kalends of each month."

"It's the sixth day before the nones two days from now," said Tancorix, doing some quick arithmetic in his head.

"What is the lady Vibiana's business in all this?" Cunedag pressed.

"Who?" the man asked.

"Vibiana, the lady up at the fort. She may use another name."

"Aye, I know who you mean, though she goes by Cordelia. She took over the whole operation when she arrived in these parts and earned Wulfnoth's favour near two months back."

"And Wulfnoth knows nothing of this?"

The man shook his head. "We'd all lose our heads if he did. It's his job to make sure the customs are paid. We've been operating under his nose for a year or so now, bringing in one shipment a month but when Cordelia, uh, this *Vibiana* of yours, took over, we grew much bolder, extending it to two shipments. She has much more influence than we do, and she can bribe whoever she wants."

"Aye, she's a dab hand at pulling strings, that one," Asaros muttered.

"What's her interest in smuggling?" Cunedag asked. "Why go to all this trouble and risk her neck just to earn some coin? Doesn't she live a life of luxury at Wulfnoth's side?"

"The word is that she wants out," said the Briton. "She's a foreigner, you see and doesn't much like the state of things in Albion. She wants to go back to her homeland, wherever that is but needs passage and capital. She gets both with the smuggling racket."

"One of the ships will take her to Gaul? When?"

"How the hell should I know? I just follow orders."

"Well, it's clear how she knew we were lying about seeing a smuggling vessel," said Tancorix to Cunedag. "Because she knows about the real smugglers who operate under Wulfnoth's nose! They would have a clue if there were others of their kind moving in their waters."

"Aye, she had us pegged for liars right from the start," said Cunedag. "But she didn't know who we were or what our game was. That was why she had us hauled before her; to find out what we were up to."

"And now that she knows we came down from Lindum," Tancorix said, "she might accelerate her plans. With the next shipment coming in two days' time …"

"We may lose her on the outgoing tide," said Cunedag. "We need to make our move. If she leaves the fort and heads upriver when the shipment is due to arrive, we might intercept her on the road."

"What about him?" Asaros said, nodding to the Briton.

Cunedag frowned. The man posed a predicament.

"He's too untrustworthy to be left alive," said Asaros, as if reading Cunedag's thoughts.

"Aye, he needs to be silenced," Tancorix agreed. "Else he'll run blabbing to anyone who'll listen. Our position here is dangerous as it is."

"No! Please!" the man gibbered, sensing that his doom was upon him.

Cunedag didn't want to hear it. The begging of prisoners as the executioner's blade hovered above them was becoming an unpleasantly familiar sound to him. Before any more words could be said, he seized the man by his hair and quickly drew his blade across his trembling throat. Blood gushed out and Cunedag let the man slump down over the spreading pool of red which seeped between the floorboards.

"Come on," he said to his companions. "We don't have much time."

Two days later, Cunedag, Asaros and Tancorix waited by the muddy road that followed the coast, their horses hobbled behind one of the clusters of trees that dotted the bleak landscape. They had spent the night there, listening to the waves of the estuary lapping the shingle shore as the tide came in. It was a dull, chill morning that dawned over the small trading vessel as it cut its way up the estuary and entered the muddy river. The three men from the north watched it pass and disappear behind an island topped by trees.

Vibiana would get to it from the southern bank of the river by crossing the narrow causeway at low tide. That meant she would be travelling along that muddy trackway sometime towards early evening. *If* she truly intended to flee Albion that day. Cunedag was confident that she would.

As the sun passed its zenith and headed across the open sky towards its destination in the west, the river turned to gold flame beneath its gaze and the receding tide left glistening mud in its wake. They ate rations of dried fish and hard tack and watched the birds poking around on the muddy banks. Somewhere, behind the hump of the island, the smuggling vessel would have finished unloading its wares which would already have been carried across the causeway and inland while the smugglers awaited the next flood tide.

The afternoon passed and the tide began to come back in, filling up the estuary with life as the boats returned. Cunedag frowned. "She'll have to hurry if she wants to make it out this evening. I hope we haven't misjudged her intentions."

"Horse coming," said Asaros, turning with his back to the setting sun as he gazed down the muddy track.

"Her?" Cunedag asked, rousing himself from the blanket they had spread over the reeds.

"Aye," said Asaros. "A woman at least."

It was indeed a woman, hooded and cloaked in the same clean, rough-spun cloth which billowed behind her as her mount made hasty progress along the riverbank.

They picked up their weapons and hurried out of the reeds and into the path of the horse. It reared as its rider reined it in, surprise written across her face. By the sluggish way the animal stepped about, Cunedag could tell that its saddlebags were heavily loaded.

"You three!" Vibiana snapped. "What do you mean by impeding my progress and frightening my mare?"

"Dangerous for a young woman to travel alone," said Cunedag, approaching the horse and patting its neck. He moved to lift the flap of a saddle bag and caught sight of the glint of coin and other trinkets within. "Especially laden with loot."

"So, you're common thieves," she replied, trying to sound stern but a fear had crept into her voice which pleased Cunedag. She would soon have cause to be far more afraid.

"We're not interested in whatever wealth you've squirreled away under Wulfnoth's nose," he said. "We're far more interested in you, *Vibiana*."

Her face took on the look of one who has received a death sentence. "You … you are from Lindum …"

"Further north, in fact, but yes, we were at Lindum. I am Cunedag mab Etern, brother of Murcho, the man you sent to be butchered by your previous master while you made your escape. There will be no escape for you this time."

"You must believe me; I grieve also for the death of your brother for it was through no doing of my own!"

"Do not shame yourself further by lying about your crimes!" Cunedag barked. "You are going to account for them so get down off that horse or I'll pull you down!"

"I set him free!" Vibiana cried. "You must believe me! I put a sword in his hand, yes, but only so he might defend himself if we were discovered! We were supposed to wait in an upper chamber of the principia until you had taken the town but your brother, damn his pride, wanted to aid your men from the inside. He climbed out against my pleas and attacked Melga …"

"Why should I believe anything you say?" Cunedag demanded. "You have made a living of lies and deceit."

She stiffened a little at this, her fear briefly overcome by a surge of pride. "Only because I am a slave and have little else to work with."

"More horses coming!" Asaros cried. "Warriors too! What the devil …?"

Cunedag glanced past Vibiana and saw a column of riders unmistakably Saxon in dress. "Wulfnoth's men! Is this your escort?"

"No!" Vibiana cried, looking over her shoulder in terror at the approaching riders. "I snuck out without Wulfnoth knowing. He must have found out that I took some items from his treasury. He has begun to suspect me, you see, you must let me go! They will slay me for betraying him!"

"That's nothing compared to what I'll do to you!" Cunedag snarled, seizing her reins.

"Please! I am sorry for Murcho's death, but I couldn't stop him!"

"Cunedag, they're almost upon us!" Asaros warned. "What do we do?"

Cunedag uttered a foul oath and let go of Vibiana's mount. "Ride on!" he told her. "Get across the causeway. We'll be close on your heels, so don't think you're out of this. Go, now!"

Vibiana kicked her mount and galloped off down the track. Cunedag, Asaros and Tancorix turned and ran through the reeds towards the trees where their horses were hidden. Several of the Saxons broke off from the column and pursued them. Quickly unhobbling their mounts, they swung themselves into their saddles and broke from cover, heading back towards the track.

Cunedag drew up and hurled his spear at one of the Saxons. There was a cry as the shaft thudded into his chest, knocking him from his horse followed by more cries of outrage from the remaining Saxons.

"I think that's drawn them off Vibiana," Cunedag said to the other two. "Come, let's lead them from the causeway and then double back!"

Kicking their mounts, they turned and headed west along the riverbank while the Saxons gave chase, yelling challenges and insults in their own savage tongue. Turning off the track, the Britons swooped left in a wide circle across the reedy marshlands, weaving to avoid patches of water and thickets of trees as they made their way back towards the causeway. The Saxons began to struggle, not being natural horsemen, and several got bogged down in the marshes or tangled in the thickets.

The tide was flowing in fast already and, as they approached the causeway, they could see that patches of it were beginning to disappear. In the distance, Vibiana had almost reached the island and, if they were to join her there, they would need to cross quickly. Water splashing around their horses' fetlocks as Cunedag and his companions hurriedly started their crossing.

Only half a dozen Saxons followed them now and charged into the water, paying no care to the incoming tide. "We need to hurry!" Tancorix said.

Urging their horses on, they did their best to follow the outline of the causeway beneath the flowing water as it grew deeper and deeper.

"Damn this!" Cunedag cried as the water rose up around their calves and their horses began to panic.

"Keep going!" said Asaros.

The shore of the island was close now, but the river was running deep and, glancing behind, Cunedag could see the Saxons floundering as they lost their way. One of them tumbled from his saddle as his mount put a foot wrong and was swept away by the current. That frightened the others, and they started to stall. That was a deadly mistake as the river surged around them, pulling at their horses and their legs. Some gave up and turned back for the shore, but it was too late. The water swept over them and soon all were flailing in the river, men sinking under the weight of mail coats and sodden clothes while horses swam off, deserting them.

It was nearer a thing as Cunedag liked, but he and his companions made it to the shore and rode up to dry land, thanking their respective sea gods for their mercy. They did not stop, even though their horses were tired. Vibiana would be making for the smugglers' camp on the other side of the island and, if she reached it, they may find that she had some armed allies.

They galloped through the woods that grew thick in the middle of the island and were able to run Vibiana down before the river could be spotted on the other side. She was not an experienced rider and lost control of her horse as they came abreast of her, Cunedag seizing her reins and bringing her animal to a halt.

"Please just let me go!" she wailed as he pulled her down from her saddle and deposited her roughly on the grass. "I tried to stop your brother from throwing his life away, but he wouldn't listen!"

Cunedag drew his sword, the thoughts of all the things he would do to this woman abandoned now that he found that all he wanted to do was give her a quick, clean death.

"Her description of Murcho does ring true to my mind," said Asaros. "He was a prideful young warrior, always keen for honour."

Cunedag turned to him. "Are you saying that you believe her?"

The Taifal shrugged. "It's up to you if you believe her or not. He's your brother to avenge. But me? I'd not take the life of somebody unless I was sure. And there is nothing about her story that seems impossible."

Cunedag ground his teeth. After all his pursuit of her, after the months of following her trail, tracking her down, now he was having second thoughts.

She knew it too and looked up at him with big, brown eyes, brimming with tears, the light of hope dim, but there all the same.

"Spare me, Cunedag mab Etern," she pleaded. "I was fond of your brother, and he was of me, I am sure of it, for the little time we were in each other's company. It was foul misfortune that meant we were not able to welcome you to Lindum side by side. I watched him die and I wept, knowing that I could not stay. Who would believe me? So I ran, aye, for the coast and sought passage to my homeland. But these damn wars you men are always stirring up forced me to remain in this land until now. I have desperately wanted to leave, knowing what I know about the future of this island."

"What do you mean?" Cunedag asked her. "What do you know about its future?"

"Only that more war is coming. Wulfnoth is inviting it. He betrays Atratinus, just as I betray him. He is preparing these shores for the arrival of more of his countrymen. Boatloads of them. They will overrun this part of the island and claim it for their own."

"When?" Cunedag demanded.

"In the spring when the sea lanes have calmed again. As we speak, a Saxon force larger than any this island has faced prepares across the sea, building boats and forging weapons."

"You lie," Cunedag said uncertainly. "The Britons' emperor, Constantinus is on the continent fighting the barbarians. He would not allow a fleet of them to sail across the channel."

"Your precious Constantinus is all but a prisoner in some town in southern Gaul. He has no control over what happens in the north. Wulfnoth is but the beginning. A Saxon horde is going to take advantage of the chaos the Britons had brought upon themselves and will be here before this time next year."

Cunedag and Asaros said nothing, both wishing that the woman spoke lies but both knew that it was the truth they heard.

"Gods alive," said Asaros. "Aurelianus must be warned."

"We'll warn him," said Cunedag, not taking his eyes off Vibiana.

"And the woman?"

Cunedag was silent for a while, his head full of conflicting thoughts. He knew himself to be no cold-blooded murderer and yet, his dreams were haunted by the faces of prisoners he had seen executed, the smuggler he had butchered in the town the latest to join their ranks. With a sigh of frustration, he sheathed his sword. He had no desire to add a woman's face to those ghostly hordes. "Get going," he told her.

"Then ... you believe me?" she asked, clearly daring herself to hope that she had been spared.

"Aye. You knew my brother well enough to paint a lifelike picture of him at least. I don't know if all you said is true, but I cannot kill you when I now doubt your guilt. Get going and don't come back."

Vibiana wasted no time in getting out from under the Votadini king's gaze before he changed his mind. She scrambled back up into the saddle of her mare and, without a word of thanks or parting, rode away from them.

"Do you think what she said was true?" Asaros asked Cunedag. "About the invasion, I mean. Or was it just a lie to buy her life with?"

"I don't know," Cunedag replied. "But too much of what she has said rings true for me. Much as I am loath to admit it, Vibiana the spy may speak more truth than we ever gave her credit for. Come, my friends, we must leave this damned island. Our business in this part of Albion is done and we have a long ride ahead of us."

"To find Aurelianus?"

"Aye, and to give him Vibiana's news and pray to all the gods that it is false."

Later that day, as the tide ebbed, a small vessel began its voyage downstream towards the coast. Gulls wheeled overhead, a stark contrast to the silence of the sailors onboard. There were no boisterous shanties being sung or harsh orders bellowed. As the ship drifted towards the sea, a sombre silence hung over it. The lookout on the headland had been bribed, but who knew how far a man's loyalty ran in these times?

Vibiana sat in the hold, the swollen saddlebags from her horse beneath her, bulging with loot taken from the fort. She had paid the sailors handsomely enough but kept a knife close to her hand all the same. They didn't know what was in her saddlebags, but they could guess, and it would be the work of a moment to turn on her and send her to a watery grave.

She had more than enough wealth to purchase a horse and an escort once she reached the shores of Gaul. And then, she would be on her way towards the mountains, towards home. She looked over the bulwark at everything she was leaving behind. As they drifted past the tip of the peninsula, the blue haze of freedom hung in the distance.

Past the headland, the wind filled the sails, and the shore of Britannia receded into the hazy distance. Vibiana looked back at the island that had been her home for many years and felt no regret at leaving it behind. God was about to visit an almighty storm on it, and she had no desire to be there when it hit.

Besides, her dream awaited. She was going home at last.

Part III

"Necton living in a life of exile, when his brother Drust expelled him, went all the way to Ireland and beseeched Saint Brigid to make a request to God on his behalf. However, as she prayed for him she said: If you return to your homeland the Lord will have pity on you: you will take over the kingdom of the Picts in peace." – The Pictish Chronicle

Chapter 17

427 A.D.

The scudding clouds drifted over the Red Hills, casting shadows over the boulders and tors that scattered the landscape, making it look like it had been the playground of giants long ago. Last winter's snow still clung to the land in the shaded dips. It held out all year in the highest spots, in this part of the land that seemed closest to the gods.

Cunedag surveyed the shattered hills that lay spread before him as they rose to craggy peaks and sank to flat, blue lochs that twinkled like gems set in rough stone. Another day and they would reach their destination as the Red Hills sank down to the woods and flat pastures of the coast. There, on a peninsular that projected into the northern sea, sat the mightiest Pictish fort and the royal seat of the Uerteru, the largest and most powerful of the Pictish tribes.

Cunedag glanced at the column of warriors behind him and the small baggage train that struggled over the uneven ground in the distance. That they were marching deep into the Pictish territories was something that he would never have believed would ever happen. That they were coming as friends, invited to Cair Uerteru by the Picts, was even more astounding.

King Talorc mab Achiuir of the Uerteru had died. If the Picts had anything resembling a high king, then it was him and he was in fact a descendant from their last high king, Gartnait. All other tribes were dwarfed by the territories of the Uerteru and their forts, bolstered by their control of coastal trade, were immensely powerful and well-defended strongholds. The Uerteru had led Pictish confederations on raiding expeditions against the Wall since before Cunedag had been born. Melga, the man who had slain Murcho had been of the Uerteru,

163

Cunedag thought grimly, the bitter sting at having lost his brother still keen after twenty years.

He tried not to dwell on old grievances. That he had slaughtered Picts by their dozens in the various wars of his youth counted for naught now that there was an even bigger threat. The Gaels grew ever stronger on the western coast of Albion and were pushing their borders eastward, threatening the Pictish tribes. If the Picts wanted to survive, then they had to band together and forget their tribal squabbles. It even meant forgetting their hatred of the lowland tribes like the Votadini whom they had always looked down on for their alliance with Rome.

The Romans were gone from Albion in any case. Nearly twenty years had passed since the Britons had proclaimed Constantinus emperor. Twenty years of war and rebellion, false hopes and shattered dreams. Cunedag had now seen almost fifty winters. He was a grandfather, had nine sons, two daughters, and more grey in his hair and beard than he would like. And he was beginning to think that there would never be peace in Albion.

The summer following Murcho's death had seen the Saxons land on the south-eastern shores in their droves. Cunedag had lent his aid to Aurelianus as they desperately beat them back to the coast, forcing them back across the sea and burning any boats that remained. It had been a brutal, bloody summer, but they had won through, and Albion remained in the hands of the Britons, for at least a little longer.

But there was much anger across the land at the failure of their homegrown emperor to protect them. What was the point of choosing their own emperor if he allowed barbarians to set out from the continent to harry British shores? In Londinium, Vitalinus took advantage of a situation he had probably hoped for all along and led a faction in overturning Constantinus's rule in Britannia. His officials were thrown out of their offices and replaced with men loyal to Vitalinus whose interests were focused on protecting the diocese, not making war on the continent. Chrysanthus, the emperor's vicarius, fled to Gaul, knowing that his position was now obsolete and his life in peril. Vitalinus replaced him as the most powerful man in Britannia and now ruled at the head of a newly formed council.

After nearly four centuries, Britain had thrown off the shackles of Rome and strove for an independent future.

On the continent, Constantinus had other concerns than losing control of his homeland. Despite forcing Emperor Honorius to recognise him as co-emperor of the west, the renegade Briton was ultimately brought down by treachery within his own ranks. One of his generals, a man called Gerontius, tried to usurp him and slew his son Constans in battle before besieging him at the town of Arelate in southern Gaul. It fell to Emperor Honorius's new magister militum to clear up the mess. He marched on Arelate in the summer of 411, sent Gerontius fleeing and forced Constantinus to surrender. He and his remaining son, Julian, were executed and their heads stuck on poles to be presented to Emperor Honorius.

The enemies of the true emperor had been defeated, but Britain was lost to him. Honorius had not the manpower to reclaim it and had his hands full dealing with the Goths under their ruler, Alaric, who had sacked Rome itself the year before Constantinus's defeat. Rome's administrative capital had been moved to Ravenna years before, but the eternal city was the ceremonial heart of the empire and to be ravaged by barbarians for the first time in eight-hundred years felt like a death knell to everything the Romans knew. Their world was crumbling.

And Britannia too, was struggling to survive without Roman protection. Saxons, Picts and Gaels harried it on all sides, just as they had done during the Barbarian Conspiracy sixty years previously. Now, even the Picts looked to the south for aid, hoping that the Votadini and the other lowland tribes would forget old grudges and stand with them against the raiders from Erin.

Cunedag would never forget. He had lost too many friends and family to Pictish blades. Yet, he was forced to see the sense in standing together against the Gaelic tide, even with old foes. But the kings of the Selgovae, Novantae and Alt Clut, while they hated the Gaels, were not so confident in an alliance with the Picts. Ride north into the wolf's den with no teulu and a small entourage? They suspected a trap to massacre the rulers of the lowlands to pave the way for a Pictish invasion of the whole island.

So Cunedag alone rode north to treat with their old enemy, bringing his three eldest sons and a small retinue of warriors with him. If it was a trap they were walking into, then they would have a hard fight and a long ride home ahead of them. He only hoped that Drustan mab Erp was in earnest in inviting him to attend.

"What else do we know about this Drustan, Father?" Tybiaun, his eldest said, bringing his horse up alongside Cunedag's and dragging him out of his brooding thoughts.

"Very little except that his father was married to the king's sister and that means he has a claim to the throne," he replied.

"Which he wants to pursue because Talorc's heir is an infant."

"Correct, but the late king was popular, and his young heir has many supporters."

Tybiaun snorted. "A child on the Uerteru throne, though! They need a strong leader to fight against the Gaels."

"Which is why Drustan has requested the attendance of the lowland kings. If it comes to civil war, which, knowing the Picts, it might well do, he wants to put in an early show of strength. Show how many supporters he has."

"And you are sure we should be supporting a man we know nothing about?"

Cunedag shrugged. "Any man who vows to stand against the Gaels is worth supporting. And as you suggested, a child leading the Uerteru is a bad idea in such times."

"Too bad the other lowland kings don't see it as clearly as you, Father," said Etern as he rode up in the company of Ruman. There was only a year between the younger brothers, and they were closer than either one was to Tybiaun who was the eldest by three years. "That even Idnerth of the Selgovae should balk at riding north with us!"

"The Picts slew his brother," said Ruman who knew the stories of their father's youth better than any. "He's hardly likely to accept the olive branch so readily."

"The Picts slew my brother too, if you'll remember," Cunedag said, a little more sharply than he intended. "But the Selgovae were ever the more timid of the lowland tribes. Even when I rode with Morleo in the old days, he was always rather hesitant and given to overthinking, good friend and soldier though he was. Still, I would have thought Cunlop would have come, at least. He is as Roman as I am. Or so they say."

"Too comfy and secure atop Alt Clut," said Etern.

"I suppose he hasn't found any more courage in the past twenty years since I helped him sit atop that rock," said Cunedag. "He was ever the foolish milksop."

He let his sons ride on to rejoin the column as it continued across the Red Hills. He was proud of his boys and thankful to the Great Mother for blessing his union with Vala with nine stout lads and two fair daughters. Vala was as fine a mother as she was a queen and he missed her dearly, though he knew he must cherish this time to get to know his three eldest sons better, for the duties of kingship pulled him from his family too often. So far, he was enjoying their company, and the trip was revealing their individual characteristics. The proud and staunchly conservative Tybiaun, the hot-headed Etern and the mild but knowledgeable Ruman. They each had their qualities, but none embodied all the qualities needed to rule a kingdom. At least not yet.

Tybiaun was his heir, and he had tried to instil the values in him that would see him rule the Votadini well once he was gone. But at twenty-eight and a father of two, Tybiaun was still too timid to take the risks needed to rule a kingdom that straddled the ruins of Roman Britain and the untamed wilds of the north. And Etern was too headstrong, too quarrelsome and quick to avenge a perceived insult. As for Ruman, he would much rather have his head in a codex or a scroll, examining the past like it was a rare plant, than deal with the present. All his sons had much maturing to do before any of them were fit to rule.

The following day, they came into view of the coast and saw the great fortress of Cair Uerteru crowning the peninsular. A series of three earthen ramparts spanned the neck of the headland and each gate was opened as the Votadini delegation passed through, dragon banner held aloft and gazed down on with interest by the Picts who stood atop the gatehouses.

The fortress itself consisted of two enclosures, the one to the west slightly higher than its neighbour. A drystone wall surrounded both with a wattle palisade atop the rampart. A similar defensive wall separated the two settlements with no gateway between them, meaning that the upper enclosure, which was reserved for the royalty and nobility, was entirely separate from the lower enclosure where the workshops and lower-class families lived.

The Uerteru's royal symbol was that of the bull and it emblazoned the banners which hung from the walls; black on red, fluttering in the breeze. As the gateway to the upper enclosure creaked open, Cunedag could see a large gathering assembled to greet them. There was no sign of a trap, and he chided himself for looking for one. He had to be confident that the invitation had been in earnest, and, for the love of the Great Mother, he must not show weakness in front of their hosts.

Not knowing any of the royal family by face, and with the king dead and the succession in question, Cunedag was unsure who to look to. There seemed to be two groups of people, each clustered around a finely dressed woman. Several druids were in attendance, their long hair blue with woad and woven with ornaments of bone and beads of glass and amber.

There was a visible gap between both camps. These, Cunedag assumed, represented the two rival claimants to the crown and, if he had to pick one of them to share a hearth with, then it would be the left-hand group for the one on the right looked on the newcomers with unwelcoming scowls.

"Greetings, Cunedag mab Etern of the Votadini," said a man of around thirty as he came forward from the left group. "I am Drustan mab Erp. Welcome to Cair Uerteru."

"Greetings, Drustan mab Erp," said Cunedag, accepting the younger man's offered arm. "I thank you for your invitation."

"Only the Votadini answered my plea for support," said Drustan. "For that, I thank you. It can't have been easy being the only king in the lowlands to accept my offer of hospitality."

My offer, Cunedag thought. The young man's choice of words left no doubt that it was Drustan and Drustan alone who wanted the Votadini here.

"The Votadini are in a position of some respect in the lowlands," he replied. "The other tribes owe us much. I am only sorry my influence did not extend to convincing them to join me."

"Yes, we have heard of the reputation of Cunedag of the Dragon Banner," said Drustan with a smile. "It is said you were raised by Romans who supported your claim for they saw in you a defender against us."

"More or less," said Cunedag, searching the man's eyes for any sign of animosity. He wondered if the Pict had any idea of how many of his countrymen he had slain. He supposed that he had.

"And now the Romans are gone, and we are all Britons once more," Drustan continued with a smile.

"I suppose so."

"Allow me to introduce you to the royal family. This is Queen Conchenn, my aunt and widow of our late king."

Cunedag bowed before the woman at the centre of the right-hand group who was flanked by two druids. She wore her hair up in the elaborate ceremonial style of Pictish queens and looked upon him with an imperious and detached gaze, betrayed only by a slight curl of distaste of her blue-tainted lips.

"Please accept my deepest condolences for the loss of your husband, Queen Conchenn," Cunedag said.

There was no reply and Drustan seemed eager to hurry things along in any case. "This is my mother, Lonceta," he said, directing Cunedag to the second royal woman. This one was clearly younger and slightly warmer than her sister-in-law. She still wore the fine clothes, ceremonial woad and elaborate hair of royalty, but, in contrast to the queen, she smiled at Cunedag as he bowed to her.

"Welcome to Cair Uerteru," Cunedag mab Etern," she said. "I thank you for answering my son's call. We have need of all the friends we can get in these times."

A small girl stood close to her, dressed in a fine gown with a hairstyle similar to Lonceta's, pinned up with bones. She was about five years old and gazed up at Cunedag with none of the shyness he was used to seeing in little girls. In fact, she seemed to be judging him harder than anybody else there.

"This is Galana, my sister," Drustan explained.

"Pleased to meet you, Galana of the Uerteru," said Cunedag, bowing to the small child.

"Come, you must be tired and thirsty after your journey," said Drustan. "Sup with us in our roundhouse and we shall talk."

The other delegation, Cunedag noticed, had started to disperse, their presence at the reception clearly a reluctant formality. Cunedag and his entourage followed Drustan and his delegation down the central avenue of the enclosure which was lined with standing stones carved with the royal bull of the Uerteru. Up ahead, stood the great roundhouse, smoke drifting from the hole in the thatch. Several smaller, though still large, roundhouses clustered around the royal residence, and it was to one of these that Drustan led them.

The sigils of several other Pictish tribes hung outside the roundhouses and Cunedag recognised those of the Venicones, Taexali and the Epidii among several others he was unfamiliar with. Many warriors were camped in hide tents in between the roundhouses and were roasting meat over small cookfires or gaming and wrestling with each other. There were enough fighting men here, Cunedag mused, to turn Cair Uerteru into a bloodbath should it come to it.

First, they were shown to a vacant roundhouse which was given over to the Votadini for the duration of their stay. While his men were settling into their lodgings, Cunedag and his sons joined Drustan in his own roundhouse on the other side of the enclosure. Lonceta and her daughter, Galana, sat at the centre of the long table with what seemed to be the family's personal druid on their left while Drustan and Cunedag with his sons sat on their right.

"You must understand, Cunedag," Drustan said as they sipped heather beer. "My cousin, Cailtram simply cannot lead the Uerteru while our tribes suffer constant attacks from the

Gaelic Coast. A strong leader is needed, not a babe at its mother's teat."

"I agree with you there," Cunedag replied. "Kings should be leaders, not merely symbols."

"Tell him about the bloodline of Modron," piped up Galana around a mouthful of honey cake.

"That's just an old tradition, Galana," said Drustan. "Most tribes don't even honour it anymore."

"An old tradition that supports our claim, it must be admitted," Lonceta added.

"True," said Drustan. He turned to Cunedag. "In ages past, a tribe's king was always chosen from the female bloodline. The crown would pass to a brother of the queen, or, failing that, a sister's son."

"That means you, brother," said Galana. "The crown is yours by right."

Drustan smiled. "My sister agrees with this particular tradition which prizes a woman's importance in honour of the Great Mother."

"And who could blame her?" said Cunedag with a smile at Galana. "Our own tribe no longer practices it, but I am given to understand that such a thing was common in ages past. But what of your people? Do you have much support from your own tribe? Do they put much stock in the old ways?"

"Difficult to say," said Drustan. "My aunt has the support of the druids, and they wield much influence."

"You seem to have one druid on your side, at least," said Cunedag, nodding in the direction of the middle-aged man with long, blue-stained hair and religious markings on his face.

"This is Vipoig, who was a friend of my father for many years," said Drustan, raising his cup to the druid.

"And now I am friend to his son," Vipoig replied.

"Does that place you in a difficult position?" Cunedag asked. "Standing against other members of your order who support Cailtram's claim?"

Vipoig nodded sagely. "Aye, a druid's path is seldom easy and sometimes he must paddle against the current. My order is not unused to disagreements and many a druid has forged his own path."

Cunedag nodded, knowing much of renegade druids but said nothing.

"Who is the druid of the Votadini these days?" Vipoig asked. "Surely old Gonar does not still walk this realm?"

"Gonar voyaged to Annun many years ago," said Cunedag. "His successor is a man called Lutrin mab Uvan."

"Ah, I know him. He is young, but I am sure Gonar trained him well. Did he support your decision in riding north?"

"He had little to say on the matter," Cunedag admitted. "He knows the advantages of a strong north if the Gaelic tongue is not to be spoken on our doorstep in the next few years."

"Better the enemy you know, eh?" said Drustan with a smile. "Especially if that enemy might now be called 'friend'."

"You did not ask Lutrin to seek the opinions of the gods on supporting Drustan?" the druid inquired.

"I did not. I chose to come here and see for myself what the situation is here in the north," said Cunedag, aware that he now had the attention of the entire roundhouse.

"And how do you find it?" asked Drustan.

"Much as I feared. The Gaels knock on your doors while you discuss rights of kingship. Action is needed, not words."

"Then I have your support?"

Cunedag hesitated, but only for a moment. Then, he raised his cup of ale and said; "Aye, Drustan mab Erp, you have the support of the Votadini, such as it is."

The roundhouse erupted into cheers and the hammering of knife hilts on tables was deafening.

Drustan rose and, setting down his cup, embraced Cunedag as a brother in arms. "Come with me," he said. "Let us breathe the evening air together and talk in private."

The assembled supporters of Drustan continued their eating and drinking with vigour now that the meal had become a celebration and Cunedag followed Drustan outside where dusk was falling, and the torches were being lit by the sentries. They headed for the steps which led to the rampart and followed it around to the northern side where the headland thrust out into the great firth. Here, the sea boomed against the rocks at the foot of the fortress walls. The other side of the firth was a black line on the horizon.

"I am glad of your support, Cunedag," said Drustan, "and if I can rally the other tribes to my banner, then my succession will be assured."

"You speak as if it will come to war," said Cunedag. "How are these disputes usually resolved in the north?"

Drustan shrugged. "If Cailtram was a man, I might challenge him to combat. But as he is naught but a child, it will come to a vote."

"Do other tribes have any say in Uerteru matters?" Cunedag asked. "I see many standards alongside our own. It's hard to believe any tribe would allow others to decide who rules them."

"My aunt and her followers believe that this is an Uerteru matter only," Drustan said. "But I believe the time has come to unite the tribes as they were united under Gartnait long ago. As long as I have enough outside support, Conchenn and her druids can't stop me."

Cunedag gazed out at the choppy waters and the distant coastline, hazy beneath the darkening sky. Gartnait had been the mastermind behind the Barbarian Conspiracy in which his own grandfather, Padarn, had been pressured into taking part. That had resulted in his father and himself being fostered by the Romans. There would be many below the Wall who would tremble at the idea of a high king of the Picts and he wondered, not for the first time, if supporting Drustan was truly the wisest thing.

"It's the only way to ensure our people's survival against the Gaels," said Drustan, apparently sensing Cunedag's reservations. "And it's not as if similar developments aren't happening in the south, beyond the Roman wall."

"What have you heard?" Cunedag asked him.

"Only that this Vertigernus is king in all but name. If there is to be a high king below the Wall, is it not only natural that there is one above it too?"

Vertigernus? Cunedag had heard the name and knew it referred to Vitalinus who sat at the head of the Council of Britannia. The word meant 'overlord', and Cunedag did not know if it was a title Vitalinus had bestowed upon himself or if it was just what the Britons in the south were calling him, but there was no denying the power that man had consolidated after Constantinus had left with the legions.

"Perhaps you are right," he said. "Though a Pictish confederation is enough to put the fear of all the gods into the Britons in the south."

"You think I harbour the same ambitions as my ancestors?" said Drustan. "Believe me, Cunedag, I seek only to protect the lands of my people from the Gaels. The days of raiding Roman territories are over. *Rome* is over."

"And when the Gaels are defeated?" Cunedag said. "Will your own people not turn their attentions south, as they have always done in the past?"

Drustan was on the verge of replying when a horn bellowed at the front gate. A party was approaching, and the iron-bound timbers creaked as the gates were opened to admit them. A small column of horsemen rode in, warriors and bold ones at that. They slid down from their mounts and flung their reins to attendants as people emerged from the roundhouses to greet them.

"Who's this?" Cunedag asked.

"A complication," said Drustan, frowning. "My brother has come."

Chapter 18

Cunedag awoke with a dry mouth and slightly pounding temples. He hadn't the head for heather beer that he used to. He got up, splashed his face with water from a jug and went outside to breathe the clear, fresh air of morning.

The arrival of Nechtan, Drustan's brother, had put a dampener on the evening and the drinking had continued, less in celebration but rather as consolation for the upset his arrival caused. The two brothers did not see eye to eye and hadn't for many years. Nechtan, Cunedag learned, was the younger brother and the wilder and more quarrelsome of the two. He had apparently spent the summer in the east, guarding the coast against Frankish pirates and now he had come to Cair Uerteru to have his say in the succession.

The only person who had been pleased to see him was his mother and, by the way they embraced and sat at table talking animatedly, her hanging off his every word, Cunedag couldn't help but wonder if he was the favourite son. Even little Galana hung off every word Nechtan said.

Cunedag contemplated breakfast while he watched the fortress rouse itself. He was approached by Tybiaun who ran his fingers through his dampened hair after having dunked his head in a nearby water butt.

"Sore head?" Cunedag asked him.

"Nothing a good breakfast won't sort out," Tybiaun replied. "The new arrivals are still slumbering, I see." He nodded in the direction of the roundhouse where Nechtan and his followers had been billeted.

"They drank enough last night to see them sleep until noon," Cunedag replied. "Just as well. I don't like the way those two brothers seem to despise each other. It does not bode well for Drustan's claim."

"Are you sure you want to do this, Father?" Tybiaun asked. "If it comes to war, do we really want to get involved?"

"Do not question my judgement, Tybiaun," said Cunedag. "I have made my decision. The last thing I want is to get involved in another war, but I believe in Drustan's dream to unite the highland tribes. It is the only way they can stand against the Gaelic storm that hammers at their gates."

"Of course, Father. I did not mean to question you. I just feel that we are so very far from home …"

Cunedag smiled. His eldest son and heir brought him great pride, but he was a conservative-minded and serious young man. He had too much in common with the other rulers of the lowland tribes, perhaps. He thought too inwardly, of the welfare of his own tribe rather than looking at the bigger picture as years of war and politics had taught Cunedag to do. He placed a hand on the shoulder of his firstborn. "This island is our home, Tybiaun. You are still young, despite having children of your own, but when you have lived as long as I and have fought in wars from north to south, you'll come to respect the notion of an island uniting against its foes."

"After all these years, Father," Tybiaun said with a smile, "you still sound like a Roman."

Cunedag grinned. He supposed his son had a point. "Where are your brothers?"

"Etern is still snoring and I haven't seen Ruman since last night. I have a feeling he snuck off with that warrior woman who was giving him eyes over dinner."

"Yes, I noticed that," said Cunedag with a smile. "I must remind that boy that he has a wife and son at home."

For all Ruman's timidness and bookish habits, he was a handsome youth with a healthy appetite for women. All of the marriages Cunedag had arranged for his sons had been political in nature, so he did not expect love and fidelity, but he did demand a certain discretion concerning such things.

Servants were sent to procure food, and they ate by the hearth, their constitutions all the better for some fresh air and full bellies. Drustan, they learned, was already up and about and came to see them on his way back from the Great Roundhouse. The druid, Vipiog walked alongside him.

"You have breakfasted?" Drustan asked Cunedag.

"Yes, thank you," Cunedag replied. "The cheese was particularly good. Goat?"

"Aye. I'll be sure to have some sent back with you. I have been in discussion with my aunt and her druids. There will be a vote, but they want to wait until all the tribal representatives are here. We await only the delegation from the Caereni."

"I thought the queen considered the succession an internal matter?"

Drustan smiled. "It seems that by recruiting my own allies, I have made her nervous and she seeks her own. All the tribes will have their say now."

"Is it likely to be a close vote?"

Drustan shrugged. "Conchenn must believe so, to postpone things just for one tribe. The Caereni are a distant people who keep to themselves. Where their vote will land, I honestly can't say."

Later, Nechtan and his men emerged from their roundhouse, boisterously declaring that they felt no ill-effects of the previous night's drinking and attempted to prove themselves by drinking more. Squabbling broke out with Drustan's men, and several insults had to be avenged by single combat. The Votadini watched with interest as two men were beaten bloody and were dragged away by their comrades, and Cunedag was glad that his own men were not involved.

But trouble found them nonetheless and it was caused by one of his own sons. Ruman eventually emerged from one of the roundhouses belonging to the Uerteru and it quickly became apparent that it was the roundhouse of the warrior woman who had been so smitten with him the night before.

This caused some grumbling among the male Uerteru warriors who did not like the idea of one of their women sleeping with a man from another tribe. One warrior in particular seemed to think that the woman was his and approached Ruman with several of his companions, their hands on their knife hilts.

"Who do you think you are, coming up here and bedding our women, *lowlander*?" the man demanded. "Maithgemm has been my lover since you were sucking on your mother's teat!"

Ruman, although pale-faced at being confronted by several angry Picts, never knew the right thing to say and only angered the man further. "That may be true," he said, "but last night she informed me that she has tired of you. She is free to choose a new lover, unless there is some highland custom I am unaware of that forbids it."

The man all but roared at the young prince's insolence and looked like he was about to hit him. Cunedag, Tybiaun and Etern hurried over, desperate to prevent what looked to be a diplomatic dispute in the making, but the woman in question had emerged from her hut and faced down her former lover.

Maithgemm was older than Ruman and clearly more experienced in warfare, for her bare arms were notched with scars and tattooed with swirling designs. Her hair was dishevelled but Cunedag could see why his son had been attracted to her. She had a fierceness and a courage that made him think of Vala.

"Back down, Ciniod!" she snapped at Ruman's rival for her affections. "You had your chance with me and have no say in who I fuck!"

"Men of your own tribe aren't good enough for you, eh?" Ciniod replied.

"What of it?" she demanded. "Would you care to test yourself against me so we can prove it? Mayhap I tire of brutes like you and fancied a more sensitive man, a man who truly knows how to pleasure a woman!"

Several Votadini warriors roared with laughter at this and Ruman's face turned crimson. The Uerteru men scowled but said nothing, not one of them willing to challenge the woman and disgrace themselves further by losing. They slunk off and Maithgemm gave Ruman a wink before retiring back to her hut.

Etern chuckled and caught his little brother in a headlock, ruffling his dark hair. "You silver-tongued devil, Brother! I think she's quite taken with you!"

"Keep it in your breeches when we are guests from now on, Ruman," said Cunedag. "I can't afford to lose our footing with Drustan just because you upset his warriors by seducing their women."

"Sorry, Father," Ruman replied, squirming free from Etern's rough handling. "I didn't know she had previous attachments."

Word of the altercation had reached Drustan and he decided to avoid any more trouble by organising a hunt in the woods around Cair Uerteru. He invited Cunedag and his sons along and dusk was falling by the time they were deep into the woods south of the fortress. It had rained during the afternoon, and the tall pines dripped down on them as they rode through the mist-shrouded woods.

Drustan seemed more subdued than he had been before his brother's arrival last night. He showed none of the optimistic bravado he had done when Cunedag had pledged his support to him. It was almost as if Nechtan's arrival had sapped his confidence in his own plans.

"There seems to be no love lost between you and your brother," Cunedag ventured by way of conversation.

"Aye, Nechtan and I have never really seen eye to eye. He is far more tempestuous than I and we fought regularly as youths."

"As did I with my older brother," said Cunedag, thinking back to another hunt in similar woods a lifetime ago.

"I forget, you know much about brotherly strife," said Drustan. "It is well-known how you defeated your brother in a civil war for the Votadini crown. I pray that it will not come to that regarding the crown of the Uerteru."

"Is that likely?" Cunedag asked. "Would Nechtan support your cousin's claim just to spite you?"

"Nechtan supports Nechtan," said Drustan with a small smile. "He would stop at nothing to thwart my own claim, but in truth, I believe he would like to see himself as high king of the northern tribes."

"A younger brother?" said Cunedag. "Choosing a grown cousin over a babe is one thing, but between two grown brothers, why would anybody support the younger?"

"Nechtan has his ways of convincing people," said Drustan. "And if it comes to a choice between the two of us, a vote won't be necessary. It would be single combat."

Cunedag said nothing and they rode on in silence for a while. He could tell that Drustan did not favour his chances in a fight against Nechtan. This brotherly dispute was worse than he had feared and reminded him much of his own troubles with Brude so many years ago.

The dogs picked up the scent of a quarry and before long, a buck with at least six tines was spotted and chase was given. They thundered through the woods and the melancholy subject of the conversation left Cunedag as he thrilled in the hunt.

The buck descended a rise and made to cut left as the horsemen crested the hill, dogs baying and darting to close it in. An arrow sang through the trees and struck the animal in the neck, making its legs buckle. The men cried out in alarm. The arrow had not come from any of them.

The dogs brought the struggling animal down but quickly forgot their quarry as a second, larger pack of dogs burst from the trees to the south. With much barking and whining, Drustan's dogs turned tail and fled, leaving the larger pack to surround the felled deer.

"Who, by all the gods …?" Drustan yelled, riding ahead and reining in his mount a few feet from the slain deer.

The party who owned the dogs came galloping through the woods towards them; twenty Picts, large and clearly warriors out for sport. "Drustan mab Erp!" cried one of them, a man only a few years younger than Cunedag, his greying hair held up in a topknot. "Our would-be king! You lost out on this buck, just as you'll lose out on the crown!"

The newcomers laughed at this, and the two parties faced each other, the threat of violence hanging in the air between them.

"You teach your men bad manners, Uvan," said Drustan. "To drive away one man's pack of dogs from the kill."

"My pack is bigger and hungrier," the man replied. "And I do not take into account the mewling of upstarts. Maybe one day you will learn that such is the way of the world. To the victors, the spoils!"

"You speak as if custom and society is unknown to you," said Cunedag, unable to prevent himself from interjecting. "

"Am I to sit and be lectured by a Roman's whelp!" Uvan snarled. "Rome is gone from these lands to which she never had any claim in the first place! You are lost, Cunedag mab

Etern! Go back to what is left of your precious wall and cower there! Aye, I know who you are and perhaps you shall know me better when I tell you that I am the brother of Melga, the man you butchered in Lindum!"

Cunedag let the hate in the man's eyes wash over him as he himself simmered. This was the brother of the man who had slain Murcho. And now he accused him of murder? It was almost more than he could manage not to draw his spatha and ram the Roman blade down this Pict's throat. He forced himself to remember that he counted some Picts as friends now and he was here as a guest of one of them.

"Melga came south to kill and plunder," he said coldly. "He got what we southerners give to such men. And it may interest you to know that he slew my own brother in single combat so perhaps we might consider ourselves even on that score."

Uvan snorted. "Even with a soft-spined traitor? I shall walk the misty paths of Annun before I consider you anything approaching my equal!"

"Damn your villainous tongue and the family that spawned you!" Etern bellowed. "My father is a great hero in the south because he held it against Pictish scum like your brother!"

"Be silent, Etern!" Cunedag bellowed.

It had been a gross breach of manners and Tybiaun and Ruman looked at the ground in shame at the middle brother's actions.

"I advise you to curb your spawn's wagging tongue," Uvan snarled. "Or I will remove it myself!" He drew a long, smoke-blackened blade from a sheath at his belt and pointed it at Etern.

"Enough of this!" Drustan yelled. "Cunedag and his sons are here as my guests and you will show them the proper courtesy, Uvan!"

"You're not my king, son of Erp," Uvan sneered. "And you never will be, so hold your threats and keep what company you will. It matters little."

Cunedag burned with anger at his son as they turned from the tribesmen, leaving them to their kill. "You will apologise to our host, Etern," he growled. "The insult you used for those who insulted me offends all who live north of the Wall and I myself have been called it more times than I like in my lifetime."

Etern stared at the trees ahead, his face burning crimson at being chastised like a small boy. "My deepest apologies, Drustan. I let my anger at that man get the better of me."

"Pay it no mind, Etern," said Drustan. "We have been called 'Picts' for so long now that many north of the Wall now consider themselves such. I do not blame you for using the term in anger. Old hatreds die hard. The process of replacing enmity with alliance is a long and slow process. Not aided by scum like Uvan."

He rode ahead and Cunedag turned to give a warning look to all three of his sons. "Between Ruman's womanising and Etern's temper, we are liable to have the whole of the north turning on us," he said. "Watch yourselves over the next few days. We can't afford any more breaches of courtesy."

Chapter 19

The following day, the Caereni arrived, riding in below their banner which showed a red roebuck on a white field. All the tribes had arrived now and there was an air of pregnant tension over Cair Uerteru as the fortress awaited the word that the vote could be held.

First, the Caereni were welcomed with a feast to which all other tribal delegations were invited. The cavernous interior of the royal residence was decorated with banners showing the bull of the Uerteru. They hung from the walls and the rafters and behind the high seat on the dais which was ominously vacant. Warriors of various delegations drank and talked below the fug of peat smoke that hung above the central hearth.

Queen Conchenn sat beside the empty throne with her son on a small chair beside her, atop a mound of cushions so he could see over the table spread with food. It was the first time Cunedag had seen Talorc's heir. He seemed a sickly thing, no more than five winters old. He plucked at bits of food from platters which servants brought within his reach, utterly oblivious to the crowds before him who were all there to either support him or disinherit him.

There was a clear division between those who stood by the infant prince and those who were there to support Drustan, with both parties keeping to opposite sides of the roundhouse. And within those parties, there were further divisions still. Drustan's men kept their distance from Nechtan's and between them, many tribal leaders seemed to mingle, apparently not knowing which party to make merry with. It did not bode well for Drustan's plan to oppose the young prince's claim.

Among Cailtram's supporters, Cunedag spotted Uvan, brother of Melga and the mouthful of mead he had just taken turned sour on his tongue. He swallowed it with a grimace, more certain than ever that he was backing the right side, fractured though it was.

Every so often, Uvan would cast a venomous glance at Cunedag and his sons and at Etern in particular. If protocol had not forbidden it, Cunedag knew that his second born would have been in danger of being challenged to a fight that night.

"Looks like you've made yourself an enemy when we are supposed to be making friends, brother," said Tybiaun, cup of mead in hand. His face showed the mirth of a jest but in truth, Tybiaun could never refuse the opportunity to barb his younger brother.

"Well at least I stood up for Father," said Etern. "You and Ruman simply sat there and dumbly let that oaf insult him."

"Take no heed of Uvan," said Drustan, overhearing them. "He is a boastful braggart of a strong warrior family, but he'll not come near you tonight. Not with so much at stake."

"I've no fear of him!" Etern said defensively. "I only wish there wasn't so much at stake so we might have at each other! I'd wipe that smirk off his face …"

"There'll be no baiting each other or any more talk of proving who's the better man," Cunedag interjected. "Drustan is right, there is too much at stake to let youthful bravado ruin all. Both of you, leave each other alone and take heed of Ruman. Now there's an example to follow."

Ruman was conversing with Vipiog about some obscure event involving an Uerteru king in the distant past. Tybiaun and Etern snorted, united for once, in their derision of their younger brother.

"Vipiog will have to be careful Ruman doesn't bore his ears off," said Tybiaun.

"I swear he should have trained as a druid," said Etern, "for he has more of a love of the past than the present."

"At least he's heeding my orders and keeping away from that warrior woman," said Cunedag.

"Aye, though she seems keen to remind him of their tryst," said Etern.

They glanced in the direction of Maithgemm who kept looking at Ruman across the crowded hall, a cup of ale in her hand and a hunger in her eyes.

Two days later, the vote was held in a sacred area south of the fort. The tribal delegations gathered beneath their banners in a clearing around a rocky outcrop. Here, some stone steps had been carved into the rock and led down to a subterranean chamber. Stone pillars supported the entrance with human skulls set into niches.

"What goes on in there?" Cunedag asked Drustan as they took their place in the assembly.

"That is a sacred spring below ground," Drustan replied. "The druids make offerings to the goddess. They are there now, asking for her blessing and advice."

It was a massive gathering and, as Cunedag looked around at the faces of the many Pictish tribes, he was struck, for the first time, at how varied the people of the north were. Tribal tattoos were as different as the symbols on the banners that fluttered above them. These were the people Drustan wished to unite and, seeing them all assembled in the cold light of day, each beneath their own banners, he wondered if it was not an impossible task.

The druids emerged from the subterranean chamber, passing up the stone steps single file, to face the assembly.

"Honoured men and women!" the eldest of the druids that were affixed to Cailtram's party said, holding his staff up for silence. "You have all come, across mountain and moor, to see a new king of the Uerteru chosen! We have asked for the blessing of the gods and the Great Mother herself to watch over these proceedings and to give their guidance in choosing the right path of the many that lie ahead of us. I know I speak for many here in saying that there is only one clear path ahead, and that is by standing with the family of Talorc mab Achiuir, who ruled the Uerteru well for many years. His son, Cailtram must be our next king!"

There was a bellow of agreement from Cailtram's supporters and much jeering from Drustan's camp. Before the old druid could continue, Vipiog stepped forward to cut him short.

"Much enthusiasm is shown here for a king who is not even old enough to be present at this gathering!" he said. "Where is he now? Napping with his mother's milk on his lips?"

Drustan's supporters roared with laughter at this.

"You must see that it is folly to place the crown of the Uerteru on the head of a child!" Vipiog went on. "Not only that, but there is tradition to think of! For hundreds of years, the crown passed down the female line of descent, not the male. This babe in arms has no more right to rule the Uerteru than Drustan here. Drustan is the son of the king's sister! It *must* be he who rules!"

Drustan's supporters shouted their agreement, doubling their effort to make up for being in the minority. From Nechtan and his men, there came not a sound.

"You speak of ways that belong in the distant past, Vipiog!" the first druid replied. "And you drag them forth purely because they support your own candidate!"

"What of it?" Vipiog replied, shouting over the murmurs of agreement from Cailtram's party. "Drustan *is* the better candidate. We face annihilation by the Gaels who sweep upon us on the winds from Erin. War will come in the spring, maybe not for the Uerteru, but certainly for the Epidii and the Creones. If they fall, then we will be next. The time for petty tribal matters is over. I say we must vote for a high king! And what better candidate than a strong man in the height of warriorhood who traces his descent along the maternal line to the great Gartnait? The gods will surely bless him as our leader!"

"If that is your reasoning, Vipiog, then there is more than one candidate!"

This last comment was from Nechtan, and the crowd fell into a stunned silence. All knew he was the younger brother of the heir's rival and that he and Drustan despised each other.

"Surely you do not suggest yourself, Nechtan?" asked Vipiog, almost pleadingly.

Nechtan strode forward to join the two druids in the centre of the gathering. "I am Drustan's younger brother, it is true, but I have the same lineage as him. I too trace my descent from Gartnait from my mother and I dare any here to say that Drustan is my better in war!"

The atmosphere was uneasy. No longer was the focus of the assembly on the rivalry between the king's son and his nephew. Now it was between two brothers and, if allowed to run its course, there could well be bloodshed before the meeting was over.

"All season, I have been patrolling the east coast, fending off bands of Frankish pirates," Nechtan continued, "while my brother has been loitering around Cair Uerteru plotting and currying favour! I have reddened my sword against our enemies while he had moistened his tongue with our late king's mead! Choose me to be your next leader and I will banish these Gaels back to Erin within the year!"

There were some scoffs and jeers at this from both sides of the gathering. The Gaels had plagued Albion's shores for more than a generation. It would take more than the boisterous words of this upstart to see them driven back across the sea and everybody knew it.

Nechtan's face coloured with anger at the insult to his pride. "Who here doubts me?" he bellowed. "You would rather have a talker and an idler than a true warrior lead you?"

"Whether you or your brother is the fitter to rule is another matter entirely," said the first druid. "First the succession of Talorc's heir must be decided. Let us vote! Those who wish Cailtram mab Talorc to succeed his father as king of the Uerteru, step forward!"

Many nobles of the Uerteru came forward, as did the leaders of several other tribes. For the first time, Cunedag saw Queen Conchenn smile. It did not look good for either Drustan or Nechtan.

"And those in favour of a son of Erp?" the druid continued.

Cunedag and several other nobles stood forth to be counted. The druids tallied the results on two sticks before declaring Cailtram the winner.

"A babe as our high king?" Nechtan shouted. "Sheep choose a lamb to protect them from the wolf!"

"Why should we follow you when you can barely unite your own family?" cried the king of the Taexali, looking from Nechtan to Drustan. "Unite the tribes? Pah! Perhaps the sons of Erp should set their own house in order before making any grander plans!"

The chorus of agreement was nearly deafening. It was decided. The tribes had chosen the young princeling over some upstart cousin. The druid held out his arms for silence.

"Cailtram mab Talorc shall be our next king!" he cried. "He will be crowned after Kalan Gayaf. A new king for a new year!"

Applause rippled through the congregation and Nechtan, uttering a foul oath, turned from them all and stalked off, his small band of followers in his wake.

"My brother split the vote and robbed me of my chance to become king!" Drustan seethed in his roundhouse that night. "If only he had kept to the coast where he belongs, I might have been chosen!"

"The vote was strongly in favour of Cailtram, my son," said Lonceta.

"Not so strong that they wouldn't have followed me if Nechtan had minded his own business. To be undone by that little shit! Always he has thwarted me, my whole life!"

"You are upset, Drustan," his mother said. "And you overreact. He is your brother."

"*Younger* brother!" Drustan snapped. "And he should mind his place!"

Little Galana, who was watching her big brother's rage with interest, was hustled off to bed by the servants, protesting loudly that she wanted to stay. Drustan ignored her and demanded more ale.

Cunedag and his sons watched the warrior storm and rage between deep gulps from his cup. Cunedag sighed. His business here was done, and it looked like his trip had been wasted. Perhaps Idnerth and Cunlop and the other lowland kings were right. Maybe there was no hope of uniting the Picts. They were even more fragmented than the Britons who had several hundred years of Roman unity to bind them together against barbarian enemies.

"I am sorry the vote did not go in your favour," Drustan," Cunedag told him.

"Bunch of fools," Drustan said. "They will come to regret their decisions when the Gaels march on our territories."

"I believe you speak the truth. But I must return to my own lands tomorrow. I have been gone long enough as it is."

"Thank you again for coming. I only wish our time here had been more productive. I did what I could to lead my people. All that is left is to fight for them come spring. Can I count on Votadini support?"

"If it comes to war with the Gaels, then you shall have it," Cunedag replied. "The north must not fall, or we will be forced to rebuild the defences the Romans abandoned. Little ever changes, it seems."

"In that you speak the truth. Gods protect you, Cunedag. Until we meet again."

The night was cold and the ground soft after a heavy deluge that had been more sleet than rain. The cart's wheels had got bogged down in the mud several times, delaying their journey by many hours. Queen Conchenn looked out of the curtained window at the blackness that closed in and the light snowflakes that danced in the air, heralding a heavier fall to come. She shivered and pulled Cailtram to her, as much for warmth as her maternal instinct to protect him.

He was to be king. It was decided. They were journeying along the firth to her sister's home of Din Moreb to spend Kalan Gayaf. Once the harvest festival was over, they would return to Cair Uerteru for the crowning ceremony.

A warrior rode alongside the carriage and knocked on the wood. Conchenn pulled the curtain aside to speak with him. He wore a heavy wolfskin cloak against the chill. "Din Moreb is about two leagues off, my queen," he said. "We had hoped to get you there before nightfall, but this weather …"

"I'm not concerned by the darkness," Conchenn snapped. "Nor am I with excuses. Just proceed with haste. My son and your king is cold."

"Yes, my queen," the warrior replied as she jerked the curtain closed. She pulled the furs up around herself and Cailtram who dozed in the crook of her arm, allowing herself to feel a touch of relief at the warrior's words. Home was not far off, and had it been daylight, she would have recognised where they were. These were the woods she and her sister had played in as children, before she had been married to King Talorc. Why then, did she feel such trepidation?

There was a small, sharp cry outside the carriage. The sound of hooves churning mud. A horse screamed in fright, and somebody cried out the alarm; "Ambush! Protect the queen!"

Conchenn jerked the curtain aside and saw her riders galloping past the carriage towards some fight on the road up ahead. Cailtram, awoken by the noise, squirmed in her grip. "What's happening, Mother?" he cried.

"Nothing, sweetheart," she said, squeezing him to her and stroking his dark locks. "There is just some obstacle up ahead. Our brave warriors will deal with it."

She wished she felt as confident as she sounded. Who would dare attack the queen's carriage? Bandits who didn't know any better? Or was it something more sinister …?

The sounds of wounded men and victorious shouts were heard up ahead. Several voices, alien to her ears, could be heard above the din, louder and fiercer than those of her own warriors. There was something about those voices … and then she realised. They were shouting in Gaelic!

Fear, the like of which she had never felt, gripped her. Gaels this far inland? It was unheard of and attacking a royal carriage? There was something foul at the heart of this, but she had no time to dwell on theories. The life of her son was in peril and, motherly instinct banishing her urge to remain in the carriage and pray to the Great Mother for protection, she tore the furs aside and opened the door, tugging Cailtram with her.

"Where are we going, Mother?" Cailtram whimpered. "I'm scared ..."

"Hush!" she hissed at him as she stepped down onto the road, the freezing mud seeping up around her slippers.

Glancing up the road, beyond the panicked horses, she could see the glint of moonlight on sword blades and the clash of arms resounded through the darkness. Pulling Cailtram down from the carriage, she hurried to the side of the road where the trees grew thick. The ground dipped down from the road and, by sliding onto her backside and pressing her back against a tree, Conchenn was able to hide herself and her son from sight from the road.

The fighting had died down now, and the Gaelic voices still burned the air, telling Conchenn that the battle had been lost. They were alone now, with the cold night and the ravaging Gaels their enemy. Horses thundered on the road above and Conchenn listened, her hand clamped over the whimpering mouth of her son to keep him from crying out.

The Gaels ransacked the carriage, tearing curtains and ripping apart the interior, cursing at finding their quarry gone. They began to spread out along the road, probing the treeline for the fugitives.

Swallowing down a sob, Conchenn knew that she had to get Cailtram away from the road and into the darkness of the woods. She desperately glanced about to see if she could recognise where they were, but all was rendered unfamiliar by the darkness and the passage of time. If they were but two leagues from Din Moreb, then they might make it on foot, though they were hardly dressed for such a cold and long trek.

Already her slippered feet were numb from the cold but she would walk until her toes dropped off if it meant getting her son to safety.

Easing herself up onto her haunches, her frozen joints screaming in protest, she made to move deeper into the woods. There was a cry from the road behind as somebody spotted her. In a panic, she tried to run, dragging Cailtram behind her.

The Gaels charged down the rise, bellowing at her to halt. She knew it was hopeless. They swarmed her and her son, hemming them in like wounded lambs. Cailtram bawled in terror and Conchenn tried to make her pleas for mercy be heard over his cries.

"We have no money but what you found in the carriage!" she said. "Take it and let us live, please!"

"We want no money, British whore!" said one of the Gaels in accented British. "And we know who you are."

For a moment, Conchenn allowed her mind to wander down the paths of intrigue. They had been betrayed, but by whom? These Gaels had been waiting for them. Sent by somebody.

"Please, at least let my son live!" she said. "Use me as you will, but my son is innocent!"

"The night is cold, and we shall indeed use you as we will," said the Gael with a grin. "But no British kings are innocent."

He drew a long knife, and the glint of his grin matched the wickedness of the blade. And Conchenn knew that there was no hope. These men had been sent to slay her son and there was nothing she could do about it. She closed her eyes and prayed to the Great Mother for a speedy death.

Drustan stormed into the roundhouse, his rage burning hotter than the glow of the hearth fire which instantly melted the snowflakes that had settled on his wolfskin mantle. "Did you know, Mother?" he bellowed.

Loncheta and Galana were playing a game of painted stones by the fire and both looked up at the noisy intrusion in alarm. "Know what, my son?" Loncheta asked.

"Surely you have heard the news by now?" said Drustan. "It was carried to me by a servant as I rode up from the harbour. The whole fortress knows it seems. Cailtram and his mother have been slain!"

"Yes, a messenger arrived this afternoon," Loncheta said, turning her attention back to the game.

"Did you know?" Drustan reiterated.

"Beforehand? How could I?"

"Mother, you have made no secret of your love for Nechtan. Sometimes I wonder if you would not rather see him as our king. I saw how close the two of you were when he was here. You were talking together like conspirators."

"You don't suspect Nechtan's hand in this, surely? Your own brother …?"

"Nothing would please him more than the death of our infant cousin. And he has been quick to act on the vile murders. Did you also hear that he has now proclaimed himself high king of the highland tribes?"

"And why should he not? Would you have acted differently had the news reached you first?"

"Maybe not, but I wished no ill to that child and his mother. They were butchered on the road, Mother! Their bodies foully used!"

Loncheta rose from the hearth and approached him, reaching out to touch his trembling cheek as she had done when he had been a child after one of his scuffles with his brother. "My son, believe me when I say that I had no knowledge of what befell the queen and her son. And I believe that Nechtan had nothing to do with it. He is just acting on the news for to do nothing would be to invite disaster. It was an awful thing, but the crown must now be taken before confusion wreaks havoc."

Drustan gripped her hand by the wrist and pulled it away from his face. "Nechtan means to rule the tribes," he said. "And I mean to fight him for the crown. I hope that you will support your eldest son, Mother. And if I find out that you had any part in what befell Conchenn and Cailtram, then I will never forgive you."

Chapter 20

Snow blanketed the hills and forests surrounding Din Eidyn. It drifted in flurries across the iron-grey firth and clung the rock base of the fortress. Smoke drifted from scores of hearth fires to dissipate in the pale sky; a welcoming sight to the small band of travellers who made their way along the coast towards it.

There was activity atop the gatehouse as the sentries called to one another, peering through the whirling snowflakes to make out who the visitors were. A banner was hoisted from the small train of warriors and pack horses; a black bull on a red field. The party was of the Uerteru.

Tybiaun, upon hearing the cries of the sentries, left his wife and newborn son, Meriaun, in their chamber, threw on a heavy winter cloak, and left the main building. Others in the great enclosure were also hurrying to the gate. It wasn't often the fortress received guests in the depths of winter and, if these visitors were truly Uerteru, then they had travelled far.

The gates opened and the snow-blasted party limped in, gasping with relief at finally reaching their destination. The lead rider, whose face was obscured by a hood and woollen bindings, tugged at the frost-encrusted material to show his face.

"Drustan!" said Tybiaun.

"Aye, it is good to see you, Tybian mab Cunedag," said Drustan. "It has been a long, hard journey but we are here at last. May we impose on your hospitality?"

"Of course," said Tybiaun. He summoned servants to stable the horses as the warriors slid down from their saddles on aching legs. "Come, to the Great Hall with you and warm yourselves with fire and spiced wine!"

As the frost melted and dripped off them in pools on the rush-strewn floor, the party of Uerteru warriors gladly accepted cups of Gaulish wine, warmed and spiced. Cunedag and Vala, emerged from their private quarters to greet the guests and found the hall already full, with most of their sons and their families come to see what the excitement was all about.

"Drustan!" said Cunedag, embracing the younger man warmly. "I am glad to receive you, unexpected though this is. What brings you down from Cair Uerteru in this harshest part of the year?"

"Cair Uerteru has fallen, Cunedag," said the warrior.

"What?" Cunedag exclaimed. "The Gaels would not attack so far inland during the winter, surely?"

"Not by Gaels," said Drustan. "It has fallen to my brother, Nechtan. He has proclaimed himself high king of the highland tribes."

"He overrules the vote of the tribes?" Cunedag asked in astonishment.

"The vote is void," said Drustan. "My infant cousin and his mother were butchered on their way to celebrate Kalan Gayaf at Din Moreb, some two months ago."

"He overrules the right of the firstborn to the throne too," said Tybiaun. "Drustan is the older brother. If anybody should be high king, then it is he."

Cunedag sat down in his high-backed chair and rubbed his temples. "This is ill news," he said. "Is it to be civil war then? I don't doubt your intentions to fight for your crown."

"Aye, it is war," Drustan replied. "I come here to you now, to ask if your oath to me still stands. Will you fight with me, come spring, against my brother who has sought to usurp me?"

The hall fell silent and looked to their king for his answer. Another war wasn't something any of them wanted. Many of the warriors present had grown up fatherless after Cunedag's wars against the Picts twenty years ago, and the thought of another campaign far from home in which more fathers, sons and brothers might be killed was a sobering one.

"I swore to support your claim to the throne," said Cunedag, "even if it came to war. This war was not of your making, but of Nechtan's and I am no stranger to conflict between brothers. I fought for my own crown against my own brother many years ago and I will fight with you for yours."

"Thank you, Cunedag," said Drustan. "You are known throughout the north as a man of your word and a fine warrior. With the might of the Votadini behind me, I know that we can win."

"And on that point," said Tybiaun, "how many tribes does your brother count as allies? Is there any indication as to how long or bloody this war is likely to be?"

"He has several of the eastern tribes," said Drustan. "The Vacomagi consider him their protector against Frankish raiders, so he has their support. Before the heavy snows came, he and a Vacomagi contingent took Din Birse with hardly a drop of blood being spilt. It is one of the Uerteru's strongest fortresses and with that as his base, he was able to march on Cair Uerteru which I was forced to surrender to him. There were just too many warriors within its walls who would prefer him as their king to me. I and a small band of loyalists, most of whom are here with me now, fled west."

"Where is it you call home now?" asked Cunedag.

"Din Moreb, the home of the late queen. It is there that I have found the most support as that family has no love for Nechtan with the rumours surrounding his part in the murder of Conchenn and Cailtram."

There were cries of disgust at this and Cunedag held up his hand for silence. "Is there any indication that these rumours are true?" he asked. "Did Nechtan murder the heir and his mother?"

Drustan sighed. "In truth, I do not know. He was quick to act on it and deep in my heart, I feel that he is capable of such barbarity."

"In any case," said Tybiaun, turning to his father. "Drustan is the rightful heir now, not his younger brother."

"Indeed," said Cunedag. "You shall have your crown, Drustan. You shall winter with us, and come spring, we march north together."

As the last of the snows melted away and trickled into the rivers and streams, the Votadini set forth from Din Eidyn beneath the dragon banner. They made for Din Moreb which crowned a wooded hill overlooking the firth. Despite being the home of the late queen, the fort was welcoming to both Drustan and his allies for they would rather see him on the throne than his warmongering brother. As the land awakened and bloomed into spring, Cunedag and Drustan planned their campaign against Nechtan.

The usurper responded by marching from Cair Uerteru and camping on the eastern bank of the White River which wound its way down from the mountains and emptied into the firth. Several thousand warriors loyal to Nechtan blocked the crossing of the river, with Cair Uerteru at their back and prevented Drustan's teulu from coming anywhere near the royal seat.

Drustan and his supporters faced them on the other side of the river, and riders were sent south, following its course, to find any possible way across that wasn't guarded.

"Every ford and bridge are held by Nechtan's warriors," said Tancorix, Cunedag's nephew and current penteulu. He was a fine warrior in his mid-thirties now and a more than adequate successor to Murcho. "There's no way across that won't result in a bottleneck slaughter. Etern led a scouting party, and they were damn near chased down."

"It was led by that Uvan fellow," said Etern.

"Melga's brother," Cunedag said with a frown. "I suppose it was too much to hope for that he would fight on our side. Not that I have any particular desire to share a camp with him."

"Damn my brother!" said Drustan. "Crossing the river is hopeless. We'll have to lure him to our side somehow and then engage him in the open."

"I suspect he's too wily to fall for a simple trap," said Cunedag. "Meanwhile, our stores run low while we sit on this riverbank counting our enemies. And I don't much like our odds in any case. Is there nobody else we can count on for support?"

"Everybody has already picked a side," Drustan replied.

"Then we must make do with what we have," Cunedag sighed. "Though feeding them is going to be a problem."

Tybiaun and Etern were tasked with procuring food for the warband and took contingents of men west to scour settlements and farms for supplies. Most grudgingly handed over what was left of their winter stores to support the war effort without too much complaint, but the settlements along the Firth were increasingly vocal about being left with nothing to feed themselves with through the seeding season.

"Gaels plundered our stores before the winter and now you come to take what's left in the spring!" one farmer complained. "Between the Gaelic Coast and Din Moreb, we are starved!"

"What Gaels?" Tybiaun asked.

"A pack of them came through here just before Kalan Gayaf and robbed us blind," said the farmer. "Maybe if the royals behind their fortress walls stopped arguing over who gets to be king for five minutes, they might spare a thought to protecting the people they rule. Gaels never ventured this far inland before. No doubt they know what they can get away with when there's no royal arse on the throne."

"Just before Kalan Gayaf …" Etern said to his brother.

"Aye," Tybiaun replied. "Exactly the time Queen Conchenn and her son were butchered. They never did find their killers."

"I don't like the sound of this," said Etern.

"Nor I. I could well understand the Gaels' desire to murder a royal, but how were they in the right place at the right time?"

They spent some time trying to extract as much information about the Gaelic raiding party as the villagers could remember before returning to camp with their news.

"I just can't believe my brother would go so far as to recruit Gaels in his plan to secure the crown," said Drustan. "Even he has more honour than that, or at least I thought so. Our own father was killed by those scum from Erin!"

"Your brother is desperate to rule the tribes," said Cunedag. "Believe me, that makes a man forget his honour."

"But to throw in his lot with the Gaels!"

"It is quite possible that he paid them like hired thugs to do his bidding and has no intention of dealing with them further."

"If word of this gets out, then he'll lose the support of the tribes!" said Drustan, his face brightening.

"We'd need proof," said Cunedag.

"Then we'll get it! I'll ride to the nearest settlement disguised as a wanderer …"

"Madness!" said Cunedag. "You are fighting for your crown. The Gaels would love nothing better than to slay an Uerteru royal and, if they are in league with your brother, then they'd sell you to him for a few bits of silver."

"I will go, Father," said Tybiaun. "Send me with a few men and we'll find out if any Gael has been paid for by Nechtan."

"I'll go with him," said Etern. "If only to keep him out of trouble. You know how haughty he gets. They'll spot him for a noble a mile off if I don't keep reminding him to keep a low profile."

"Your mouth and hot temper are more likely to get us into bother," said Tybiaun.

"Enough," said Cunedag. "You shall both go and watch over each other. Find out what you can but in no way place yourselves at risk."

"We'll pose as Britons looking for strongarm work on the Gaelic coast," said Etern. "That's the best chance we have of falling into the same circle that supplied Nechtan with his hired murderers."

Chapter 21

After attending to the finer details such as clothing and handpicking half a dozen men to accompany them, Tybiaun and Etern set off the following morning, riding west, towards the lands that rang with the Gaelic tongue rather than the British. Instead of finding themselves in a landscape stripped and ravaged by war, they passed settlements of Britons who seemed to live peaceably side by side with the Gaels.

By asking locals, they were able to head towards the largest nearby concentration of Gaels. That seemed to be the likeliest home of the murderers of the queen and her son. The fort was in the form of a large stone tower with several levels, surrounded by a ring wall which also enclosed several thatched and turfed dwellings.

"Best if we leave the men on the outskirts," said Tybiaun. "We don't want to draw a lot of attention to ourselves by marching in with an armed escort."

"Aye, you lads wait here," Etern told the six men they had brought with them. "And be ready to help us out if we need it. This might turn sour at any moment."

"Not if we keep our heads and our tempers," Tybiaun warned.

Etern rolled his eyes, and they left their escort and headed down into the settlement.

This 'broch' as the Gaels referred to it, was an ancient Pictish fort, claimed and refurbished by the men from across the sea and served as a power centre for the local area. There were many warriors there, and it was an unnerving experience entering the gate in the ring wall, though visitors did not seem to be an uncommon occurrence. There was trade to be had, and smiths and craftsmen worked at their forges and anvils, while sheep were traded in one of the pens. Here was a thriving community, not a fort geared for war.

They took an ale in a smoky turf-roofed hut which seemed to be the social hub of the settlement and glanced around at the clientele.

"When was the last time we had a drink together?" Etern said.

"You always drink plenty in Father's feasting hall," said Tybiaun.

"No, I mean just the two of us. When was the last time we rode out together or even just talked? It's been years."

"We have a mission to accomplish," said Tybiaun. "This isn't a social occasion."

Etern rolled his eyes and took a deep draught of beer. "Fine lot of fun you are," he said, wiping the foam from his mouth with the back of his hand. "I was only trying to make conversation."

"Fine," said Tybiaun with a sigh. "Let's talk, then. How's Briallen?"

"Doing well, thank you for asking," said Etern. "I only hope we return before she gives birth. I missed the birth of our last one, you see."

"Here's to a boy," said Tybiaun, holding out his drinking cup.

Etern clinked his against it. "Aye, the gods must bless me with a son sooner or later and, with three girls already, it certainly seems to be later. How is your fair lady and little Meriaun?"

"Both well, I thank you. We are expecting also."

"Really? You never said!"

"It's early still, so we haven't told anybody. But, as we are making friendly conversation, I thought maybe you could be the first to know."

"Thank you, Brother," said Etern, feeling quite touched. "Father will soon have more grandchildren than he can count. And our sisters are not yet married."

"Father will soon find Teguid a husband," said Tybiaun. "She's nearly fifteen. And Gwen is not far behind her."

"Barely a noble house in the north remains that does not have a member of the line of Cunedag in it," said Etern with a smile. "Father has damn-near conquered the north with his blood."

But Tybiaun wasn't listening anymore. His eyes were on the alewife who was a large woman with a stained apron and a face like a ham. She seemed to be on jesting terms with everybody present and would certainly know who they might approach to get them an audience with whoever ruled these parts.

Tybiaun and Etern attempted to strike up conversation with her but, having little Gaelic between them, only served to identify themselves as Britons in a distinctly Gaelic environment. As they pressed her for information, the smile fell from the alewife's face, and she shut up like a clam while the atmosphere in the ale hut grew decidedly chillier. Tybiaun and Etern supped their ale and wondered what to do next but before long, two warriors entered the room and headed towards them.

"Britons, are you?" they asked in accented British.

"Aye," said Tybiaun. "What of it?"

"What's your business here? You are warriors to look at you."

"That's right," said Etern. "King Nechtan sent us."

Tybiaun glanced at his brother in alarm, wondering what the damn fool was playing at. Why say Nechtan had sent them? The Gaels frowned at them and for a moment, Tybiaun was convinced that there was going to be violence.

"The chief will want to see you then," one of them said. "Come with us."

They got up and followed the warriors out, all eyes on them. Tybiaun had to admit, though his heart was still in his mouth, that Etern's recklessness had paid off. It had been a fast and easy way to ascertain if friends of Nechtan were welcome here. It seemed that they were, but it had been a hell of a risk, and he wasn't sure if he could forgive his brother for taking such a chance.

They were led up to the stone tower and in through the low door at its base. A peat fire smouldered in the hearth, the smoke coiling up the centre of the tower and out through the vents in the thatched cone that roofed the building. It really was a remarkable construction, with several timber floors and a staircase that spiralled up between inner and outer walls.

Faces peered at them through the fug of smoke as Tybiaun and Etern were led to the centre of the room and made to stand on ceremony while the chief of the settlement emerged from a wicker-doored cell at the base of the stairway.

"Fergus mac Eochaid, ruler of Dun Trodan," somebody announced in Gaelic, simple enough for Tybiaun and Etern to understand.

They both bowed their heads as if in the presence of a king which, given the paltry nature of the settlement, they highly doubted. He was an aging man who had most likely led an active youth given the scars on his face and bare forearms which were now mottled like old leather and jingled with gold and silver ornamentation.

"What do British warriors in my lands?" Fergus said, easing himself into a highbacked chair that he probably considered a throne.

"Lord Fergus," said Tybiaun. "Greetings. We are warriors of King Nechtan of the Uerteru. We come before you with a further proposition." He supposed that seeing as Etern had already cast them in these roles, they had better play them to the fullest.

"Proposition?" the old Gael grumbled as a servant filled a horn for him.

"After your men so effectively helped our king before Kalan Gayaf?" Tybiaun hadn't meant it to sound like a question, but he was floundering in the dark, trying to get this old villain to confirm their suspicions.

"*Samhain*," Fergus corrected them, using the Gaelic name for the harvest festival. "Weren't my services enough? Does Nechtan still struggle to place the crown upon his head even after his rival has been dispatched?"

Tybiaun resisted the urge to glance at his brother. *So, it was true! Nechtan had used this Gael's men to murder his way to the throne!* "Another rival has stepped into the child's place," he said. "Nechtan's brother, Drustan."

"I told Nechtan's last envoys," Fergus said, "I cannot afford to get embroiled in a war with the Britons. Lending a few warriors to grease the wheels of succession is one thing, but I have enough problems with other leaders of my own people. A war now would be disastrous."

"Believe us, the last thing *we* want is war," said Tybiaun in all earnestness. "But if Nechtan does not defeat his brother, then all will have been for naught. And Drustan would be a much more aggressive neighbour than Nechtan."

"Do you seek to intimidate me?" Fergus bellowed. The warriors in the hall roused themselves and suddenly the situation looked a lot more dangerous.

"Not intimidate, not at all!" said Etern. "Merely to make you aware of the disadvantages of seeing Drustan on the throne as well as the advantages of helping his brother."

"What advantages? I've seen none yet, despite my help. He seems to be incapable of winning his crown even after I've dealt with one of his rivals."

"Drustan must die!" said Etern. "But it can be arranged and with a little help from you, we can win this war before summer is upon us!"

"What then?" Fergus asked. "What would Nechtan have of me now?"

"Drustan is vulnerable," said Etern, taking control of the situation. "He is leading a small contingent south, across the White River to try and invade Nechtan's territory while the bulk of our forces hold the river further north. We have not the men to close the gap behind him but if you send fifty warriors, then …"

"Fifty?" Fergus interrupted. "Perhaps you'd like me to lead every man, woman and child myself into battle on the whim of your would-be king!"

"Less then," said Etern. "If fifty is too much then say thirty or twenty even. You are only required to hold the ford and stop Drustan escaping back to his lines. We will finish him when he is cut off from his teulu. He'll be like a cornered hare!"

Fergus stroked his grizzled chin. "I have only to hold the ford? Not engage Drustan's warriors?"

Etern shook his head. "They will be to the north, their hands full with our diversion. We plan to let Drustan slip into our lands thinking he has the better of us. All you must do is pull the noose taut!"

"Drustan will be slain and Nechtan will be our irrefutable king," said Tybiaun. "And he will be most generous to his Gaelic neighbour who helped him win his throne."

"How generous?"

"I'd say his control of the coast and trade with Gaul would be open to you," Tybiaun went on. "You'd be the first of the Gaelic chieftains to have access to shipping on the eastern side of the island."

Fergus grinned at the prospect, his greed and hatred of his own rivals overcoming any suspicions he might have had. "Well, then," he said. "I'd require something up front, not just the promises of an envoy …"

"A talent-weight of silver," said Etern. "For holding a ford for less than a day."

Fergus was silent as he digested this offer, and the rest of the hall blinked and looked to one another in surprise. A massive sum of silver had been offered to their chief and greed hung in the air thicker than peat smoke. Tybiaun did not dare look around at the shocked faces for fear he might break the spell, and he wondered if Etern had not overdone it to the point of making the offer too incredulous.

"You can't say that's not a generous offer," Etern pushed. "Our king offers enough to feed you and your men well into next year."

Fergus barked a short laugh of triumph. "Your king must be desperate indeed to see his brother thwarted. Done! For a talent-weight of silver and access to his ports, I will send my men to block the ford. I just hope your king will keep his word and ensure the battle remains in the north."

"Then it is agreed," said Etern. "Send your warriors to the ford two days from now. That is when we will trick Drustan into crossing."

"Will you remain here tonight and drink with me?" Fergus asked, his newfound wealth suddenly making him a lot more hospitable to the Britons.

"With the greatest respect, Lord Fergus," said Tybiaun, "time is short and we must return to our king with the news that you will aid him in his victory. He will be most eager to hear it."

"Fine, fine!" said the Gael. "Get you gone and see that all is ready. I will prepare my warband and they will set out tomorrow."

Cunedag had hoped that the approaching riders would be his returning sons, but, as the small troop of horsemen entered the camp, he could see that it was a group of northern tribesmen, apparently come as friends.

"Aniel?" Drustan said as he emerged from his tent to greet the new arrivals. "Is that you?"

"Aye, it's me, Brother," said a tall, rangy man in a long, wolfskin cloak as he dismounted. "Come to offer you my sword arm, for what it's worth."

"Brother?" Cunedag wondered aloud as the two men embraced. They were of a similar age and looked alike enough to be closely related.

"One of the late king's indiscretions," explained a nearby tribesman in a hushed tone.

"Not another potential rival for the crown, I hope," Cunedag said.

"Not at all," the warrior replied. "Aniel is Talorc's bastard son and half-brother to Drustan and Nechtan. He is not of the line of Gartnait and therefore has no claim."

"I see," said Cunedag. It was common enough for men to sow their oats in fields afar. His own sons had fathered the occasional bastard, even if he had always been faithful to his wife.

"Come, let us drink together," said Drustan, walking towards his tent with his arm around Aniel. "Cunedag, you too! We must celebrate the addition of another ally to my cause."

"I fear I can only add ten men," said Aniel.

"That's ten more than we had this morning!" said Drustan, his mood greatly improved by the arrival of his half-brother.

They drank and talked, and Aniel was eager to learn of the situation. "You appear to be on the cusp of battle," he said. "I can see the smoke from Nechtan's fires on the other bank."

"If battle can be avoided, so much the better," said Drustan. "I have no desire to kill those who should be my subjects. Besides, we are locked in a damned stalemate with neither side daring to wet their feet by crossing the river. But we have a plan in motion that might break Nechtan's ranks irreparably."

Drustan told him of the mission of Tybiaun and Etern in the west and Aniel swore black thunder at the treachery of his other half-brother. "That Nechtan should stoop to murdering royal blood! The man was ever the black sheep. Even I, bastard though I am, feel more loyalty to you than he."

"Evidently," said Drustan. "That much is clear by your very presence by my side. But you see what we are up against. Nechtan has split the tribes nearly fifty-fifty. If it comes to a battle, the losses would be catastrophic."

"We may yet have our salvation," said Cunedag, rising from his seat. "For, unless my ears deceive me, more riders approach. I pray that it is my sons with good news."

Chapter 22

"And you are willing to swear on your word that what you say is true?" Drustan asked Tybiaun and Etern once they had been admitted into his tent and provided with ale to quench their thirst after their long ride.

"Drustan, the word of my sons is good enough for me," said Cunedag who stood by their side, proudly.

"But will it be good enough for Nechtan's supporters?" Drustan asked. "I apologise for giving any offence, but they do not know your sons as I do and may easily say that they have concocted a lie to sow division."

"Then I will challenge any of them to single combat to prove otherwise!" Etern said testily.

"And I will swear before the Great Mother or any god they care to name that we speak the truth," said Tybiaun.

"Let us hope then, that it will be enough," said Drustan.

"What is your plan?" Cunedag asked.

"I want to invite them to parley. We'll talk terms. Nechtan knows he has a bloody battle ahead of him, so he won't sneer at that. You will be there, Cunedag, and your sons too. When we have our say, your sons can impart what they have found out."

"And then?"

Drustan smiled. "We watch the seed of doubt sprout in Necthan's followers. We'll see how eager they are to follow him once they learn what he has done. I can scarcely credit it myself, but my brother has ever been a stranger to me."

Envoys were sent across the river and a parley between the two rival claimants took place on the east bank, beneath a large, hide tent in which crackling braziers kept the morning chill at bay.

Drustan, Cunedag and their followers waited patiently as Nechtan and his men filed into the tent, looking pleased with themselves. *They think we've come to surrender*, Cunedag thought to himself.

Nechtan seated himself before them with a twirl of his fur-lined cloak, looking every bit the king and conqueror. Uvan was there, along with Nechtan's other top warriors, and he scowled at Drustan and his men in turn.

"Well, you come before me at last, Brother," Nechtan said. "I am eager to hear what you propose in way of terms, though, by the looks of things, you have little to bargain with."

"You look good, Nechtan, I have to admit," Drustan replied with a smile. "You really play the part of the king well. But I didn't come here to play the subject and the only terms I wish to discuss are the terms of your surrender."

Nechtan looked to his men, and they chuckled together as if Drustan had lost his mind.

"I'm glad you swaggered before me today with the leaders of the factions who support you," Drustan continued. "Because we have something to say that they should all hear. The men to the left of me are Tybiaun and Etern mab Cunedag, princes of the Votadini, and they have something to say."

All eyes in the tent looked to Cunedag's sons. It fell to Tybiaun, the eldest, to speak. "A couple of days' ride to the west," he began, "is a Gaelic broch ruled by a chieftain called Fergus mac Eochaid. My brother and I visited him two days ago because we had suspicions that this Gael played a part in the murder of Queen Conchenn and her son, Cailtram. Our audience with Fergus not only confirmed this, but he also confirmed that he had been paid to murder the mother and her babe by Nechtan of the Uerteru!"

The uproar was instantaneous. Nechtan's cries that Tybiaun was a liar were drowned out by the oaths sworn by his followers. They didn't believe it and Cunedag hadn't really expected them to. This was only the initial declaration. Convincing them that their candidate for the crown was a liar and a murderer would take time. And Nechtan wasn't about to sit by and let it happen.

He rose from his chair, and it tumbled over behind him as he flung out a pointed finger. "Execute the lying traitors!" he bellowed, this time loud enough for his followers to heed him.

Drustan, Cunedag and the others leapt up, reaching for their sword hilts. Nechtan was clearly desperate to silence the truth which could lead to his downfall. It was more proof of his guilt than anybody needed, but his followers were too blind and outraged to see it in the heat of the moment.

"Surround the king!" Cunedag shouted, drawing his sword as the men in the tent converged on them, Uvan grinning at the prospect of finally wetting his blade in the blood of these upstarts.

Cunedag, his sons and the other warriors formed a ring around Drustan and slowly edged their way out of the tent. Outside, chaos was unfolding as Nechtan's cries to murder his opposition were taken up by his followers who turned on Drustan's men. Fighting broke out just as Cunedag and the others escorted Drustan from the tent.

Cunedag glanced over his shoulder at the ford where the horses waited, nervously stepping about at the sound of clashing blades. "Don't let them cut us off!" he bellowed. "Make for the horses!"

Drustan's warriors held off Nechtan's contingent admirably, keeping them from attacking their king and giving him enough time to reach the ford. Swinging up into their saddles, they turned and escorted Drustan back across the river. Cunedag, whirling his spatha in the air above him, yelled to the remainder of Drustan's warriors who still fought off

Nechtan's men and were slowly being overwhelmed. "Back across the river!"

They turned and ran towards the riverbank. Cunedag and his sons rode towards them and swung their blades, cutting down any warriors who gave chase. When the last of the warriors were splashing their way across the ford, they turned and fell in behind them.

Nechtan's men were mounting up and preparing to give chase. On the other side of the river, enough of Drustan's men were forming up to meet the attackers and it looked set to become an all-out battle.

As Cunedag and his sons rejoined Drustan's men on the western bank, they turned to face the ford and the men swarming across it. Horns bellowed and war cries were shouted. Nechtan's riders drew up, the river still flowing over their horses' fetlocks as they reconsidered giving chase. They would be massacred if they set foot on the west bank and they knew it. To the jeers and taunts of Drustan's warriors, they turned tail and headed back to their camp.

"I had hoped that would go better," said Drustan as he accepted a cup of wine from a servant back in the safety of his own tent. "Your lads didn't even get the chance to give their word or accept a challenge of single combat."

"Your brother wanted to massacre us all," said Cunedag, entering the tent and unlacing his cuirass. "He knows we speak the truth, even if his followers do not. But we must be patient. We have planted the seed of doubt, now we need only watch it grow."

"You are by far a more patient man than I, Cunedag," said Drustan.

Later that night, Cunedag was roused from resting in his tent by cries that horsemen approached. His servants hurriedly strapped on his armour, and he headed outside as he buckled on his spatha to find Uvan and several other warriors dismounting in the centre of a ring of Drustan's men. *Surrender? Impossible!* Uvan was the wildest, most haughty of Nechtan's followers. But could that pride really be the cause for this late-night visit?

"Lord Drustan," said Uvan, his face rigid as the words, apparently so hard in coming, came from his lips. "I come here to offer you my support."

"Uvan," said Drustan, approaching the small group of warriors. "This is most unexpected. Why the change of heart?"

"Not long after the debacle this afternoon," Uvan said, "your brother's men ran into a party of Gaels who have camped at a ford far to the south, on its eastern bank. There was a short battle and they fled back across the river, but not without leaving us a couple of captives. We pressed them for information as to what Gaels were doing this far west, and they said that they were warriors of a Fergus mac Eochaid."

There was a murmur of gladness from Drustan's men at this and Uvan looked to Etern and Tybiaun with none of the hostility he had previously shown towards them. "We squeezed them harder, and they admitted that their chieftain had been approached by Nechtan's envoys who had asked him to hold the ford and play their part in a trap to ensnare Drustan. They also admitted that this was not the first service they had done for Nechtan."

There was silence as all awaited his next words. The big warrior looked to the ground, unable to meet Drustan's eyes. "It is as the sons of Cunedag said. Nechtan hired Gaels to butcher our queen and heir."

"Then you stand with me and support my claim to the throne?" Drustan asked Uvan.

Uvan met his eyes. "Aye. I'll not stand with a murderer of women and children and nor will many of those whom your brother once counted on for support."

There was a cheer at this and Drustan offered his embrace to Uvan who clumsily accepted it.

"I would celebrate with you, Uvan," said Drustan. "But we must keep our heads clear and our wits sharp. For tomorrow, I intend to cross the river and claim my crown!"

The next day dawned on a camp marching to war. Vats of animal fat were tainted blue with woad and the Picts smeared designs on their bare chests and arms to the chanting of the druids.

Cunedag and his sons watched this tradition that stretched back to Britain's distant past before the first Caesar set foot on its shores. Drustan, his entire face blue and wearing a helm adorned with a raven, offered them some of the blue body paint but they politely refused.

"The Votadini have long since departed from that tradition," Cunedag explained. "Perhaps we are too Romanised to return to it now.

"Suit yourself," said Drustan. "But already I can feel the strength of the ancestors coursing through my veins! At last, we are to war!"

They set off under clear skies and fresh breezes which gave further hope to the followers of Drustan mab Talorc as he and his riders led the column of warriors towards the ford.

Nechtan's men gaped in terror at the approaching warband and deserted their posts, leaving the ford clear for Drustan to cross. Mere days before, such a move would have been unthinkable for Necthan's teulu would have converged on them and trapped them in a bottleneck to pick them off damn near one at a time. But Nechtan's force had been dealt its death blow and nobody came to meet them as they stormed the east bank.

"I can see the banners of Nechtan's camp!" said Cunedag, shielding his eyes against the morning sun. "The bull of the Uerteru, but not many others!"

"Most of the other tribes will have deserted him," said Uvan, riding up alongside him.

"Headed back to their own lands?"

"Some. Though some might have stayed to show their support of their new king."

"Where are they then?" Drustan asked, annoyance showing in his voice. "So much for ruling the north as a high king. This civil war my brother stoked has ruined our chance of uniting."

"Perhaps not, my king," said Uvan. "Look!"

He pointed towards the trees in the hazy distance north of their position. From the wooded coast of the firth, several banners could be seen emerging from the treeline with many warriors clustered behind them.

"I see the Taexali and the Venicones!" shouted Drustan. "And look! The Vacomagi! My brother's biggest supporters have turned on him!"

The various tribes of the north rode towards them, blowing horns and chanting the names of Drustan and of the Uerteru. The air crackled with ecstatic joy as the two forces converged and the newcomers saluted their new king with great shouts to the sky.

Up ahead, the camp of the usurper looked small and pathetic. Warriors were running about trying to form shield walls and mount what little defence they might, but it was hopeless. Drustan led the charge against Nechtan's remaining loyalists, his desire to end this war burning hotter than ever before now that victory was within his grasp.

Cunedag joined in the bellowing war cry as the front ranks of horsemen lowered their spears and charged the camp. No mercy was given to the last remnants of Nechtan's rebellion. They had had their chance to flee and join the true heir and they had chosen to remain and die. The riders surged through the camp, swamping it like the waves over a rock at high tide. Blades scythed through the air and blood spurted as men went down under hoof or were picked up on the ends of spears and hurled to the ground.

Once the camp was overrun, Cunedag reined in his horse and rejoined Drustan who was ordering his warriors to search the dead and question the prisoners as to the whereabouts of his brother.

"There's no sign of him," Drustan said. "Surely he would not be so cowardly as to flee?"

Cunedag and his sons joined in the search, tearing down what remained of the tents and herding the surrendered prisoners together like cattle. Uvan was particularly thorough, his disgust at his former comrades who, unlike him, had not sided with Drustan all too apparent as he manhandled and threatened his way about. Cunedag recognised what was coming. If the prisoners remained uncooperative, then torture would be employed, and he had a feeling that Uvan would truly excel at that.

Fortunately, one of the prisoners also saw that hot knives and pincers were not far off and spoke up.

"He rode south as soon as our banners were spotted," Uvan reported to Drustan. "Damned coward!"

"He can't think to hide from me," said Drustan. "Why suffer the indignity of being ridden down like a dog?"

"The Gaels!" said Tybiaun. "They will still be at the ford. He'll most likely be making for them seeking their protection."

Drustan swore and mounted his horse. Cunedag and his sons mounted theirs and the hunt took off, the final blow in this war yet to be delivered.

They rode south as hard as their already exhausted horses could be pushed, following the river as it snaked through woods and glens. When they reached the ford, they found the remains of the Gaelic camp on the west bank, the cookfires still warm.

"Do we pursue?" Cunedag asked, looking westwards towards the land of the Gaels.

"No," said Drustan. "I have not the men to spare engaging the Gaels and risking another war. Let him go and find what friends he can in the west. "I have my crown. It is enough."

Part IV

About this time a deputation from Britain came to tell the bishops of Gaul that the heresy of Pelagius had taken hold of the people over a great part of the country and help ought to be brought to the Catholic faith as soon as possible. A large number of bishops gathered in synod to consider the matter and all turned for help to the two who in everybody's judgment were the leading lights of religion, namely Germanus and Lupus, apostolic priests who through their merits were citizens of heaven, though their bodies were on earth. – Constantius of Lyon, *The Life of St. Germanus*,

Chapter 23

429 A.D.

In a villa on the outskirts of Venta Belgarum, some seventy miles west of Londinium, a wedding was taking place. The British nobles from every town and hillfort in the south-west, had gathered at the country estate of Ambrosius Aurelianus, the Comes Britanniarum, to see his son be bound to Publia Drusilla, the daughter of a high-ranking member of Britannia Prima's elite.

The groom – seventeen-year-old Ambrosius Aurelianus the Younger – nervously awaited his fifteen-year-old bride on the steps to the main house, the assembled guests at his back. Night had fallen and the entire villa was lit up with candles and oil lamps. Out in the darkness, a train of burning torches could be seen approaching along the road that led from town and Ambrosius felt a tightening in his gut.

It was silly. He had known Drusilla since childhood. Their families had been close, and it was only natural that the two youths would one day be married. But he had dreaded this day all the same and now that it was here, everything seemed to be passing in a syrupy haze, like it was all a dream and not quite real.

Drusilla approached the villa at the head of the procession of torch bearers. She had ridden in a carpentium most of the way from town but walked the last mile on foot as part of the ancient tradition. Her family and attendants lit the way with torches while slaves threw nuts to farmers and shepherds and their families who clustered by the side of the road to watch the procession.

She wore a saffron stola with a flame-coloured veil and a crown of flowers she had handpicked herself. She walked slowly, her head down, the living symbol of virginity and fidelity. Stopping at the gates to her new home, a female slave handed her a small pot of pig fat with which she anointed the posts of the household. Two of her male attendants lifted her over the threshold to ensure she didn't trip, and, with a gentle nudge from his father, Ambrosius descended the steps to take her hand.

Applause broke out as he lifted the hand of his new bride and led her up the steps and into the cross hall of the villa. His nerves seemed to settle a little with her by him and he could almost sense her own embarrassment mirroring his own. This all just felt so silly and unnatural. They had played together as children, often inventing imaginary games and now that were stepping into the roles of husband and wife, it still felt like playacting, albeit in front of a large audience who took it all seriously.

She turned towards him and lifted her head, just a little. He took that as his signal to lift her veil. The face that greeted him caused a fresh flutter of nerves and excitement deep within his belly. She had always been pretty, but the white lead and kohl that had been applied to accentuate her features suddenly made her look every inch a woman when he had only known the child before.

He tried to stop his eyes wandering down to the elaborate knot on her belt which symbolised chastity and which he would have to unpick as part of the consummation ritual after the feast. He both looked forward to it and dreaded it, not knowing if his fingers could delicately pick apart the knot without causing too much embarrassment for the both of them.

"Welcome to our household, Drusilla," said his father, approaching them. "That is the last time I will say that, for it is your household now."

"And welcome to the family," said his mother, taking Drusilla's hands in hers.

"Thank you, both," Drusilla replied. "I know that I will be very happy here, as I always was as a child."

"Then let us feast and raise a toast to the unification of our families!" said Aurelianus.

The feast was an elaborate one with much attention paid to Roman tradition and taste. Dishes had been prepared with unusually exotic sauces and wines imported from far flung provinces of the empire at no little cost. Even the marriage rituals had painstakingly conformed to old Roman tradition. It was all deliberate. Indeed, many of the older guests commented on the nostalgia the proceedings conjured for more prosperous times, when Britannia had been part of the empire. Aurelianus entertained a circle of noblemen who longed for those days and in the wedding feast of his son, had spared no expense in paying homage to them.

Ambrosius and Drusilla sat at the head of the table with their families on either side, picking daintily at the dishes and counting down the hours with a mixture of dread and excitement. Before the feast had begun to wind down, a soldier entered the cross hall. His armour had been polished especially for the occasion and Ambrosius watched as he spoke into his father's ear before the two of them left together for the privacy of the gardens.

Ambrosius politely remained seated for a time, listening to Publius, his bride's father, tell an amusing story about a recent hunting episode, before discreetly excusing himself. He found his father in the gardens giving orders to a slave that his horse should be saddled.

"You are not leaving, Father?" he asked.

"Would that I could stay and see the festivities through to the end, my son," Aurelianus replied, clapping him on the shoulder. "But you are a man now and are ready to be head of this household in my stead."

"You speak as if you are going on another campaign."

"In a manner of speaking, I am. But a spiritual campaign, rather than a military one, but no less important for Britannia because of it. Bishop Germanus has arrived in Rutupiae."

"Bishop Germanus?" Ambrosius exclaimed. It had been rumoured that the Gaulish bishop had been sent to Britannia. Something to do with the Pelagian heresy.

"He has been dispatched by Pope Celestine himself," said Aurelianus. "To turn peoples' souls away from the teachings of Pelagius and back to the Augustinian doctrine."

Ambrosius knew little of the Pelagian heresy for his father had done his best to shield him from heretical teachings, but he understood that it all had something to do with denying the concept of original sin.

"But Rutupiae …" he said.

"It is some distance, I know, but His Eminence will require a strong bodyguard if he is to travel this island and do God's work. He will have many enemies here and I trust no other to safeguard him. I must go myself. Besides, Bishop Germanus is the most exalted visitor Britannia has received since the rebellion of Constantinus."

Aurelianus winced at his father's use of the word 'rebellion'. Certainly, the election of Britannia's homegrown emperor was referred to as such on the continent, but here in Britannia, there were many who saw Constantinus's failed bid for the purple as a noble, though flawed cause.

"We must establish good relations with the Gaulish clergy," his father went on, "if this island is to entertain any hopes of rejoining the empire."

"Is that your wish, Father? I thought you said Lord Vertigernus—"

"Lord *Vitalinus*," his father corrected him, "sees Britannia's status as a lone candle fluttering in the wind as a good thing. There are many of us who fear that she may be snuffed out at any moment. Connections with the continent are vital to our survival, believe me."

"Your intentions of befriending the bishop go beyond stamping out the heresy," said Ambrosius, noticing the sly look on his father's face.

"Yes. Our pleas to the emperor have fallen on deaf ears. Only through the clergy can we have any hope of receiving support from the continent. Germanus has good relations with the Roman military."

"Father, you speak of defying the Council," said Ambrosius. "Of bringing a foreign army here to reclaim Britannia for the empire …"

"Calm yourself, Ambrosius," said his father. "These are not things you need concern yourself with yet. Not tonight at any rate. You have a new bride to bed. Return to her now. Just know that all I do is for the good of our island."

Ambrosius nodded dutifully and watched his father leave for the stables. He had an uneasy feeling in his gut. All his life, his father had dutifully served the Council of Britannia. Now it seemed that he was going behind their backs and his words were uncomfortably close to his idea of treason. Bring the Roman army back to Britannia? It would mean civil war. Many, Lord Vertigernus included, wished to keep their independence and would not give up their powers without a bitter fight.

As he returned to the wedding feast, he found that his nervousness concerning the impending consummation of his marriage had dissipated. Deeper concerns plagued his mind. He worried for his father, and he worried for Britannia.

Four days later, the rain hammered down on the shingled roof of a mansio on the Londinium road. Sodden sheep bleated in the nearby pasture and chewed disinterestedly as they observed the small troop of horsemen who came along the muddy road.

Aurelianus reined in his mount and bellowed for the stable boy to come and tend to the horses. Swinging himself down from his saddle, he glanced up at the ramshackle mansio, the smell of cooked food tantalising his nostrils after four days of hard riding in filthy weather.

He had travelled with six of his personal guard, each cloaked in red, with crested helms and mail shirts. Such a sight had caused quite a stir on the road and the effect was the same on the patrons of the mansio as they headed inside, the rain dripping from their cloaks onto the tiled floor.

Travellers in various modes of dress glanced up from their cups of wine and ale at the soldiers who were removing their helms and shaking the moisture from their cloaks. Aurelianus scanned the room and spotted a group of hooded figures in the corner who had a clerical look to them. He ignored the stares of the other patrons as he led his men through the room towards the far table.

"Bishop Germanus?" he asked.

The hooded men looked up at him and the eldest of them, a man in his fifties with greying hair and a close-cropped beard said; "Aye, I am Germanus, my son."

"Your Eminence," said Aurelianus, bowing his head and kissing the ring on the bishop's offered hand. "I am Ambrosius Aurelianus, Comes Britanniarum. I have been searching the Londinium road for you ever since I heard that you had landed on our shores. I am glad to find you safe at last."

"Safe?" the bishop replied with a smile. "How could I not be safe when God is with me? We have been tested on our journey, it is true, but prayer got us through. Allow me to introduce you to my associate, Bishop Lupus of Tricasse. He was appointed by the synod in Gaul to accompany me and aid in my mission here in Britannia."

A slightly younger man offered his own hand, and Aurelianus kissed the ring on it.

"Please," said Germanus, "join us for food and wine. It is meagre fare, and the local wine leaves a lot to be desired, but it must suffice, given our surroundings."

Aurelianus and his men gratefully sat down at the table and the landlord fetched them bowls of pea stew, coarse loaves and a fresh jug of wine.

"The weather in this country is as bad as it is reputed," said Bishop Lupus. "Since we landed on the coast, we have been fairly drenched every step of the way."

"The spring rains are the worst of it," said Aurelianus. "Summer improves, though the temperatures remain low."

"God willing, we will not be here long enough to see the summer," said Germanus. "Tell me, Aurelianus, is the situation here really as bad as we have been told? Ever since Emperor Honorius banned Pelagianism ten years ago, Britannia has become a haven for heretics fleeing persecution and seeking shelter beyond the boundaries of the empire."

"Pelagianism is rife, I fear," said Aurelianus, "though the greater threat comes from the barbarians who settle within our borders. Saxons in the east, Scots in the west and Picts in the north."

"Yes, we saw the Saxons up close in Rutupiae," said Germanus. "They almost seem to have the run of the place. I thought those great big forts on the coast had been built to keep them out?"

"As well try to keep the tide from washing up the shore," said Aurelianus with some embarrassment. "Unfortunately, the Comes of the Saxon Shore has been forced to rely upon Saxon mercenary bands to keep the peace. The Saxons are a divided lot and regularly fight each other, so that plays to our advantage."

"The shepherd employs the wolf to guard the sheep," said Germanus. "As long as they stay divided, it might work."

"There are occasional uprisings and raids from their countrymen, but on the whole, Cantium is defended."

"And the Picts and the Scots?"

"Regular troublemakers, though we do have allies in the north. The tribes of the lowlands, beyond the Wall of Hadrian, are partially Romanised and keep the true Picts of the highlands in check. Both hate the Scots as much as we do, and the fighting is mostly confined to the lands beyond the Wall."

"Mutual hate breeds a delicate balance of power," said Germanus, grimly. "If Britannia is to remain the stout anvil against which these heathen hammers rain, then its soul must be purified and the land brought closer to God. Tell me of the Pelagians. I understand they look to one Agricola as their preacher."

"Agricola is the leading culprit in the spread of the heresy," said Aurelianus. "He is the son of the Bishop of Eboracum and travels the land spouting the lies of Pelagius."

"With his father's support?"

"Yes, Your Eminence. Bishop Severianus of Eboracum is a Pelagian himself."

"Am I right in thinking that the north is the hotbed of the heresy, as its spiritual leader is a heretic himself?"

"Oddly no," said Aurelianus. "The heresy has found more support in the south and in Londinium in particular. It is among the wealthy that Pelagian thought has found its home. The north is wilder country where paganism is still rife. Bishop Severianus is content to hide behind Eboracum's walls while his son preaches heresy in the south."

"Paganism in the north and heresy in the south while barbarians sit on the doorstep," said Germanus. "Britannia certainly has its problems. If only they had not rebelled against Rome and thrown off her protective embrace."

"That is the problem at the heart of the matter," Aurelianus agreed. "And not one easily remedied. Many of the high-ranking nobles support independence from the empire and none more so than Lord Vitalinus, praeses of Maxima Caesariensis."

"And he is the most influential man in Britannia?"

"Yes. King in all but name. Is there any hope that Rome might send military aid? Reoccupied forts and repaired defences might persuade the nobles to look to Rome once more."

Germanus and Lupus shared an uneasy look. "Times are difficult for our fledgling emperor," said Germanus. "As well as the usual problems with Goths, Vandals and Huns, there is yet another damnable civil war raging in Africa between the emperor's generals. No, my son, Britannia's salvation is in our hands and only by converting people to the true faith can it be saved. If Londinium is the hotbed of the heresy, then it is to Londinium we must go."

Chapter 24

Vitalinus dreamt that he was sitting on a throne before a long hall. He didn't recognise the building but had a notion that it was Londinium's basilica, considerably refurbished and repainted, for it looked nothing like the ruined shell that was currently being used by Bishop Lentilus to address his flock.

There was a vast congregation before him. Everybody was there, from petty nobles to the members of the Council of Britannia. And they were all looking at him, or rather, at what was resting on his head.

He felt the weight of it. It was a comforting weight, pressing on his temples. He reached up and his fingers brushed against cold metal. *Could it be …? A … crown?*

Suddenly, everybody was gone. The hall before him lay empty and the pleasing weight of wealth and power on his head had vanished. He clutched his scalp and felt only his own thinning hair.

No! It had been such a pleasant dream!

There was only one other person in the hall, faint, but coming ever closer. Vitalinus squinted and felt his insides freeze as he recognised him.

"Brutus?" he whimpered. "You're … dead …"

The young man continued walking towards Vitalinus who felt speared to his own throne by the dead man's gaze. As he approached, he could see rotten flesh hanging from a pale skull in strips. A fiendish light blazed within hollow, sunken eye sockets and Vitalinus screamed.

He woke up, sweat making the bedclothes cling to him. His wife, Cordelia, stirred beside him, disturbed by the pitiful yelp which had escaped his lips but had sounded like a roar of terror in his nightmare.

He sat up and swung his legs down to rest his head in his hands. A nightmare. Nothing more. He was not a king, more the pity, but Brutus, his brother, was long in the ground. Good riddance. *He* ruled Britannia, not Brutus. It was time to get up and continue to rule it.

He left his wife slumbering and moved through the palace, his robes flowing, as slaves attended to his morning rituals. He ate a breakfast of cheese, honeyed figs and porridge while reports were brought to him for his attention. By the time he had seen to most of them and finished his breakfast with a cup of wine, the bad memory of his nightmare was almost forgotten. That was for the best, for he had many things to apply his thoughts to.

There was the discussion of military action to be taken against the force of Picts and Scots who were ravaging the far-flung corner of Venedotia. The Scots had settled there over a generation ago, claiming the island of Mona and much of the peninsula that jutted out into the Hibernian Sea. Now, it seemed, they had joined forces with a band of renegade Picts.

A year had passed since word had come down from the north that the Pictish tribes had united behind a new high king. Such news was always disheartening for the Britons below the Wall, but Vitalinus had it on good authority that Cunedag of the Votadini supported this High King Drustan, and had even helped him gain his throne.

There were many councillors who had suggested to him that perhaps Cunedag had forgotten his loyalties to the south these past two decades since he had helped Aurelianus defend these shores from Saxon and Pict alike. Vitalinus didn't think so. Cunedag was too much the Roman to turn on the diocese which had made a man of him. He owed his very crown to his Roman connections. Besides, according to his information (which was far better than anybody else's), this Drustan had exiled his brother, Nechtan, in the family squabble for the

Pictish crown and it was Nechtan who had now joined forces with the Scots to invade deeper into Britannia Prima.

Then, there was the issue of Bishop Germanus.

With the backing of several officials in Londinium, Bishop Lentilus had sent an appeal to a synod in Gaul, claiming that the Pelagian heresy had grown to rampant proportions in the diocese. If left untended, the whole island would turn from the true word of God and in so doing, lose its collective soul. Perhaps these constant barbarian incursions were God's punishment for straying from the true path?

It was all greatly exaggerated as far as Vitalinus was concerned. There had always been Pelagians in Britain. Pelagius himself had been born here. But Pope Celestine had dispatched Bishop Germanus, an aging firebrand who had been a military man and lawyer in his youth and had lost none of his bullheadedness, to Britain to address the heresy.

For weeks now, that old goat had been travelling the diocese, preaching the Augustinian doctrine and engaging in heated debates with Pelagians. Vitalinus had hoped that they might make a martyr of him, but no such luck. The Pelagians were a peaceful lot and every bit as God fearing as Germanus so for all the world, Vitalinus couldn't fathom what all the fuss was about. So what if Pelagius had denied the concept of original sin and placed greater emphasis on man's free will? It was a theology that somewhat appealed to Vitalinus (though he would never admit to being a Pelagian) and it was little wonder the heresy had taken root in Britannia which was trying so hard to exert its own brand of free will and independence.

The worst of it was that Aurelianus, the man who held Britannia's military in his grasp, was utterly besotted with this Gaulish bishop and had taken it upon himself to play the part of his personal bodyguard! As if the island didn't have more pressing concerns, the Comes was escorting this upstart from town to town and safeguarding him from harm.

Things had almost boiled over to violence during a heated debate in Londinium's basilica less than a week ago when the Pelagians, under their spiritual leader, Agricola, had descended on the town to debate Germanus in public. A huge crowd had gathered to witness this theological battle and both sides had blustered and ranted until they were purple in the face. Germanus's arrival in Britannia had whipped its people up into a sort of anti-Pelagian hysteria and Aurelianus's soldiers had been forced to press the crowds back to stop the basilica being stormed. Eventually, Agricola and his cohort of priests and deacons had been forced to cut a hasty retreat with most of them scurrying back north.

Germanus, practically hailed as a saint in his own lifetime by the townsfolk, had been insufferable in his victory. He had declared that some rest and distraction were in order after his efforts and had gone off with Aurelianus to visit the shrine of Saint Alban at Verulamium. Vitalinus only hoped some tragedy would befall the upstart Bishop on his travels for the greater his successes in Britannia, the closer its people began to feel to the Roman world they had left two decades ago.

By the time Vitalinus left his study, Cordelia and the children were up. God had blessed their marriage with two: the nine-year-old Senovara who was fair and pretty, and the eight-year-old Vortimer, dark and obedient. Whenever Vitalinus looked at them, he felt his determination to bring this island under his control increase tenfold. He would be its king one day, and Vortimer would succeed him. The line of Vitalinus would rule Britannia for a hundred generations!

It would take time, of course. In twenty years, the island was struggling to hold itself together, independent from Rome and ravaged by barbarians who scented weakness like the wolf closing in on a lame lamb. If only the fools in Londinium could see that their only route to survival lay in independence! But four centuries of Roman rule had instilled in the Britons a distrust of kings and crowns. Saxons, Scots and Picts were hammering at their doors, and they wanted to run screaming back into Rome's embrace like frightened children!

The very thought made Vitalinus's blood boil. After all they had worked for and achieved, the notion of rejoining the empire was downright treasonous to his mind. Appeal after appeal had been sent by lily-livered politicians, begging the emperor to send military aid. Such intervention in British affairs was unthinkable and Vitalinus had done his utmost to stamp out these cowardly attempts to bring the Romans back. When their pleas to the emperor fell on deaf ears, those spineless wretches had turned to the church for help.

Vitalinus cared little for the spiritual battles that raged on British soil but if they continued to draw the attention of the clergy on the continent, then more 'aid' might be sent. That would seriously disrupt his plans and the more he thought about it, the more convinced he became that Germanus must be removed from British interests altogether. A tragic accident would cut short his meddling and would raise little suspicion in Gaul. These things happened, even to living saints. After all, how else were martyrs made?

With a smile, he called for his scribe and, as the pattering of the man's feet echoed through the palace hallways, the contents of the letter he was going to write were already forming in Vitalinus's mind.

Fire raged through the small settlement like a hungry god devouring sacrifices. The thatched roofs blazed in the early light of morning, blackening the sky with smoke and reflecting off the surface of the nearby lake like a mirror of Hell.

Bishop Germanus started in his sleep, his dreams of fire and brimstone made appallingly real by the crackling of burning buildings and the screams of the villagers outside his hut. He sat upright on his pallet and saw orange light shining in through the cracks around the doorway. He crossed himself. The village was burning!

As he struggled to scramble out from between his sheets, Bishop Lupus across from him and several of the deacons were stirring, their own dreams shattered by the steadily increasing clamour.

"The village burns!" Germanus cried. "Offer your prayers to God and lend your aid to me!"

His leg, bound between two splints, would be a considerable inconvenience in escaping the burning village. He had injured it after falling from his horse on their way back from Saint Alban's shrine. It had significantly impeded their progress and had necessitated an overnight stop at this simple village between Verulamium and Londinium. Now, it seemed that his misfortune might be the death of him.

The terrified Lupus and a deacon helped Germanus up from his pallet while two others opened the door. Scorching heat soared into the little hut like the breath of the devil and the deacons fell back, shielding their eyes. Before them, a roaring inferno blazed as dozens of huts and workshops burned.

"God be merciful!" one of the deacons cried. "It's all around us! We're trapped!"

"Onwards!" Bishop Germanus insisted. "Trust in God to protect us!"

At the urging of their leader, the small cluster of holy men staggered out into the muddy street in their night shifts and looked up and down at the fire that seemed to encircle their hut. Distant screams could be heard as the villagers fled, carrying away as much as they could but here in the centre of the inferno, there were no voices, only the roaring, crackling fire that hemmed them in on all sides.

Germanus closed his eyes and knelt down. There was no escape. "Kneel now, my brothers," he said. "Our time of judgement is upon us. Kneel and pray to God to accept us into his embrace!"

Whimpering, the holy men knelt in the mud and bowed their heads in prayer as Germanus led them through the Pater Noster, ignoring the agony in his leg as it supported his weight. The Latin words, spoken with such passion and conviction, rose up amid the smoke, rivalling the sound of the crackling of burning buildings.

The door to a nearby hovel, its roof ablaze, was kicked open and a figure emerged, a wet cloth held to his face. It was Aurelianus.

"This way!" the Comes bellowed. "There's a way through! Help the bishop!"

Two of his soldiers hurried past him and helped Lupus and the deacon carry Germanus towards the door. Black smoke filled the interior of the hut and glowing embers fell down on them from the smouldering roof.

Germanus and his followers hacked and coughed as the smoke filled their lungs. Wet cloths were pressed over their mouths and noses, and they were told to hold them in place. It was difficult to breathe through the wet material, but it was better than getting a lungful of the awful burning smoke.

Through the hellish blackness Germanus was carried, and they emerged on the street on the other side. Here, buildings were burning too, but they were beyond the worst of the blaze and villagers ran back and forth with buckets of water and soaking blankets in an attempt to save at least a few of the hovels.

Germanus removed the damp cloth from his face and breathed the slightly better air more freely. "My thanks," he said to Aurelianus. "God must have sent you in place of an angel. We would have been done for were it not for you."

"We searched for an alternate way through to you when we learned that both ends of the street were blocked by fire," said Aurelianus, his face smeared with soot and his eyes red-rimmed. "That hut was the only way to you and it's impassable now. We got through just in time."

They watched as the roof of the hovel they had just passed through came crashing down, its timbers eaten through by fire. The heat drove them back and they retreated to the village's outskirts while Aurelianus's men aided the villagers in saving the last remaining hovels. It seemed an impossible task. Thatched with reeds as they were, it would be a miracle if any survived.

"Is there any indication as to how the fire started?" Germanus asked, easing himself down into a chair which had been hurriedly fetched for him. He stretched his injured leg out and tried not to show how much it pained him when there was so much pain and loss all around.

"The inferno seemed to have broken out in several places almost simultaneously," Aurelianus said. "And on all sides of your hut. The very work of the devil, perhaps."

"Perhaps," said Germanus, deep in grim thought as the village burned. "Perhaps."

"God be praised that you survived!" said Vitalinus as he swept into the cross hall of the palace to greet Bishop Germanus and Aurelianus. "When I heard, I knelt down and gave thanks to God."

"As did I," Lord Vitalinus," said Germanus. "It was a lucky escape. Were it not for Aurelianus …"

"A miracle!" Vitalinus interrupted. "God was surely watching over you. Please, come and be seated. I heard about your leg. Such misfortune! Does it pain you greatly?"

"Less and less each day," the bishop replied. "I am fortunate to rely upon Aurelianus's surgeons."

Vitalinus turned from them as he led them to his private office, partly to hide the rictus grin on his face which was wearing thin. *Damn that Aurelianus!* If he didn't insist on escorting the Gaulish bishop everywhere like a loyal hound, then he would have been rid of the troublesome old fool! But, when one door closed, another was opened. He had been playing the game of politics long enough to firmly believe that now.

While Germanus and Aurelianus had been away making their devotions to dead saints, a new barbarian threat had emerged. The alliance between the Scots and Picts in Venedotia was now brewing war as they raided their British neighbours and took ever more land. Fortunately, this damnable marriage between military and clergy was eager to set out and reclaim north-west Britannia Prima and Aurelianus and Germanus were here to discuss just that. It suited Vitalinus just fine. Wars had a way of seeing inconvenient people come to misfortune.

"And how many Picts have joined in this invasion?" Vitalinus asked as one of the palace slaves poured them some more wine.

"My scouts report that they are in the hundreds, rather than the thousands," Aurelianus replied. "Though in truth, it is hard to tell the difference between Pict and Scot. The Picts don't always paint themselves as their name suggests."

"Strange that they should ally themselves with the Scots," said Germanus. "I had been led to believe that the two peoples were mortal enemies with the Scots taking much land from the Picts in recent years."

"Correct," said Aurelianus. "It is a strange move, but the word is that these particular Picts are exiles from their own lands. They must have nowhere else to go but over to the Scots and help them in their conquests. Damned traitors to their own people."

"No doubt this Nechtan of theirs intends to build a powerbase in Venedotia with the aim of taking back the crown of the Picts from his brother," said Vitalinus.

Both Aurelianus and Germanus looked surprised and Vitalinus allowed himself a small smile of pride. "I have my own sources of intelligence, gentlemen." He only wished he still had Vibiana as one of his agents, but she had long since vanished into the mists of the north. Killed most probably, though there had been some indication that she had betrayed him in the end. Just as well she had met a bad end. He placed much pride in his network of spies but trusted none of them overmuch.

"Perhaps this brother of his might be useful in putting down the invasion," Vitalinus continued. "Use the Picts to fight the Picts, that sort of thing. It would certainly save a lot of your men from being killed, Aurelianus."

Both Aurelianus and Germanus frowned. "I'm not sure that inviting another horde of Picts to infest our diocese would really be the answer, my lord," said Aurelianus. "What's to stop them from turning on us and picking up where their countrymen left off?"

"Cunedag," said Vitalinus, with a smile. "He is on good terms with Drustan of the Picts. Helped him win his throne, in fact."

"Can this Cunedag be trusted?" asked Germanus. "I have heard he is little more than a Pict himself."

"But one raised below the Wall," said Vitalinus. "And he served as a cavalryman in the Roman army and has fought alongside Aurelianus."

"Cunedag is a good ally and a trustworthy one, it is true," said Aurelianus. "But he is aging now and has many sons. The strength of their loyalty is unknown to me."

"This is a perfect opportunity to put them to the test," said Vitalinus. "Rome spent much effort on cultivating good relations with the tribes directly north of the Wall. It would be a shame if we were to lose them through lack of use. Besides, we may not have the men to oust the Scots from Britannia alone."

"While I agree with your logic in maintaining peaceable relations with your northern neighbours," said Germanus, "I am not overly fond of the idea of using barbarians to fight barbarians. Especially pagan ones."

"We cannot afford to be too picky, I fear, Bishop. I will write to Cunedag and ask him to be our middleman. He will rein these Picts in on a short leash, I feel."

Aurelianus and Germanus shared a look, neither of them liking Vitalinus's decision, but knowing that they could not challenge it. He was head of the Council and the most powerful man in Britannia. And, as Vitalinus sent for his scribe, Germanus did not take his eyes of this self-styled *Vertigernus*, not liking how much of what went on in Britannia was in the hands of one man.

Chapter 25

"An irony that we must now make for Eboracum," Aurelianus shouted to Germanus over the din of the marching host. "The very place Agricola scurried off to after you trounced him in public less than a month ago."

"Irony or God's will?" the bishop replied. "I have come to learn that they are often one and the same."

"Perhaps. No doubt Agricola and his father will be thinking it too. For too long has the north been a refuge for Pelagians. Now it is an army of pagans who have summoned us north. Inconvenient for the Pelagians on both fronts."

"Mayhap we will kill two birds with one stone," said Germanus. "Both pagan and Pelagian should tremble at our coming!"

Germanus's leg had healed almost fully but the weather had slowed their progress. Spring rains had plagued them as they marched north, rattling off the helms of the cavalrymen and drenching their cloaks. Provisions were spoiled and cartwheels got stuck in the mud-clogged ruts in the poorly maintained road that led from Londinium to Eboracum. By the time they reached the capital of Britannia Secunda, the men were hungry, exhausted and soaked to the bone.

Their reception was not a warm one. Bishop Severianus seemed to be the voice of authority in the town and Aurelianus believed that he would have barred the gates to them had they not arrived with the largest war host Eboracum had seen in a generation. Once the men were billeted in the crumbling fort, Aurelianus and Germanus crossed the river into the town to confront the renegade bishop and his son.

"What right do you have to march into this town and occupy it like an invading force?" Severianus raged in the hall of the old praeses' residence. "The Roman legions left these shores twenty years ago, but you are doing a very good job of impersonating their arrogance!"

"We are here for this town's protection, Your Eminence," said Aurelianus. "Surely even a Pelagian can appreciate that."

"And what's that supposed to mean?"

"I mean, with the greatest respect, that this horde of Scots and Picts will butcher everybody within these walls, whatever their interpretation of the word of God is. I doubt they even know what a Pelagian is. So, harping on about independence from Rome and spitting in the eye of its military will do you little good when you require the aid of a Roman-trained army to save your hides."

"You are not a Roman anymore, Aurelianus," said Severianus. "Only the muscled arm of a self-styled dictator!"

"I am still the *Comes Britanniaum* and the defence of this island is my sworn duty!" Aurelianus snapped. "And were I you, dependant on somebody to prevent those painted savages from skinning and boiling me alive, I would show that man some proper respect!"

Bishop Severianus was a short, tubby man with a face that was given to red flushes when he was angry, but the red flush on his features paled somewhat at Aurelianus's raised voice echoing around the hall. His son, Agricola, stood by, almost ignoring Aurelianus, but his eyes were like daggers on Bishop Germanus who had so humiliated him in Londinium.

"And I suppose the presence of *His Eminence* in your company is merely down to chance?" Agricola said. "You wouldn't possibly be using this barbarian threat as an excuse to march your soldiers into Eboracum and convert us to the Augustinian teachings at sword point?"

"Gentlemen, I can assure you that my presence here is merely as a guest of our brave Comes," said Germanus. "And his presence here is to fight the barbarians. But, while I am here, I will turn as many away from the Pelagian heresy that you two have fostered here as I can, merely with my words and the words of Augustine."

That hardly seemed to satisfy the two Pelagians and they departed the hall in a bluster of outrage. As they exited, a soldier came hurrying in through a side door, his hobnailed sandals click-clacking on the tiled floors. "Sir!" the soldier said, saluting the Comes. "Our scouts have returned from the west! The enemy approaches!"

The walls of Eboracum were hazy in the distance, the fug of battle obscuring them like a dream. They may as well have been a dream to Cunedag as he looked on the town of his youth and the home of his wife. How many times must it be threatened? How many times must he ride to its defence? He was old now and knew he didn't have many battles left in him. His sons were good warriors and Tancorix was a fine penteulu, but none of them had the same loyalty to the south as he did. What of Britannia once he was gone? Would his dynasty keep their attention on the north and leave the lands below the Wall to fall prey to Gael and Saxon?

He forced himself to focus on the present. A combined army of Gaels and Picts were massed on the western side of the town, their camp a slapdash affair of hide tents and smouldering fires beyond arrowshot of the parapets. The siege had been short but brutal and the walls of the town showed the evidence of hard fighting.

It had been a quiet year in the north since Nechtan had vanished behind Gaelic lines. Many thought that had been the end of him but both Drustan and Cunedag had feared that something like this would be brewing. What Nechtan had promised the Gaels in return for helping him usurp his brother was unknown, but he knew that whatever it was, it would be bad news for the north. The Gaels already had a strong foothold in Venedotia, but this spring had seen them increase their aggression tenfold.

It was clear that Nechtan and his supporters were attempting to help them enlarge their territories below the Wall with the aim of taking the whole northern part of the diocese. Once that was complete, they could march beyond the Wall and claim the lowland tribes and finally the highlands with the mighty fortress of Cair Uerteru as the final prize. Nechtan and the Gaels would divide northern Albion between them. It had to end here. Eboracum was the largest town between the enemy host and the Wall. If it fell, then this hellish alliance of Pict and Gael would storm the north.

Aurelianus held the town but had waited behind its walls until the Votadini and the Picts under the High King Drustan, came down from the north. With the enemy's attention turned on the new arrivals, the western gates to the town and fortress were creaking open and Aurelianus's cavalry were streaming out to form ranks at the feet of the walls. The enemy were now caught between two armies but there was enough of them to make a confident stand.

Tancorix bellowed orders to form ranks as the enemy marshalled itself to meet them. Drustan and his Picts held the right flank with the finest Votadini riders on the left. Cunedag and his sons occupied the centre behind ranks of horsemen with the dragon banner fluttering behind them.

Horns bellowed as warriors hurried to find their places. And then, almost simultaneously, the two hosts charged forward to meet each other. Cunedag felt the old thrill of battle warm his stiff bones and he drew his spatha, holding it aloft to a cheer from the warriors behind him.

The two hosts met in a thunderous clash of steel, bodies and foaming horseflesh. Blood spurted and warriors screamed death cries as they hacked into each other in a swirl of mud, woad and gore. From above, where the ravens wheeled, looking forward to their grisly feast, the line of battle looked like a wavering snake, rippling as flank pushed against flank, gaining ground, only to lose it before fighting back and claiming it once more.

"Pull the left flank back!" Tancorix yelled, his horse rearing up beneath him. "They're too exposed!"

Hooves churned in the mud and the penteulu's orders were relayed to the bellowing of horns. The Picts and Gaels roared their defiance, encouraged by the sudden retreat of the forces pressing on their right.

Cunedag, his spatha red with blood, turned in his saddle and saw the left flank of the Votadini host turn and ride back. *Good lad*, he thought, thoroughly approving of his nephew's restraint. Too often battles were lost by headstrong aggression. By drawing the enemy closer, they increased their chances of outflanking them.

On the right, it was a different story. The Picts under Drustan were showing no such restraint and were hurling themselves at the enemy as if it were their last stand. It was no wonder the Roman army had conquered these lands and a hundred just like them. Nobody, it seemed, matched the Romans' orderly sense of discipline. For the Picts, pursuit of personal glory on the battlefield always trumped working together as a unit and that had always been the downfall of unromanized peoples across the world.

"Damned fools won't let up," he shouted to Tybiaun over the din of battle.

"If we don't keep up with them, we risk losing our right flank," Tybiaun replied. "And Drustan too if he's not careful. I can just about see him in the thickest of the battle."

Cunedag grimaced. He well understood Drustan's wish to see his brother slain or captured and end his uprising, but if Drustan fell in battle, then Nechtan would get exactly what he wanted; a clear path to the Pictish crown. All this would be for naught if Drustan was killed.

"What are those buggers waiting for?" Etern yelled, pointing in the direction of Aurelianus and his troops which remained motionless below the walls of the town.

"For us to fence the enemy in," said Cunedag. "If they charge now, then they risk being outflanked. We need to bring our wings around. Tancorix knows what he's doing; look! He's reinforced the left flank and the Gaels are falling like ripened wheat!"

From the centre of the line, Cunedag and his sons watched as the left flank of Votadini riders, pressed forward, turning their retreat into a feint and driving the attackers back so they fell over themselves in confusion as they tried to make it back to their lines.

"Both wings are in a strong position now," said Cunedag. "If Tancorix is worth his salt, then he'll give the order for the centre to advance any moment now."

"The Romans, Father!" said Tybiaun. "They're moving forward."

"Aurelianus sees the trap about to be sprung," said Cunedag. "He ever was the canny soldier. Wait for Tancorix's order to advance!"

The order wasn't long in coming. Tancorix came galloping along the rear lines, three riders with him. "The Romans prepare to trap the enemy, my king!" he shouted.

"Aye, good job holding that left flank, Tancorix!" Cunedag replied. "I suggest a forward advance?"

"It must be now, else we risk letting the enemy slip around on one of our flanks. Drustan's side would be my guess, for it's a fucking shambles over there."

"I agree. He can't hold that flank if the Gaels are pressed against him by Aurelianus's men."

"Carry my orders to the wings!" Tancorix said to his riders. "We advance at my signal! As one!"

His riders galloped off and Tancorix pushed his way through to where Cunedag stood with the dragon standard. Horns bellowed and men cheered as the advance began.

"Albion!" Cunedag bellowed, holding his bloodied sword in the air, cutting a striking and inspiring picture against the rippling banner of the red dragon that billowed behind him; Romans and Britons united on a single field of red.

A single line of iron-hard horsemen, trained in Roman tactics by their king, disciplined and keen for slaughter, pressed forward, driving the rag-tag Gaels and Picts before them. Swords scythed through limbs and shoulders, blood spurted up shields and across knuckles. The press of Aurelianus's troops at their back made space tight with little room to manoeuvre. Most of the Gaels were on foot and the charge of the Votadini horsemen squashed and trampled them.

A massive Gael in a tartan cloak was wielding a two-handed war hammer to deadly effect, crippling horses and then slamming the iron head down onto the heads of their riders as they fell, crushing helms and skulls with ease.

"Watch that bastard!" Cunedag yelled, pointing at the Gael with the tip of his spatha.

A circle had grown around the battle-crazed warrior as the Votadini horsemen tried to keep out of the reach of his massive weapon. Uttering an oath, Etern lifted his spear and hurled it at the Gael. It thudded into his shoulder, knocking him back a pace, his hammer swinging wildly by one hand. Etern took his chance and urged his horse forward, pushing through his own men. The Gael recovered his stance and, with the spear still jutting out of his shoulder, took a vengeful swing at him. Etern made his horse sidestep the blow and then brought it back again, ramming his cavalry sword deep into the man's neck, sinking the blade in as far as he could reach.

The Gael gasped and the war hammer tumbled out of his grip to land with a spatter of mud and blood. The Votadini cheered. Their prince had slain the giant! Etern ripped his blade free and kicked the dying man to one side. He twisted and tumbled to the ground and disappeared beneath a flurry and stamping and stabbing from the warriors he had held at bay.

Cunedag's heart swelled with pride to see his second-born excel himself in battle. He had always been the better fighter of his sons, a quality marred only by his bullheadedness. But today he had shown caution while still proving to be a formidable warrior. Perhaps he was learning after all.

"Father!" Tybiaun yelled. "They're breaking! We have them!"

Cunedag glanced up and saw the left flank of the enemy trying to force their way through Drustan's Picts who were already so mixed up and fragmented, that they were proving no decent defence.

"Damn him!" Cunedag said, cursing the Pict's keenness to reach his brother and challenge him to singe combat. "They're forcing their way right past him!"

With an avenue of escape open to them, it became a full-scale retreat. The mounted Gaels and Picts charged the breach with the warriors on foot struggling to keep up. The chaos before them meant that the Votadini couldn't stop the enemy leadership from slipping away. All they could do was cut down stragglers and they reaped a bloody harvest until Aurelianus's front lines were close enough to hail.

"Eboracum is saved, Aurelianus!" Cunedag yelled at the red crest of the British general which bobbed about behind shields emblazoned with the Chi Rho of Christ.

"Thanks to your timely arrival, Cunedag!" Aurelianus bellowed back.

"We lose the enemy leadership! Shall we pursue?"

"Cut down as many as you can, but don't chase them all the way back to Venedotia," Aurelianus replied.

Cunedag grinned. It had been meant as a joke but in truth, he knew that the war would have to be taken to the Gaels. The day had been won, but they squatted on the fringes of Albion and would strike again as soon as they regrouped. And as long as Nechtan was still alive, Drustan's throne was at risk.

They drank wine in the fort's praetorium, still in their bloodied armour, while the wounded were treated and food and lodgings were found for the newly arrived warriors and their horses.

"May I present Bishop Germanus of Autissiodorum," Aurelianus said, indicating the elderly man in the leather cuirass Cunedag had seen by his side in the battle.

"A bishop warrior?" Cunedag exclaimed.

"Yes, I was in the military in my youth," said Germanus. "But turned my attentions to the church in my middle years. I was sent here by the Pope to put down the Pelagian heresy but found many other problems afflicting this island. Pagans on all sides, seeking to overrun the diocese. Hardly surprising, given the weakness found in much of the British leadership. Eboracum itself is in the hands of a Pelagian. Speaking of which, I wonder where that rascal has got to. Cowering in a hayloft, no doubt. Somebody had better go and tell him that the danger has passed. For the moment."

"Bishop Severinus has taken it upon himself to rule Eboracum in place of your late foster father," Aurelianus said to Cunedag. "Cunedag grew to manhood in this town, you see, Your Excellency. He was fostered by Praeses Colias."

"Ah," said Germanus, narrowing his eyes at Cunedag. "And good Colias no doubt instilled in you the word of Christ."

"Not as such, no," said Cunedag, meeting the bishop's stare. "I follow the religion of my people."

"I see."

Their conversation was cut short by a bout of jovial shouting in the cross hall. Drustan and his high-ranking warriors roared into the room, a jug of wine between them and many jests and boasts on their lips. Their blue woad was smeared, and they were spattered with mud and blood which matted their hair and beards.

"Gods damn us, Cunedag, but that was a mad scramble!" Drustan greeted Cunedag. "When your Roman friends pressed the advantage, we were damn near trampled by my brother and his allies as they sought to get away! But we'll catch him, if not tomorrow then the day after. We'll chase those Gaels back into the sea if that's what it takes!"

"Perhaps if you had held the right flank in some sort of order," Bishop Germanus said, "you might not have been so easily overrun."

Drustan blinked comically as his wine-blurred vision took in the armoured bishop. He didn't speak much Latin but understood enough to know that he was being criticised. "Who the devil is this and what does he mean by that remark?"

"This is Bishop Germanus," said Aurelianus, hastily. "He is on a mission to Britannia from the Pope himself."

"I care not who sent him, but no man insults the actions of me or my men."

"I only meant to say," Germanus went on in good but accented British, "is that there are more nuanced ways to fight a battle than by charging headlong into the enemy ranks like wild animals."

"Damn this prattling priest!" Drustan exclaimed in his own language. "He wears the armour of a warrior so perhaps he'd like to exchange sword blows instead of words!"

"Settle down, Drustan!" said Cunedag. "He is on our side, and you can't go challenging priests to single combat."

"Maybe not druids, but he's a priest of no religion I recognise."

"Friends, please!" said Aurelianus. "We have just won a great victory. Let us not spoil it by squabbling among ourselves! Tonight is a night for celebration and tomorrow, we need to focus on our next move."

"I agree," said Cunedag. "I suggest we take the fight to the Gaels before they can reorganise themselves."

"But the question is, where to stop?" said Aurelianus. "The Gaels control most of the northern coast of Britannia Prima. The peninsula and the island of Ynys Mon are teeming with Gaelic settlements. We have not the forces nor the time to spend on a long campaign. Not with the Saxons causing trouble in the east again."

"Drustan's brother is the key to this whole problem," said Cunedag. "As long as he lives, he presents a threat to peace in the north. I don't doubt that he's stirred up as much unrest as possible among the Gaels and incited them to war. They've never struck so deeply into British territory before."

"Aye, my brother will have promised them land and alliances in exchange for helping him steal my crown," said Drustan. "Land and promises he can't possibly fulfil."

"But they don't know that," said Cunedag.

"It seems to my mind," said Germanus, struggling a little to understand the conversation that was being conducted in British, "that we must deal with this Nechtan as our first priority. Perhaps the Gaels might be pressured into handing him over. After their defeat today, their spirit for bloodshed will have been dampened somewhat. They have no desire to get bogged down in a lengthy war any more than we do."

"The bishop speaks the truth," said Cunedag. "I suggest we march west quickly and fall upon them with a large show of might. The Gaels are a warlike people and will not surrender easily. But they might be open to a way out of this situation that does not threaten their honour."

"Then we march on the morrow," said Germanus. "Nip Nechtan's rebellion in the bud and let God sort out the rest."

Chapter 26

On the eastern fringes of Gaelic territories, less than twenty leagues from the old Roman legionary fortress of Deva Victrix, the two camps faced each other. Each occupied a hill on opposite sides of a tributary that flowed to the River Deva in the east.

The banners of the Gaels fluttered atop a tree-studded hill. They were around seven-thousand strong, some mounted, but most on foot, armed with either spears or slings. This valley was the gateway to the territories their fathers and grandfathers had claimed from the British and they weren't going to give them up without a fight.

On the opposite hill, the building of the British camp was well underway with trenches being dug, tents erected and firewood and game foraged. Cunedag made his way to where Aurelianus and Germanus were overlooking the valley. A deputation from the Gaels was approaching and steadily making their way up the hill. There looked to be at least three tribal leaders as well as a man in woad whom Cunedag recognised.

"Nechtan comes with the delegation himself," he said. "He must be feeling confident that they won't just hand him over."

"Where is Drustan?" asked Aurelianus.

"Overseeing the defences surrounding the baggage train."

"Somebody had better fetch him. We are about to negotiate with his brother."

The parley was held under the open sky with the Gaelic chieftains and their Pictish ally sitting with their backs to the river and a group of their warriors on hand with their horses to aid their escape should negotiations get too heated. It was clear that they didn't really want to fight, despite outnumbering the Britons. The disciplined units of Aurelianus and Cunedag promised a hard and bloody battle.

The Gaels spoke no Latin and their British was poor, though their own language was something of a cousin to it and, through the occasional use of interpreters, the negotiations proceeded. It was put to them that Nechtan was a criminal and should be subject to Uerteru law and that, if they handed him over, the British host would leave the valley and there would be no need for violence.

They had a druid with them who spoke on their behalf, and he explained in no uncertain terms that they had pledged their allegiance to Nechtan's quest to reclaim his throne which had been stolen from him by his brother.

"Damn him, he's my *younger* brother!" Drustan exclaimed. "The crown was mine by right!"

"The crown belonged to our cousin, as he was the son of the late king," said Nechtan. "After tragedy befell him, the tribe voted for the next best man to rule. They chose me."

"Tragedy which you engineered!" Cunedag snapped.

"Lies!" Nechtan retorted. "Again, you spread this slander, you Votadini meddler!"

The Gaels watched this heated exchange in British with bored expressions. Cunedag had no idea if they knew anything about Nechtan's hiring of their northern countrymen to do his dirty work. It might have some effect on their decision to support him if they did, just as it had lost him the support of most of the Picts. It was worth a shot.

"Do any of you know the Gael Fergus mac Eohaid?" Cunedag asked the druid.

"Aye," said one of the chieftains, understanding the question at least. "He is my wife's cousin. What of him?"

"His lands border those of the Uerteru," said Cunedag. "Would you say that your wife's cousin was a man of honour?"

There was indignant rumbling at this once the druid had translated his words. "He wants to know what you mean by insulting his wife's family with such a question," said the druid.

"He might also like to know that his wife's cousin was recruited by his new friend Nechtan to slay a child and his mother in order to secure his way to the crown of the Uerteru."

"More lies!" Nechtan protested.

"You harbour a traitor, a kin slayer and a murderer of babes and mothers," said Cunedag, looking directly at the Gaelic chieftains. "There can be no dishonour in handing him over to us and ridding yourself of the stain he represents. There is no need for us to fight."

One of the chieftains stood up, angrily. "You come into our territories with lies and threats," he said in heavily accented British. "The dishonour is yours!"

The other chieftains rose and turned to leave the camp. Nechtan flashed his brother a grin of triumph before following them to the horses.

"Well, that didn't go so well," said Aurelianus. "Why did you offend them, Cunedag?"

"It was the only way to get them to question their support of Nechtan," said Cunedag. "Besides, they would never have handed him over to us based on anything we said to them. But now they have something to think about. The seed of doubt has been planted, just as it was before the battle on the banks of the White River. Nechtan's position among the Gaels might not be as secure as it was before they climbed this hill. That, at least, is something."

"Then, God willing," said Germanus, "there might be no battle."

Night fell and pinpricks of light on the opposite hill could be seen as the enemy cooked their meat over their fires. Cunedag glanced at them as he made his way to his tent, aiming for an early night. Battle might be upon them at daybreak, and he needed rest. He and Aurelianus had been discussing tactics over wine in the latter's tent and already he felt woozy. Age seemed to sap the strength from him as well as his tolerance for drink, even for the watered-down Roman stuff.

Others had similar thoughts, and a lull fell over the camp as most bedded down and tried not to think of what might happen tomorrow. Cunedag dreamed of Din Eidyn and of Vala and how much he missed them both.

He awoke with a start, disturbed by shouting from outside his tent. His oil lamp burned low, and the night was dark beyond his tent flap. Surely the enemy weren't attacking in the middle of the night? His armorer had been awoken too and was picking items off his armour stand, ready to gird his king for battle.

Cunedag ignored him and seized only his spatha before running out of the tent. He found several of Aurelianus's soldiers outside Germanus's tent. Bishop Lupus was there too, and a few of the deacons, one of whom appeared to be wounded. Lupus was holding his bleeding arm and attempting to bind it with linen to staunch the flow.

Two of the soldiers held a man between them and the bleeding side of his face showed that he had already received a pacifying blow from one of them. He looked to be a camp follower and wore the simple attire of a craftsman. Bishop Germanus emerged from his tent looking shaken but putting on a stoic face.

"What happened?" Cunedag asked, belting his spatha around his middle.

"This scum snuck into the bishop's tent and was about to murder him," said one of the soldiers.

"My life was saved by Deacon Sergius, here," said Germanus, indicating the wounded cleric.

"I was awoken by a shadow falling over me," said Sergius, clutching his bound arm through which several spots of blood were blooming. "I've always been a light sleeper, God be thanked, for otherwise I might not have seen the assassin creeping up on His Eminence."

"The brave man tackled my would-be killer and took an injury meant for me," said Germanus, looking on his colleague gratefully.

Aurelianus came hurrying over to them, wearing only his tunica but, like Cunedag, carrying his sword with him.

"Does anybody recognise this man?" he said, once the alarming events had been relayed to him.

"Aye, Sir," said one of the cluster of soldiers who had quickly gathered around the disturbance. "He's a fletcher."

"How long has he been with the army?"

The soldier shrugged. "Couldn't say, Sir. At least since Eboracum."

"A plot has been foiled," said Aurelianus. "This assassin was no doubt following somebody's orders. We will find out whose come dawn, have no doubt of that. I have some very skilled interrogators in my army. Fetch him along!"

The failed assassin was dragged off to a secluded tent where his interrogation would be conducted. While the irons were heated in a brazier, Cunedag and Aurelianus shared a quiet word.

"Who could be behind such a plot?" Aurelianus said. "To murder a bishop! Surely no Christian could be behind it …"

"I have trouble believing it could be anybody from the Gaelic camp. Why would they care about a bishop? You or I would be a much better target."

"Agreed. I think we can rule out Nechtan and his allies and must look to our own side for the culprit."

"A Pelagian, then? Germanus has certainly made some enemies during his short time here in Albion."

"But Pelagians are God-fearing men, all the same," said Aurelianus. "I doubt even Bishop Severianus would stoop to murdering a fellow man of the cloth, no matter their differences."

"Could be a personal matter. A grudge of some sort."

Aurelianus shook his head. "A lowly fletcher with a grudge against a bishop and a foreign one at that? No, this reeks of intrigue. I feel that there is more to it, some hidden hand behind it all …"

There came a cry of alarm from the direction of the interrogation tent. Cunedag and Aurelianus ran over to it and found several soldiers peering in through the flaps.

"He's dead, Sir!" one of them reported. "Somebody slashed his throat and snuck off."

"Raise the alarm!" Aurelianus snapped. "I want the murderer found! Where is that guard I posted?"

"No sign of him, Sir."

The guard. Cunedag had noticed the man in simple armour of boiled leather and iron cap. Not one of Aurelianus's professional veterans, but an auxiliary fighter recruited from one of the militias. He had been hanging around when the attack on the bishop had been foiled and Aurelianus had posted him on guard outside the interrogation tent.

"Blast him!" said Aurelianus. "How could I have been such a fool! He was clearly the assassin's accomplice and was hanging around to see the job done and help him get away."

"But after he was captured, the accomplice's mission changed," said Cunedag.

Aurelianus nodded. "To silence the assassin. He knew the man would reveal the name of their employer once the hot irons were applied to him. This conspiracy infests my camp like a sore!"

The entire camp was raised and the sentries placed on high alert. Riders were dispatched to scour the surrounding woods, but it was hopeless. The murderer had got away into the night. Angry and suspicious of more treachery, everybody headed back to their tents to catch what little sleep was left to them.

The dawn came cruelly fast with the bellow of horns in the valley signifying that the enemy were on the move and advancing. Strapping on his armour, Cunedag hurried to the crest of the hill where Aurelianus was already surveying the scene below them. Hundreds of Gaelic tribesmen were emerging from the trees and making their way across the small river towards them, beating on their brightly painted shields with the butts of their spears and hilts of their knives.

"So much for negotiations," said Aurelianus as he tightened the strap on his helm. "Battle is upon us, it seems."

Orders were hastily carried to every corner of the camp and the British host arranged itself at the crest of the hill. British, Votadini and Pictish cavalry formed a line facing the advancing enemy with the infantry at the rear. To avoid a repeat of Drustan's impetuousness which had nearly cost them the last battle, Tancorix had put him and his Picts on the left flank under the command of Etern while he commanded the right with Aurelianus's cavalry. Cunedag and his other sons held the centre with Aurelianus in front of the baggage train.

"We send the cavalry against them while we hold the ridge," said Aurelianus, "and see if we can't drive them back across the river. That might be enough to break their spirits."

"Let's hope so," said Cunedag. "What's Germanus doing?"

The bishop and his followers were riding along the ranks, a large cross carried between them while Germanus made the sign of blessing with his hand. His words were barely audible over the wind and stirring of the men and horses, but he seemed to be delivering a sermon in Latin.

"Baptising the men," said Aurelianus.

"Aren't most of them baptised already?" asked Cunedag. "I thought most of your lot were Christians."

Aurelianus gave him a sidelong smile. "On the cusp of battle, a second baptism can't hurt. Soldiers need all the divine help they can get."

"I would much rather have ridden with the first wave alongside Etern," Tybiaun said to his father, "instead of waiting up on this hill."

Cunedag smiled. "Part of being a king is learning to hold back and let warriors do their job. It's a hard lesson to learn, believe me."

"But you rode into battle even after you were king," his son protested. "I've heard the stories of your war against the Saxons with Aurelianus and of how you and Asaros and Tancorix snuck around the Saxon Shore pretending to be mercenaries. You never cared overmuch for your own safety."

"That is true," said Cunedag. "But I was a young man then. Much as it pains me to admit it, I am no longer the rider nor the warrior I once was. Better men must lead the charge now."

"Men like Etern, you mean."

Cunedag understood his son at last. He was jealous of his younger brother. "You are my heir," he said, clapping his hand on Tybiuan's shoulder. "And it is you who must learn the hardest lessons of all."

Tybiaun nodded, but Cunedag could see the distaste written on his face. He sighed. He missed being a young man himself, but at least he had those memories to think back on.

What did Tybiaun have? It was as if he had spent his life fighting and killing just so his own children could grow up only to envy his own youth. The gods were a callous bunch with a twisted sense of humour.

The enemy were close now and Bishop Germanus seemed to have finished his mass baptism and was now delivering a rousing speech. Cunedag couldn't hear the words at such a distance, but the bishop seemed to be encouraging the men to repeat a word after him.

"Alleluia!" the bishop cried.

"*Alleluia!*" came hundreds of voices.

"Alleluia!" Germanus repeated.

"*Alleluia!*"

"ALLELUIA!"

"*ALLELUIA!*"

The soldiers were whipped up into a frenzy now as the enemy began climbing the hill below them. They beat on their shields in anticipation, eagerly awaiting the orders to charge.

At last, the orders were given and, before the horns had ceased to blare, they were off with a roar of war cries, charging down the slope, using the angle of the terrain to give them speed and a deadly advantage. The Gaels, who were halfway up the hill, looked up in alarm and raised their shields to meet the oncoming charge.

Leading the left flank, Etern bellowed and hurled his spear at the closest enemy warrior, just as he had done when he had finished off that giant Gael outside the walls of Eboracum. As before, he scored a good hit and the spear punched through the man, skewering him to the earth where he stood, transfixed like a grotesque scarecrow, before the rush of horses knocked him down.

The sudden charge was not what the Gaels had been expecting, not being great cavalry warriors themselves. They had perhaps expected a hail of arrows and spears from which they might crouch behind their shields, but a downhill cavalry charge took them by surprise. Shields were shattered and men cut down as the horsemen swept down the slope and the Gaelic right flank fell back to the river, splashing through it in a full-on retreat to the woods.

"Pursue!" Etern yelled, holding his sword aloft. "Their camp is undefended! Run them down and destroy their baggage train!"

From atop the hill, Cunedag, Tybiaun and Aurelianus watched the Gaelic line buckle and collapse on their right flank as Etern broke through and sent them scattering. Their left flank still held strong, however, as Tancorix and Aurelianus's cavalry struggled to gain much ground.

"Your son is quite the cavalryman," said Aurelianus. "I've never seen a charge quite like that one."

"He took to his lessons well," said Cunedag. "But is often overkeen to throw himself into danger where there is glory to be won."

"Often a trait in the young," said Aurelianus. "Although today, it has to be admitted, it has won us the advantage."

Tybiaun said nothing but gazed at the wake of bodies and bloody destruction his younger brother had left on the hillside with the compliments of his father and Aurelianus hanging in the air like a thundercloud.

On the right flank, things were looking bleak. Tancorix bellowed orders to hold the line and not get drawn off into small skirmishes. Twice already he had remarshalled the cavalry wing and charged the Gaels and the horses were now exhausted. The enemy had held firm, digging in behind their shields and clustering together to form small islands of barbed obstacles. Every time they got close to them, a spear was hurled, felling a rider.

"Form up!" Tancorix yelled. "We make another pass but steer clear of those spears!"

What few riders were closest to him, forced their mounts back up the hill and wheeled around to ride down on a cluster of Gaels. Gripping a spear overarm, Tancorix readied himself to take aim at the first Gael who poked his head above his shield. If picking them off one by one was the only way to wear them down, then so be it.

They thundered past the tortoise-like bulge of shields and spears, willing the enemy to break formation and open a gap in the armour. As Tancorix passed close, one of the Gaels could not resist temptation and lifted his shield to throw a spear. It was a small gap, but an opportunity nonetheless and Tancorix hurled his spear with all his might at the same time the Gael threw his.

The spears passed each other in the air. An angry curse boiled up in Tancorix's throat as he saw his own clatter off the shield of the man next to his target. He had missed! The curse did not have a chance to leave his lips as the spear thrown by his enemy thudded into his neck, the finest throw he had ever seen. Had one of his own men made it, he would have congratulated him heartily.

He choked as the iron head punched through the back of his throat and the wooden shaft slid through his neck, the force of it hurling him from his saddle. He heard the cries of his men as he landed heavily on the grassy hill, neck twisting awkwardly as the length of the spear forced his head to one side. Blood filled his throat, and he began to suffocate.

"Tancorix is down!" Cunedag said, leaning forward in his saddle, his face twisted into anguish at seeing his penteulu and brave nephew tumble from his saddle, a Gaelic spear lodged in his throat.

The enemy on the right flank roared in triumph as the Votadini cavalrymen fell back, dragging their penteulu with them, shielding him with their bodies and their horses, with anything to keep him from further harm.

"Damn this waiting game!" Cunedag cursed in a strong contrast to his acceptance of his role earlier in the battle. "Aurelianus, we need to reinforce the right flank. My men are leaderless and discouraged."

"I agree," said Aurelianus, and he dispatched orders to draw what was left of the cavalry to form up with the infantry behind. Bishop Germanus drew his sword and loudly offered more prayers to God to see them safely through this new development in the battle. The Christians cheered, convinced that God was on their side while the pagans grimly muttered their own prayers to their various gods, hoping that they would side with the Christian god for once.

Tybiaun gripped his spear, the sight of Tancorix's fall burning in his gut and making his shame at not having been part of the charge all the hotter. He swore he would make up for it now, and, if Tancorix had been slain, then to avenge his cousin.

With further bellows from horns and one last round of 'alleluias', the mounted host set off, following the ridge of the hill to come upon the enemy from their left while the infantry steadily marched down the slope, shields overlapping and spears pointed downwards.

On the opposite hill, Etern led his men through the Gaelic camp in a havoc-wreaking charge that cut a bloody swathe through tents and men alike. The enemy leadership, having seen five-hundred-odd riders cresting the hill, had deserted the camp and ridden down the other side of the hill and into the valley, presumably to seek the safety of their warriors who were still storming the other hill.

Those who had been pursued through the woods and up the hill, made a last-ditch effort to stand and fight and were hacked down where they stood. Cook fires were scattered and men leapt down off their horses to pick up burning brands and hurl them at tents. Soon the sky was marred by the black coils of smoke as the enemy camp was destroyed.

"My lord!" one of Drustan's Picts cried, riding over to Etern at a gallop. "The battle does not fare well on our right flank! Your father and the Roman leadership are entering the fray to reinforce them!"

Etern galloped towards the clearing which provided a view of the valley below. Beyond the river which now ran red with the blood of the corpses that clogged it, there was a desperate fight on the side of the hill. The left flank of the Gaels was still strong and had all but overwhelmed Tancorix's cavalry. Squads of infantry were marching down the hill to engage the enemy while the remainder of the British cavalry were harrying the left flank, the banner of the Votadini held aloft alongside Aurelianus's standard and the cross of Germanus.

"Gods, those don't look like good odds," said Drustan.

"Mount up!" Etern bellowed to his men who were currently helping themselves to the camp stores. "Our people and allies need us on the other hill! Mount up and ride at my signal!"

Drustan yelled similar orders to his own men and within seconds, Pictish and Votadini tribesmen were swinging up into their saddles, ready to charge once more. Etern led them down the steepest portion of the hill, through the trees and towards the river. His horse panted and gasped beneath him, already exhausted. He ground his teeth in frustration. They would need plenty of energy to get up the hill on the other side and would be engaging the enemy rear at a disadvantage, but there was nothing else to be done.

They thundered across the river, trampling bodies and kicking up sprays of pinkish water, forcing their mounts up onto the muddy bank on the other side.

"Albion!" Etern roared as the rear ranks of the Gaels turned around to gaze at them with widening eyes.

Charging an enemy uphill was a poor strategy, but this enemy were already tired and were facing away from them, engaged with the iron-hard infantry of the Romans. The mounted leadership which were hacking away at the left flank of the Gaels cheered to see Etern and Drustan charging into the enemy ranks and carving a bloody path despite their exhausted mounts.

The Gaels knew that the tide had turned and were now hemmed in on three sides with only their right flank left open. They began to move to the east, dropping away from the battle. The leadership, mounted and in the centre of the press, bellowed to their warriors to stand firm, but it was over. Etern's final charge had broken the courage of the Gaels, and many knew that this whole battle could have been avoided had they only handed the Pictish exile over to the Britons.

"Keep at them!" Aurelianus bellowed, his Chi-Rho standard wavering in the hands of his standard bearer.

The Gaels began to retreat en masse but the Britons and Picts were too tired to give much of a chase. Nechtan and the Gaelic chieftains eventually realised that they were defeated and rode back down to the river to escort their retreating warriors up to the smouldering remains of their camp.

Etern and Drustan forced their way through their own men who were seeing to the wounded, aiding their own and dispatching the Gaels with ruthless efficiency. "We have them, Father!" Etern cried.

"Aye!" Cunedag replied. "Your charge saved us all, my boy!"

Etern caught a glimpse of jealous contempt in Tybiaun's face and ignored it. "The enemy leadership is slipping away," he said.

"Little matter," Cunedag replied. "The battle is won and we are in a much stronger position now. Time for another round of negotiations."

Chapter 27

With the ravens descending on the valley of the slain like a black cloud come to devour the dead, Aurelianus, Germanus, Cunedag and Drustan met with the Gaelic chieftains atop their own hill to discuss terms. There were enough Gaels left alive to mount a considerable defence of the opposite hill if the Britons wished to attack but both sides hoped it would not come to that. All that remained was to negotiate the peaceful retreat of both sides from the valley.

Nechtan was curiously absent from the meeting and Cunedag had the notion that the Pict was feeling somewhat in danger of being handed over to his brother by his allies in order to buy their way out of the situation.

"We put it to you again," said Aurelianus to the Gaels. "We want Nechtan. This whole ugly slaughter could have been avoided had you simply surrendered the traitor to us."

"This *Cruithin* must have great value to you," said the chieftain who had the better command of British, though he used the Gaelic word for 'Pict'. "So many have died today so that you might claim your prize."

"We only wish to avoid bloodshed," said Aurelianus. "He represents a threat to peace on our island. Will you now hand him over to us?"

There was much discussion in Gaelic between the chieftains until finally, the more vocal of them said; "We cannot besmirch our honour by handing over a man we are allied to."

"You've just suffered defeat, man!" Aurelianus exclaimed. "Would you fight to the death atop your hill to save a traitor who sought only to use you to gain power?"

"We value our honour perhaps higher than you do yours, Roman," said the Gael. "But another solution presents itself.

You say Nechtan represents a threat to peace so long as he remains on this island."

"True."

"Then what if he is allowed to remain a guest of our people, but not in *Alba*."

Aurelianus shared a surprised look with Drustan and Cunedag. "You mean take him to Erin?"

"Aye. He would have a place in one of the great households of *Ériu* and would be of no further trouble to you."

Cunedag smiled. These Gaels were as keen to be rid of the troublesome Nechtan as much as the Britons were, but their honour forbade sacrificing an ally to save their own hides. Better that he be squirrelled away somewhere in their own ancestral lands.

"So be it," said Drustan. "My brother must sail for Erin as soon as possible and must be known for an exile. If he should ever set foot in Albion again, then his life will be forfeit as will the lives of any who protect him."

"I support this request as Comes Britanniarum," said Aurelianus. "And will enforce it if need be. Nechtan will be slain if he ever returns to Albion."

Once the negotiations had concluded, the Gaels returned to their camp where they would presumably inform Nechtan of the decision made concerning his future. While the Picts were pleased with the outcome of the battle, the Votadini were in mourning for their fallen penteulu. Tancorix had died of his wound before the reinforcements had reached him. The spear had been removed from his throat and his body had been placed on a cart where it was currently being washed and wrapped by some of the female camp followers for its journey back to his homeland.

"I don't know if my sister is ever going to forgive me," said Cunedag as he and his sons shared a wineskin and watched the women dress Tancorix's corpse.

"He was our penteulu," said Tybiaun, "and a warrior. Aunt Alpia understood this."

"But she never understood my loyalty to the south," Cunedag replied. "Always she resented my decisions to fight the wars of others. She did not see the bigger picture, as I do. This will break her."

"Will we take him back to Din Eidyn?" asked Etern.

"Yes. I will not allow him to be buried in southern lands. He must be laid to rest in the north, near his family. We are going home, boys. Another war is over, and Albion is a little safer, at least for the time being."

"You sound tired, Father," said Ruman.

"I *am* tired," Cunedag replied. "I'm tired of fighting to hold this island together. I've been doing it all my life and now, as my winter years approach, I have to ask myself; what has it really achieved?"

"The battle for peace is a fight that is both paradoxical and unending," said Aurelianus behind them. He was stripped of his armour and was wearing a fresh tunic and cloak. "Rome understood this. And so do you, I think, Cunedag. We are the last guardians of Rome's light on this island. We fight on because we have to, and the torch will be passed to our sons to fight on in our name. In Rome's name."

"What about in Albion's name?" said Cunedag. "Every winter that passes, Rome seems more distant. Fight on we must, but for ourselves, not for Rome."

Aurelianus seemed somewhat displeased with this answer but did not press the issue. "As long as we fight, that is what counts," he said, before leaving them to see to his own officers.

"And now, I must choose another penteulu," said Cunedag.

"So soon, Father?" asked Ruman. "Tancorix is barely cold on his bier …"

"As Aurelianus said, the fight goes on. Unceasingly. And our warriors need a commander. One who is both fearless and cunning in battle." He looked to his three sons "You have all grown so much in the past two years and I am proud of you all. Tybiaun, your sense of justice reminds me so much of myself as a youth. Etern, your hot-headedness is familiar to me too, but always your cause is just, and no man holds their honour in higher esteem. Ruman, your thirst for knowledge will serve you well, as will your way with women." He smiled as Ruman blushed and his brothers smirked. "All of you would make fine leaders, but only one of you will be my penteulu. I have decided that Etern shall succeed Tancorix."

"Father, I …" Etern began.

"Your quick thinking won the battle today," said Cunedag. "And I can see now that your impulsiveness has been tempered with age and experience. I want you to lead my teulu."

"I can't thank you enough, Father!" said Etern, beaming.

"Go and get yourself cleaned up. There will be drinking tonight for, though we mourn Tancorix, we are victorious. We must drink to his shade and all the others who now make their voyage to Annun."

"It feels somewhat like a hollow victory," said Ruman as Etern headed off towards his tent.

"Most victories do," said Cunedag. "You will come to learn that. Go on, you get cleaned up too. Drink heartily tonight but stay away from those Pictish warrior women!"

Tybiaun remained by Cunedag's side, and they watched the women continue to tend to Tancorix for a while in silence.

"Do you have something to say?" Cunedag asked his eldest son.

"Father, why Etern?" Tybiaun asked. "He's my younger brother and, as you said, he's impulsive and hot-headed …"

"You are my firstborn," said Cunedag. "And therefore my heir. I know it is hard, but you must learn to let your younger brothers do their jobs so that you may do yours. One day, you will be king of the Votadini and will choose your own penteulu. Until that day comes, Etern will lead our warriors on the field of battle."

"But …"

"I have made my decision," said Cunedag with finality. "Do not question it further."

After the dead were buried, the last of the wine and ale was drunk in a victory celebration that lasted until dawn broke over the hills of Venedotia. The Gaels had gone back to their lands in the west after burying their own dead and the bloodstained valley seemed quiet and melancholy in the wake of the battle.

They returned to Eboracum where Aurelianus hosted his Votadini and Pictish allies, much to the consternation of Bishop Severinus who refused to attend. Germanus was there and gave a sermon to God, preaching the Augustinian teachings with special vigour in this nest of Pelagians. Already he had won many over to the church's approved doctrine and the power of men like Severianus and Agricola seemed to be waning.

Cunedag spent most of the feast in deep conversation with Drustan and Tybiaun wondered what the two of them were plotting now. The sting of Etern being made penteulu when he knew that he was the better man for the job still hurt and he drank deeply to dampen the feeling of betrayal.

When the feast seemed to be at its apex, Cunedag rose from his seat and asked to be heard. He had an important announcement it seemed.

"Friends! Allies! Fellow defenders of Albion!" the Votadini king said. "War has a way of bonding men together, even former enemies. Ten years ago, who would have believed that the tribes of the highlands would join forces with those of the lowlands and the Britons below the Wall to fight a common enemy? We have fought together to keep our island safe, but what of the coming years which, all gods willing, will be peaceful? It is bitter irony that peace all too often causes allies to drift apart and forget bonds of fellowship. Therefore, King Drustan of the Uerteru and I have reached an agreement. With the aim of binding our tribes closer together, we have decided that he will marry my eldest daughter, Teguid! A Votadini princess will become an Uerteru queen!"

There was much cheering at this and hammering of knife hilts on tabletops. Tybiaun frowned. Teguid was a high-spirited girl and wouldn't take to the idea of marrying a man she did not know and going off to live with him in the far north. But it was what it was, and Father had made his decision. Another family member who had no say in their future.

The wine was making him melancholy and brooding and he knew of no way out of it other than to carry on drinking. He eventually passed out, as did many other revellers, to dream of the mighty feats he would accomplish in the years to come in order to win his father's favour.

Two weeks later, Aurelianus escorted Bishop Germanus and his entourage to Rutupiae from where they would sail back to Gaul. They had done much in their short time in Britannia and could depart with hearts content that they had done God's work in defeating both Pelagian and pagan alike.

The gulls cawed and wheeled over the grubby docks where many Saxon vessels were moored, and Aurelianus watched the small trader beat out across the whitecaps, the wind filling its small, square sail. He hoped that the bishop would carry word to higher authorities of the dire straits Britannia now found itself in. A visit from the most respected members of the clergy had done wonders in cleansing the soul of the island's faithful, but military intervention was rapidly seeming like a necessity.

And it wasn't just the barbarians that surrounded them. There was something not right in the leadership of the diocese. Something rotten at its core. Twice, Bishop Germanus had nearly been killed during the summer and it hadn't been by the blades of the barbarians. That there had been an actual plot to assassinate him banished any doubt that the fire which had nearly killed him had been an accident.

Vitalinus.

Aurelianus was sure that the self-styled 'Vertigernus' of the isle had been behind the plot to kill the bishop. It had taken Aurelianus many years to see Vitalinus for what he was; a cold-blooded and immoral tyrant. The Council of Britannia was little more than the bureaucratic arm of his rule and any who opposed him or caused any kind of problem, came to misfortune as Bishop Germanus had nearly done.

The more he thought on it, the more he wondered how many people Vitalinus had done away with over the years to cement his rule. If he was capable of trying to assassinate a bishop, then he had probably been murdering people right from the very beginning.

And then he remembered Brutus.

Vitalinus had not been intended to rule Britannia at all. His father, who had been every bit as ambitious, had married

Sevira, the daughter of the usurper, Magnus Maximus. Their son, Brutus, had been Vitalinus's younger half-brother, but, as the son of a British chieftain and a Roman Emperor, had been groomed to rule the island from birth.

The failure and execution of Maximus had dashed those hopes. Nobody was interested in serving the grandson of a failed usurper. But Brutus remained his father's favourite and stood to inherit his lands in the west. He had died, not long after Maximus, in somewhat suspicious circumstances. They said that he suffered from the falling sickness and had choked to death on his own tongue shortly after dinner one night. What was curious was that nobody had been around to aid him. The servants later claimed that they had not heard him for they were outside the hall on various errands.

The only person who had been anywhere near Brutus, was Vitalinus, his envious half-brother.

Dear God, could it be true? Aurelianus pondered the thought as he watched the vessel carrying Bishop Germanus disappear into the blue horizon. Vitalinus was a monster. A tyrant who had wormed his way into power through murder and deceit, backing one usurper against another and playing men against each other like game pieces, including Aurelianus.

He had to be stopped, and Aurelianus was determined to be the one to stop him. He had control of the army, such as it was, but removing Vitalinus from power would be like opening a sack of snakes. The power vacuum could easily turn into civil war and then there were the various allies Vitalinus had curried favour with. How would men like Cunedag and his sons react if he were to wage war on Vitalinus?

Politics had never been Aurelianus's strong suit, and the problem presented a political nightmare. He was a simple soldier at heart and if he was going to bring Vitalinus to ruin, then he would need political allies. There were many who despised Vitalinus but forming an alliance with men who hated one another without being detected by Vitalinus's considerable spy network, was going to be a difficult task.

His head blossoming with conspiracies, he rode back to his villa in the west. He had promised his son that he would be home by midsummer, and he intended to keep that promise. After a turbulent spring, he looked forward to some lazy days with his family. He must take advantage of any lull in the troubles of the island, for he knew that another storm was not far off and it threatened to be the worst one yet for the small island of Albion.

Cunedag will return in *The First Pendraig*; the final book in the *Dragon of the North* trilogy. If you are enjoying the series so far, please leave a review on the platform of your choice. Reviews are a massive help to authors!

Printed in Great Britain
by Amazon